⋛ Perils of ⋚
Ms. Apple

⫷ Perils of ⫸
Ms. Apple

Justin Jones

ⅭiUniverse®

PERILS OF MS. APPLE

iUniverse books may be ordered through booksellers or by contacting:

iUniverse
1663 Liberty Drive
Bloomington, IN 47403
www.iuniverse.com
1-800-Authors (1-800-288-4677)

ISBN: 978-1-4917-6752-8 (sc)
ISBN: 978-1-4917-6751-1 (e)

Library of Congress Control Number: 2015908211

Print information available on the last page.

iUniverse rev. date: 06/10/2015

To my wife, Peggy. Through your avid and voracious appetite for horror and fantasy, you encouraged me to pursue my own wild imagination, resulting in *Perils of Ms. Apple*.

CONTENTS

PART ONE

C H A P T E R 1

Life Interrupted

"**B**oard up your houses, or head to the Osage Hills—'cause this here's the big one! Get the hell in, and let's go face the bastards on their side of the tracks!" a group of young Negro men yelled as they piled into an old rusty car. Their rifles hung out the windows, clanging against the chrome door moldings. The car spun out, throwing gravel and dust toward the sky.

Another group of men ran past her. Apple had been hiding for hours. She had changed her hiding place several times since the retreat started. She did not know who was fighting, but there was definitely a war raging, and people were retreating. Her dark eyes flashed between the tall blades of johnsongrass and other weeds, which provided an additional layer of cover between the low-hanging, untrimmed elm limbs and the partially graveled ground. She was already drenched in sweat from making her usual daily rounds. Humidity clung around her like an earthbound cloud of rain. The morning doves were usually gone this time of day and replaced with crows or an occasional pair of scissor-tailed flycatchers. Her favorite, however, were the mockingbirds. They could be anything they wanted to be. Apple thought of herself like a mockingbird. She could fit into any crowd that happened to be around. She could cuss with the old men at the pool hall or talk scripture with the church ladies who visited the pool hall to harass the old men. She called it harassment when the ladies would demand that the old men repent or burn in damnation to hell or something like that. Even though she was a chameleon, imposing beliefs on others was not her way.

All her neighborhood feathered friends had been seen earlier, flying north toward the Osage Hills, but the doves appeared to follow Apple wherever she went this day. No one had to tell Apple that doves mated for life. She had never seen these two that followed her today separated.

No matter which family she was staying with, this area of the street was where she always returned. It had always been safe for her. There were many hiding places and areas to let her imagination run; however, today was different. It seemed that grown men and women were hiding in all her secret places. She approached the pile of rusty sheet iron propped up against the abandoned clothing shop, her favorite place to play hide-and-seek with imaginary friends.

Today, what appeared to be a complete family lay still and silent with only the lowering and rising of their chests indicating they were alive. Their faces buried into one another. Only after a couple of seconds of staring did any buried face move or rise to see who had entered. One of the small boys stared back at Apple. His large, round dark eyes looked like marbles as they darted back and forth from his father to Apple. Apple understood the dilemma. Should he come out and play or stay with his parents? Or was it different from that? She wanted to speak, but this was such a strange day; she thought better of it. She looked up, and the doves were watching.

"Get the hell out of here!" screamed the hidden mother. "You will give us away. They will kill us—kill us all!" The mother's face protruded from the rusty tin shadows. It was then that Apple recognized her as one of the maids she had spoken to on several occasions. Just last week the maid mother had been at the grocery store complaining about how tired she was from traveling across Tulsa to clean houses for the rich white oilmen. Jobs around Greenwood did not pay much.

Apple was an orphan who had roamed the north side of downtown Tulsa for all her ten years. This was her territory, Greenwood, that was now being invaded by what appeared to be insane strangers.

A sweaty man with a torn shirt ran down the middle of the road. "Kid, get the hell out of the street. Don't you know when to run?"

Apple gave him a discerning glare and moved on with her routine.

She had lived with many families in the area who took pity on her. Mary Johnson was her current and favorite make-believe mother. Apple had been with her for two years now. Mrs. Johnson had even allegedly conducted some research on Apple in an attempt to find out where she came from and if she had any family in Tulsa. Apple always used the word *alleged* since *trust* was not a word she knew. Mrs. Johnson explained to Apple how her mother had died giving birth to her. She was named Apple because she was the apple of her mother's eye.

Tom Duke, the wizard of Greenwood Street, had given her a different account of her short life. She knew he really wasn't a wizard, but he looked the way she imagined a wizard should look. Tom had a growth of beard that surely reached his knees if he ever stood up. She was sure he stood up sometimes, but she had never seen it. Of course this was just another make-believe aspect of her life. Tom did stand up, but it was a rarity. He was never without his sunglasses. His clothing consisted of overalls that were at least four sizes too large and a plaid shirt made from a flour sack. Mrs. Johnson had explained how people shrink when they grow older and how old Mr. Duke had worn the same set of clothes for fifty years. Mrs. Johnson had always cautioned her about making fun of people who looked different. Old Mr. Tom Duke was different, with a gap in his front teeth that a truck could drive through. Most people commented on his gap—but not Apple. Tom Duke's face had ridges and crevasses deep enough to create suspicion for what might be hiding in them. At least Lizzy

Raines thought so. She was the food store owner on this street. Apple thought Lizzy had a crush on Tom Duke even though Lizzy always talked bad about him. Apple learned early in her life that just because someone spoke badly about a person, it didn't mean she didn't love or want him around. Apple had been in enough foster homes to figure this out. These types of deductions helped her survive.

Most people in this area of town wore clothing made from flour and feed sacks, and nobody made fun of that. Mrs. Johnson would always let Apple pick out the flour in the prettiest sacks. Apple would count the days until the flour was gone; once the sack was empty, it could be magically transformed into a new dress.

Tom Duke's attire was topped off with a purple velvet hat and high-top, lace-up sharecropper boots. No matter how early she went by his spot or how late she stayed, he never stood up to greet her or anyone else. He just sat on his straw-backed chair, leaning against the front porch of the local moonshiner's house. He would tap the bottom of his powdered snuff tin can as if the last speck of powder was essential to sustain his life. The gap in his teeth served as the device to spit a stream of snuff powerful enough to kill any grasshopper or cricket brave enough to come within ten feet of Old Tom. Come to think of it, she had never seen an insect close to him. They were everywhere, especially this time of year, but not close to Old Tom.

Apple's mind was racing. She did not understand why her thoughts were not focused this day. All her acquaintances were coming in and out of her thoughts. He had told Apple that her mother had given into the evils of the times and had run away to escape her demons. She suspected Tom knew she could cut through his bullshit, but he was too much of a gentleman wizard to just lay it on the line.

No one really understood how street-smart Apple was. Her interpretation was Mom was a heroin addict and prostitute who probably left town in lieu of being sent to Big Mack. Big Mack was a nickname for the state prison, which was about a hundred miles or so south of Tulsa—or at least that was what she had been told. When she would present this theory to Tom, he would just drawl, "Oh well." Many of the young men in her part of town had spent time behind those granite walls at the state pen, and that is what they told her. She had often thought Big Mack was much closer.

Shaking her mother from her thoughts, Apple continued to watch in amazement as more and more people ran past her. She started to see blood on the faces and clothes of some of those running. Black and gray smoke came rolling down the street, giving chase to the runners. Apple heard the popping next. She knew they were gunshots because guns were common in Greenwood. Many in the neighborhood shot possums, skunks, and other varmints if they wandered into the area. On New Year's Eve, everyone who did not own a gun borrowed one to shoot into the dark winter sky. Celebration of a new year was as good a reason as any to shoot a gun. She guessed possums weren't necessarily varmints since most of the residents ate them, and she had acquired a taste for the barbecue version. She found her thoughts separating between guns, varmints, Old Tom, and other aspects of her life. This was her way of coping with, or at least compensating for, the chaos of the day.

"Get away from my store, Apple!" screamed Lizzy. "Go hide. Run as fast as you can!" Lizzy had closed the curtains to her shop and was now locking the door from the outside.

"Why should I hide?" Apple backed away from Lizzy's store. "Where you going, and why can't I hide with you?" Apple scooted her feet across the dusty road as she continued to move back and away from the store. She kept asking questions along the way. Slowly, she leveraged herself in a small crawl space between two buildings across the street.

Apple ran across the street and quickly shimmied up a blackjack tree, not caring that the rough bark scratched her legs. The doves were in the treetop. She did take care to pull her yellow-and-pink-roses flour-sack dress up in an effort to minimize the damage.

To the south, she could see men running toward her. They were going straight north. As they came closer, she recognized several of them as having run from the north earlier. This time, they were toting hoes, rakes, and guns. To the south, there was a gathering of people about two blocks away. This was close to the train tracks where Negro meets white. Her chosen perch was great for seeing all the chaos.

"Apple girl, get your damn self out of that tree, and come here!" Apple glanced down, and to her amazement, Tom Duke was looking up at her. "I said, Apple girl, get downs here now!" Two things amazed Apple. First, she had never seen old Tom Duke standing so straight, and second, she had never heard him cuss. Apple thought, *This is my chance. I will jump down if you will play the blues for me.* Tom always had an old, handmade guitar with only a speckle of varnish remaining. He had taught her what he explained as the five and only essential chords to play every true blues song ever written.

"Apple!" Tom's gravelly voice yelled.

That was enough for Apple. The blues was not in him today. There was urgency in his voice. She jumped into his arms without warning.

Tom may have been older than dirt, but he was as quick and strong as any man. "Girl, I'm glad you only weigh about as much as a sack of sweet potatoes." He grabbed her hand and led her across the street and down south a block or so to the corner of Archer and Pine. The late-spring wind was always fierce, but it was outdoing itself that day. With the wind assisting, Tom's feet left a trail of dust rising like a rooster's tail.

"Where we going, Mr. Tom?" Apple asked in a curious but insincere tone. "I didn't know you could walk, much less run. Are you okay? You sure we can't sing the blues? How about this? 'When the Lord gets a ready, you gots to move,'" she sang.

Tom paid her no mind. He led her to stairs leading up to a narrow two-story building. Apple was one of the few kids in the area who could read, and she could read extremely well. All her caretakers had read to her, but Mrs. Johnson had instilled in her a curiosity for the written word. Apple found reading was a great way to escape the streets and all the misery and heartaches she had experienced and witnessed. "Beene and Holmes, Lawyers," she read aloud from a sign swaying from chains on the front porch. She read it once again to remind Mr. Tom she could—and to one-up his control of this short journey.

"Sits here, Apple, out of the way of all these crazy people. They all crazy. They don't have a chance. I knew this was going to happen. Negros gettin' too rich, and I knew the whites wouldn't be takin' it too long. Time to move on."

"Mr. Tom, you crazy. What you talking about? It's just the Fourth of July, ain't it? Or maybe New Year's. People just celebrating and having fun." Earlier she had thought it was a war, maybe a play war. But now, thinking it might be the Fourth of July helped. Both knew it was not the Fourth. She had to cope in her way, and he had to ensure their survival.

She never addressed him in the same way twice. It was Old Tom, Mr. Duke, Old Mr. Tom Duke; that was the point. It was a game to her and also a way to keep him guessing for the next time. She would see him and start to address him by one of these names, and he would say, "Halt. Who goes there?"

"Why, it is me, Miss Apple Lewis, at your service. And what shall I be calling you this date?"

He would always ask, "What is your pleasure?"

With that, they would both simultaneous yell out one of the variations of his name. If they called out the same name, he would win—and Apple would always have to fetch him a cola or something from the food store. Of course he always bought her one too. If Apple won by not matching the name he called out, she would win a new story. Tom Duke never told the same story twice. His stories were always about slavery, Indian Territory, or a fairy tale combining the two subjects. He liked telling of a lost tribe of misfit Indians. Sometimes, she felt the stories were not stories at all but the truth. Tom always denied this and was insistent he made them all up.

Apple had an unorthodox but effective way of dealing with the oddities and drama in her life. She had already rationalized all she had witnessed so far this day. What she could not rationalize, she eliminated from her memory. The family huddled under the rusty, sheet iron hiding place had to be driven from her memory. It made no sense and could not be rationalized. Therefore, she never saw it; therefore, it didn't happen.

"Girl, you not understanding. This here is all-out war. I knew this would happen. It may have been the Negro and Indians this land was opened up for, but this ain't going to be no different than anyplace else. I should have taken forty acres and a mule and not citizenship. Those whites need to keep us in our place and north of those tracks. Girl, this is war, and war is bad. I got to leave. You will be okay here. If things get really bad, those same stairs going up go down to the cellar." Tom motioned with his hand to illustrate his instructions.

"What about Miss Johnson? She going to be all right? I need to go get her. She can stay in the cellar with me." Her words started to sound like those of a girl her age. She prided herself for calculated talking by choosing big words and speaking adult. She would circle words in her books and ask everyone she met what they meant until someone told her. Some of the words were circled but not really with a conventional circle design. Many had abstract designs of demons while others were circled with angel designs, and then there were those unexplainable circular doodled words. No matter what shape the identified words would take, Apple identified them with a firm wrapping of all her fingers around the pencil. She was oblivious to the world while doing this. Tom just stood there for what seemed like an hour to Apple and stared at her innocence.

"I'll be back," he said, with an air of confidence she would always remember. She grabbed his skinny old legs and squeezed with love and desperation.

"Girl, it will be all right as long as you stays on the porch."

Apple watched as Old Mr. Tom Duke effortlessly shuffled his feet across the sandy road, appearing to place only the slightest of weight on the grains of sand. A whirlwind twisted around him. Tom raised his hands, appearing to lift the baby wind dusting twister off him and tossing it into the heavens. For the first time, Old Tom truly appeared magical. Not in the way when he was referred to as the Wizard of Archer Street, but in a real magical way this time. She continued to watch him until he appeared to float into a cloud of dust at the next intersection. Somehow, she felt, he would never be seen again, not in this life anyway. Dismissing this thought from her mind, a fantasy of his returning as a king or knight suppressed all other emotions. She would hold on to his promise of returning.

Apple grew restless as she walked back and forth across the front porch of the lawyer office where Tom left her. No one was with her, and it didn't appear anyone was coming. Playing "Don't Step on the Crack" soon bored her. She stopped to peer in the window, with nose and lips smudging the glass. She saw rows of well-dressed black men in photographs encased in rusty metal frames and broken glass. It was obvious to her they must have been from Black Wall Street. To her, Black Wall Street was just another area of Tulsa to play in and find hiding places. Sure the men dressed like they were white, but Tom had said there was more to it than dress. He explained that a Negro man could never be white, and a white man could never be Negro. She never really understood what he meant.

Some of the picture frames hanging had no photographs in them at all. They had no rust and were fancier than the others. She drew pictures of flowers, moon faces, and stick men with her fingers in the dust-covered front window. Tom must have known what he was doing bringing her there. There was nobody in the street running to or away from the fire south of her. She was relieved not to see any more guns or hear screaming, scared people. It was her space, and she was relieved no one was hiding around there.

CHAPTER 2

War

A loud noise, sounding like water being forced into ears when jumping headfirst in a pond, resonated above her. Apple heard the noise, but before her eyes opened, she saw a great flash of fire through her closed eyelids. Instinctively, she rolled backward off the front porch bench and away from the fire flash. She had fallen asleep on the porch bench while drawing pictures in the dust.

What was that smell? Her face was burning as she reached up to wipe it. Between her fingers, she felt the rough but delicate remains of burnt, matted hair. Her eyebrows were nonexistent. She continued to roll across the porch as flames climbed up her cotton sack dress. She slapped at her head as embers of burning hair fluttered away. The woodened porch made sounds like a train rumbling down the tracks as Apple rolled across its surface. Again, a flash of light; then another and another. *Where are they coming from?*

The roar of engines drowned out all other sounds. For a second, she heard people screaming, then nothing but the engine sounds. She did not recognize them. Automobiles were not that loud. She peered up through a burnt hole in the front porch roof to catch a glimpse of a low-flying airplane. It appeared to her in slow motion. She saw two men in the convertible plane. One was driving, and the other was tossing out flaming bottles. The lawyer's office was ablaze.

Bombs, she thought, *they are throwing out bombs.* Apple scrambled to her feet and ran into the street. *The same stairs that go up go down.* She heard Old Tom's voice in her head. She stopped dead in her tracks, turned, kicked off both her shoes, and ran for the stairs; however, she did not make it very far.

Apple felt a pinching pain in her left arm and then her right one. Instinctively, she pulled her arms down and away. Apple had been grabbed many times by the arms while roaming neighborhood streets. Sometimes a wino would grab in an effort to force change from her, and sometimes an adult would mean her harm. She learned quickly that grips controlled by a thumb were easily and simply broken by a twisting motion of the arm.

Her freedom was short-lived; a second later, she felt the pinching grab again on both arms. Again, she pulled free, but before her feet could catch a grip and stop spinning on the dusty porch, a slapping sting radiated across her face. She saw it coming but was unable to react in time. Like the slow-motion bombing airplane, a huge open hand darkened her eyes, and a moment later, the sting followed. Purple and blue would find a nesting place under her eyelids. The sound of the impact rang in her ears.

"Be still, you little naggar bitch!"

Apple was face down on the porch. *Hit me again, and I won't cry. Hit me again, and I will watch you die.* She had no idea where the thought came from. Even under the most difficult circumstances, she had never thought of killing anyone.

Apple rolled over, drawing her knees up and wrapping her arms around them. She felt more protected in that position. As she glared at the two men standing over her, the taste of blood acknowledged itself in her mouth. She reached up and wiped a meandering trickle of blood from the corners of her mouth. She remembered the taste of blood from pulling several of her teeth. The two men glared at her. They appeared as giants with the largest of feet shoved into aged leather work boots.

Apple glared back with round, dark eyes. She had put the bluff on many a person in these streets, and even though she had never encountered such large and white men, she would do the same with them. She possessed a mastery over her eyes. She could make them change shapes and grow darker. Now she stared hard enough to imagine them as two black round marbles glistening as if they were sprinkled with glitter.

She scrambled to her feet and squared up against the two. Instinctively, she dug her toes into the porch surface for better gripping. They were several feet in front of her. As she glanced from the corner of her eye, she saw her two doves perched on top of the lawyer's office porch. The two men also saw her looking at the doves. In a flash, she heard gunshots and saw the two doves fall in a flutter of feathers. The feathers capriciously rose upward to greet the clouds before being swept away by a wind gust. Once again, all moved in slow motion. The birds floated to the ground while the disengaged feathers reached for the heavens. Apple watched as the birds fell to her side. When they reached the ground, the world regained its true motion. The birds hit with a deadening sound for only her to hear. Blood oozed from the buckshot pellets.

At least they died together, Apple thought.

Apple reached down to touch her friends, forgetting for a moment the two six-feet stacks of angry white flesh standing a few feet away. As she reached to touch the doves, a leather heel ground into her hand.

"That stupid bitch!" one of them said.

Regaining her survival instincts, Apple turned and ran for the stairs. She was quick enough to gain a head start, but not quite quick enough to stay totally out of reach. One man reached for her and came up with a piece of her burnt dress. She kept her feet churning and ran out of her dress. In T-shirt and boxer shorts two sizes too large, Apple ran for her life down the stairs, only hitting every third step. With every stride, she recited, "The same stairs that go up, go down." Apple gasped as she ran harder. *I hope this is one of his riddles 'cause if not, I am in trouble.*

The two men were close behind her when she hit the basement door with both arms extended and palms up. The double door swung open without hesitation, and when she turned to close it, the door was already closed. A long block of wood had fallen into place, locking it.

"You little nagger bitch, you can't stay in there forever. We know where you're at, and we ain't going away. We are going to wait right here for a few minutes, then we are coming in to get your young black ass!"

Apple could hear the men breathing hard, and she took pride in outrunning them to this safe haven. She was so glad she had guessed right; Tom really had made this safe place part of a riddle.

"You still in there, sweetie? We really don't mean you no harm. Come out and play with us. We are going to have dove for supper," one of the white men said in a mocking tone.

Not only do you fools run slow, you must also think the world is dumber than you, which is an impossibility. She suspected that maybe part of what Tom was talking about in coming back, meant he would come rescue her.

It was cold in the basement. As the men outside grew silent, she looked around only to find true darkness. It was darkness like she had never seen or felt before. She had been in many dark places in her young life but nothing like that. When she sometimes closed her eyes and concentrated, little floating specks of light appeared. With eyes wide open, this place had no specks of light. She felt the darkness with its thickness and dampness. She could even taste the oldness of this dark hole she found herself in. The odor of old dust filled her nostrils. Not the smell of clean or new dust that would flow across the street when cars drove by the dusty roads on the east side of Tulsa.

"Damn it. Come out of there!" *Bang, bang, bang.* The men hit the door with the butts of their guns.

Apple backed away from the door while facing it. With her hands feeling the air behind her, she stepped backward into the darkness. Her feet felt the coolness of the dirt floor. No it wasn't cool; it was cold, cold as ice. Slowly she stepped backward as the banging on the door grew louder.

"Step away from the door, you little varmint. We are going to blast it." A deafening shotgun blast preceded the pellets hitting the door. Her feet shuffled backward until she tripped and fell.

"Fucking door! We didn't even make a fucking dent in that wood. What kind of damn wood is that anyway?"

Apple fell backward and landed on something that felt like a cushion of clouds. She had never felt anything so soft. She stayed motionless, her arms and legs spread out as if she was making a snow angel.

"Frank, we got work to do. We can't wait all day on this little catch. Besides, man, we got shit to burn and naggers to kill. We can come back for this little dessert later. Go fetch a hammer and nails."

Tom will be here soon. Apple allowed the moment to come. That moment where she followed her muse and let her mind drift. It was another of her coping and surviving skills. The hammering that came later never interrupted her muse.

Apple had no idea of the historical significance that was occurring on this thirty-first day of May 1921 while she was hiding in the dark basement. History would record that her neighborhood, known as the Greenwood District and also referred to as Black Wall Street, was burned to the ground with thirty-five city blocks destroyed and more than ten thousand left homeless. No one would ever know how many died.

Apple relived her life to date. Of course she always added some fantasy. She often thought of her life as a biography of fact and fiction. Biographies were her favorite type of books. She read everything she could get her hands on. She found many a book in the trash. She was grateful for people throwing away books, but she never understood why. All books were wonderful, and it was unimaginable to not keep every one she found. She had hid them everywhere in Greenwood. Some were under the board sidewalks, others were in hollow trees, a few were under ledges—just about anywhere else she thought was safe. She kept only the ones she was currently reading with her at Mrs. Johnson's house. There were several reasons for this. The main one was trust. She had been moved from one home to the next too many times, and most times, she was not allowed to take anything with her.

Apple allowed her newfound friend, the cloud, to tickle her palms as she surveyed the softness with them. Her palms found a home behind her head as she stared into the blackness, only occasionally making out an outline of something clinging from the ceiling. However, she did have doubts about seeing any true outlines in this darkness. It was darker than any closet she had hidden in before. This thought caused her to remember her second or third adopted family. The Joneses had a son who was about fifteen years older. Apple had been five or six years old at the time. Rufus was supposed to watch after her while Mr. and Mrs. Jones worked downtown. Mrs. Jones was a maid, and Mr. Jones was an elevator man. They worked at the same downtown hotel, across from the courthouse.

Rufus would throw Apple in the closet and push an old dresser up against the door. This enabled him to run around all day or just hang around the house without being bothered by Apple. Sometimes she could tell he had a girlfriend in the house. The house had only one bedroom; Apple and Rufus slept on two couches pulled into the hallway at night. Her closet dungeon, as she referred to it, was a few feet from the only bed. She could sometimes feel and hear the bed rocking accompanied by sounds that were odd to her. It wasn't until a few birthdays later—and several new families—before she understood all the sounds. She was later somewhat thankful for the closet episodes as the darkness enhanced her sense of hearing. The closet also assisted in the development of an unsurpassed imagination. She still had this elevated sense and was utilizing it now. She paused from her thoughts and listened to the darkness. She sometimes felt she could hear the darkness replacing itself. She imagined darkness would strengthen her. Once it started to become light, her strength would need to be replaced.

Rufus was not all bad. He had taught her how to kill chickens, skin rabbits and squirrels, and make cracklin' corn bread. They had only a couple of acres but made good use of it. Apple attributed her lack of fear and disgust for blood to Rufus. She would place the chicken's head and neck on an old board, press her foot on the head, and jerk with all her might while gripping its feet. If all went well, the chicken was relieved from the rest of its body. The body would continue to thrash about for ten or fifteen minutes. Rufus never allowed the thrashing to last very long. He would make her hang the chicken on the clothesline so it could have a proper bleeding. "Bleeding," he would say, "keeps the meat clean."

Sometimes Apple would hold a fruit jar underneath to catch the blood. She pretended it was magic and could bring things back to life. Maybe blood would bring her doves back to life. She also used it as paint to draw pictures on rocks. Rufus always said playing with blood like that was damn crazy. Skinny squirrels and rabbits were not as much fun. She had to hold the legs and pull while Rufus used his pocketknife to slit the skin and pull it back. If done correctly, all the fur and skin would be wrapped around the animal's head. She liked this technique since it covered the animal's eyes, and the eyes could not curse her. She still had a couple of lucky rabbit feet and a few squirrel tails hidden in an old well on the north side of Archer Street.

She knew now that she'd had a crush on Rufus. She now wished he had put her on the bed as his girlfriend to make those odd noises with. She did not know for sure what happened on the bed, but her curiosity led her to believe it was magical. Mr. and Mrs. Jones had said Rufus ran away from home. She was not sure what happened to him, but she was damn sure he didn't run away. She had heard stories about young black men who would just disappear. She had no idea where they went, but it must have been a magical journey. Or he could be at Big Mack.

Apple migrated from past thoughts to fantasy. Her eyes closed, and she could feel her body lift off her cloud. Her fantasy was created and not dreamed. Apple would not let herself fall asleep. Her instincts for survival were unsurpassed. She was resolved to the fact; her survival was hers and hers alone. Apple took everything she liked in life and wrapped it around her fantasies. She would be a great writer, married to a man who would create a home for all the children they would adopt. They would adopt them all. She would pay Old Tom Duke to come by and tell them stories. She would have hundreds—no thousands—of doves. Hiding places would be created everywhere. She would be a pillar of the community, just like Mabel Ramsey. She had never met or seen Mabel Ramsey, but she had read a great deal about her. She was in all the society newspaper pages that Apple would dig out of people's trash. Married to an oilman, Mabel was the talk of Tulsa. Apple enjoyed reading about her donating to charities and holding big parties. Obviously, Mabel was white, but Apple didn't care. If Mabel could live such a life, so could she.

Although a child, Apple understood that her survival was hers and hers alone. She understood survival completely. A booming voice shattered her fantasizing.

While Apple was immersed in her world, her pursuers had attempted to gather the support of several more men to join the capture of Apple. Most other men were more interested in the total destruction of homes, churches, businesses, and the Negro population than focusing on one little Negro girl. The men were frustrated by the lack of attention they were receiving; they perceived the capture of Apple as a fine sport and a necessity.

"Hey, you little shit, are you in there?"

Apple was starting to feel hunger pains when the sound of her hunters jolted her back to reality. She had no way of knowing how much time had passed. Her survival mechanism of fading into fantasy to escape reality was not designed for that type of survival need.

CHAPTER 3

The Meeting

"Hey, you little shit, are you still in there?" The voice was even louder this time.

"Hell, you know she is. There's no way out."

Apple's fantasy came floating down like a capricious wind trapped on a dead-end street. Her head was swirling as her fantasy crashed into oblivion.

She heard hammers again, but this time, they were clawing. She heard the stretching and screeching of nails as they were being forced away from the wood.

With reverberating indignation, she screamed, "Come get me if you can, you fucking monsters!" Apple was surprised by her anger and eagerness to harm. Sure she had heard such language but seldom used it—and certainly not in anger. Sometimes she used it to fit in or to impress her friends; she used the words maliciously, but never as encouragement for evil.

Time must have passed quickly. Maybe she fantasized longer than suspected. She gazed in the darkness toward the splintering noise. The splitting sound of an ax falling on the door was deafening. Again, again, and again, she heard wood splitting. Darkness had turned to gray. *The door is cracking,* she thought. *Night must have arrived.*

She could see shadows across the room. With her eyes adjusting to the darkness, she could peruse the room she might soon die in. First, she examined the cloud. A black or purple fuzzy spread covered it. Her hands explored a headboard cut in shapes of a bear, a cat, and other creatures. She squinted and felt the two poles at each end of her cloud. "Snakes," she whispered, "wood-carved snakes." Forked snake tongues protruded from the end of the posts. The tongues were smooth as if all polish or varnish had been worn off. They felt like one of Old Tom's pipe stems after he had whittled on them. There was a roughness to all the scuffed, worn carvings.

"Almost there, you little bitch! Here we come. Coming to get you; ready or not, here we come." They were almost singing.

Apple's eyes zipped around the room. She could see clearer by the moment. Her mind raced, and her feet followed. Running around the cloud, she realized reality was a bed and reality was survival. She frantically searched for something to place against the door. The room contained no dressers or end tables. There was nothing. Her hands could feel engravings on the walls but nothing else. She reached under the bed. She felt damp dirt, sticks, and rocks piled underneath. She dug and pushed enough of it aside to position her small frame underneath the bed.

Her imagination was fleeting. Apple's ability to control her fear and thoughts, her ability to cope, her ability to survive, and her ability to explain everything vanished. It was not the Fourth of July, and it was not a war. That family in her hiding place was there because of this evil. This evil at the door would soon be inside.

Apple's mind was unique. In a matter of seconds, she was calm. Death was not a bad thing. It was the beginning of another journey. Sure, she wanted to grow somewhat older, but she didn't believe people always got what they wanted, needed, or wished for. That being the case, Apple was prepared for death. She would not go peacefully. She found a large rock and a small stick. The stick was plenty big enough to inflict pain. She had seen her friend step on a much smaller stump, and it had gone through her foot. Apple spent the next few minutes chewing on the end of the stick to increase its sharpness.

When evil arrived, it arrived quickly and with a bang. She watched from her hiding place while the door crashed open. The two white men looked uglier in the twilight than before. Cautiously, they entered her violated sanctuary. Apple thought the men were somewhat amusing, entering so cautiously. Were they really afraid of such a little girl—or were they just afraid of the dark? She peeked at them and instantly recognized coal oil lamps in their hands. They were used in the coal mines: tin cans with wicks. She had played with those types of lights many times. She would find them discarded in trash heaps. Many times, they had just enough fuel to light.

"Come out, come out, wherever you are." They slowly walked toward the bed, holding their lights higher in an attempt to illuminate the entire room. She could hear the sweat dripping off their hair, sliding down their necks, and pooling on their shirts. She watched with enlarged eyes, but she felt no sense of panic or urgency.

They moved faster than she anticipated. A grimy hand reached in, grabbed her by the back of the neck, and pulled her out from beneath the bed with one simple motion.

Apple struck his ankle with the rock and stabbed through the foot with the tooth-sharpened stick. She expected him to fall. Part of him did, but not the part she expected. She rolled to her side, but the fallen object still hit her. She looked up at the stick embedded in his foot.

The fallen object smashed her face against the floor. It stunned and hurt her. The impact cut her, and blood dripped across her face. She thought it was her blood, but when she felt the side of her face, all she felt was a bump.

She realized the dead calm and quietness were present for a reason. Slowly she opened her eyes. Her sight was parallel with the floor, and she met the stare of her attacker. Confusion reigned. How could he be looking at her and still be bent over and maintaining his grip on her neck? She stared into his frightened eyes only to realize the eyes were connected to a severed head. *Did I do this?* She jerked so violently his hands released her. The body fell over and struck against its head just enough to cause it to roll face over face, slowly away from her.

Apple's heart was racing and pounding loudly. Slowly she gathered enough reality and strength to look up. Attacker number two was staring straight ahead, past her and through her. His eyes matched the fright in the eyes of the disengaged head of attacker number one. Slowly, he fell to both knees. He tried to speak, but his lips were paralyzed. Blood oozed from the corners of his mouth and then spewed forward with the strength of a bent water hose.

"Well, you boys wanted to play rough with this little girl here. What's the matter now?" a deep voice said from behind the dead men.

"I say there, young man, cat got your tongue? Are we still big and strong? Want to play some more? Guess not."

With the sound she associated with tearing a sheet, a hand thrust through her attacker's chest. The ugly white man's light fell to the ground and flashed across his chest. Fingernails protruded out of his chest and cut down to his waist. The fingernails disappeared back into his body, and blood gushed out. The second white man fell to the ground, staring straight into Apple's eyes. She spit in his face as he died.

"My, my, my. What do we have here, Jesse? She's a mean one."

"Oh, I don't know, Bobby. She just seems a little pissed off right now."

Apple reached for the lamp and held it out to get a better look at her new attackers. While doing this, she wiggled back under the bed. *This is not right.* The realization she had just witnessed two men killed in a matter of seconds—with no defense provided—frightened her more than the ugly white men had. How did the head come off, and how could anyone stab through a man with a bare hand? These were just many of the thoughts escaping from her fantasy to reality. She knew it was not the Fourth of July; it was a war, and the men were frightening.

"We are not going to hurt you, little one," the taller man said.

"Here. Take my hand," the shorter one said.

Apple looked cautiously from one savior to the next. Her mind was racing with the realization that her two attackers had been destroyed. With the light, she could see the two black men. This gave her some ease even though she had also known mean black men. They wore matching wide-striped suits like businessmen and lawyers wore.

Apple was careful not to place her left hand into the pool of blood spreading from the headless body. The two pools of blood were mixing; the stabbed man's blood seemed to be reaching for his partner's blood. She raised her hand, and the man called Jesse pulled her off the ground. Her feet touched down on dry ground, a foot or so from Jesse.

Jesse bent down on one knee and looked her in the eye while cupping her face in his manicured hands. *He may be the shorter one,* she thought, *but he is still so tall, skinny, and muscular. His hands are very cold.*

"How did you get in this predicament?" he asked in a deep, piercing tone. She realized his eyes were yellow. As she stared into his eyes, they seemed to turn brown like hers. She felt strong and determined to make a quick exit, but when she tried to speak, only a squeak emerged.

"Bobby, I think she is a little shook up." Bobby walked over and knelt down beside Jesse and Apple.

"I don't know, Jesse. She looks more like she is ready to kill both of us."

"Either that or she has already peered into our souls and knows us. Children are like that, you know. They're able to see things with innocence and purity. Adults are callused after years of surviving and living."

"I ain't innocent, and I ain't pure, you bastards!" Apple forced the words from her mouth with ferocity; only a scream would have been louder.

"Now, now, little one. There's no need for attitude. You're safe with us, and besides, what choice do you have? If you go out there, the Klan will kill you, and what you have seen in here will probably pale in comparison to what is happening in Greenwood tonight."

"Come on, Jesse. With talk like that, you will scare the child."

"Scare her? You think maybe running your hand through Mr. Child Attacker wasn't scary?"

"I can't believe you would say that. Hell, your little decapitation was enough to scare me. I have told you before: no showing off."

Apple watched and listened while the well-dressed saviors, killers, or whatever they were debated nonsense.

Jesse, still kneeling and looking into her eyes, continued to debate his partner.

Bobby produced a candle from somewhere and lit it. The illumination was brighter than anything Apple had ever seen from one candle. The light allowed her to see the blood dripping from Bobby's hand and his blood-soaked sleeves.

"I didn't need no help," Apple explained. "I was fixing to handle the situation. The bastards were as good as dead."

"Well, excuse me, oh mighty one," Bobby said with a hint of tartness. "I did not know you were a killer also."

"I do what I has to do," replied an indignant Apple with her small hands on her hips.

"And you're not scared of us and what you witnessed a few moments ago?"

"Should I be?" Apple asked with bravado most grown men would never be able to demonstrate.

"Bobby, we better move away from the door and go on through to the caverns before more Klan comes our way." The caverns had been cut from rock and Oklahoma red clay. The walls were sticky to the touch, and black bugs scurried up and down, looking for hiding places. Spiderwebs hung from the top. An occasional tree root reached out through the cavern's sides. Apple walked with the two until they faced the back wall.

"Come on, my little warrior. We can't fix that door, and it probably wouldn't keep the Klan out anyway." With a wave of Jesse's hand, the wall slid down with a loud squeak. The wall was made of thick, cracked wood. Metal whiskey barrel bands hammered out to run straight held the wood planks together. They walked through to a tunnel that had four immediate recesses. The wall hissed as it quickly went back up after they stepped across the tunnel threshold. They took the route to the left, turned right, and then the three descended dirty rock stairs into a perfectly assembled sitting room.

To Apple, the sitting room was more like a parlor. Mrs. Johnson and several other foster parents had them: places where people could read, entertain guests, or just sit.

Jesse sat on a fluffy cushion tied to the seat of a rocking chair, and Bobby sat on a small sofa.

Apple stood in the middle of the room and spun in a slow circle to get a lay of the land. She was used to memorizing and checking out anything new in town. Her survival instincts were still on high alert.

Bobby took his jacket and shirt off. "Damn blood," he said. "Another good suit ruined."

"You can sit or stand, makes no difference to me, but you aren't going anywhere for a while. I have a strong feeling the war, riot, or whatever history may call it will last a day or so," Jesse explained.

Apple stared at Bobby's bare chest. "Nineteen, twenty, twenty-one," she silently counted scars on Bobby's chest. She sat on the floor, crossed her legs underneath her, and rested her chin on her hands. Her big eyes lit up when she noticed the large bookcase about to break from the weight of what must have been a thousand books. There were more books than she had ever seen in one place. She would never have been able to hide all those books around Greenwood.

"If we are going to spend some time together, don't you think we should get to know one another?" asked Jesse. Apple had already decided Jesse was the brains, and Bobby was, well, something less.

"Go ahead and talk about yourselves," answered Apple. "You won't bother me. Are all those books yours?"

"Yes, and there are many more in the other caverns. This cavern you are in is one of many we have created in this area of town. We did not want to appear too prosperous to the white man. Great amounts of our more fancied possessions are hidden in these caverns. Besides, we all knew someday that what is happening outside would happen," explained Jesse.

While Jesse talked, Bobby was cleaning the blood from beneath his long, polished fingernails with a small, spear-like object. Even though she was listening to Jesse, her eyes stayed glued to Bobby with an occasional glance toward the bookshelf.

"Bobby and I are lawyers." Jesse leaned toward Apple because he knew she was not listening.

"I didn't see any weapons," Apple stated with annoyance. "How did you kill those men? I didn't see any weapons. How did you cut his head off?"

"Slow down, little girl. Jesse will get to all that stuff. Give him time." Bobby was picking at his teeth with the same tool he used on his fingernails. Apple may have spent a majority of her young life on the street, but disgusting and strange hygiene was repulsive. Apple was more disgusted by Bobby than the carnage they'd produced.

"Did you know I was in your basement, or was I just lucky you came along?" Apple asked with sarcasm.

Jesse shuffled in his seat, and Bobby leaned forward.

Apparently, I have your attention, she thought.

Jesse was flying through the pages of several crusty leather-bound books while the others talked. Apple occasionally glanced at Jesse, not allowing herself to believe he could be reading that fast.

"For such a little girl, you appear somewhat more intelligent than your years should allow," Jesse retorted.

"I would say more than a little. I bet I can read better and spell better than you two killers, lawyers, or whoever you are. How come he has all those scars?" Apple pointed with a demanding finger.

"Okay, we need to start over. It's obvious you have a lot of questions, and I am not sure we need to tell you everything. Would you prefer to ask questions or allow us to speak and maybe, just maybe, your questions will be answered?" asked Bobby.

"I would prefer, gentlemen, to just leave, but for some reason, I have a feeling that possibility does not exist."

"You sound more like an adult, the more you speak. Yes, you are correct. For the time being, you are stuck with us. For your information, Apple, we promised Tom Duke to watch over you until the riot moves out. Oh, now you look surprised." Jesse chuckled.

"The killing, blood, and other events of the day appear to daunt you less than us knowing a little bit about you. Yes, we know your name, Apple," Bobby said.

Apple was beginning to think she had misjudged the two; maybe Bobby was smarter. "Sure. Go ahead. What do I have to gain? I ain't got nowhere to go anyway," she said, turning her head and attempting to decipher the book titles.

"Tom trusted us to look after you. He knew this was going to be a day from hell. Tom left town, but he told us where you would be," Jesse began to explain.

"Jesse, have you no manners? We should start with formal introductions. I am Bobby Beene, and this here is Mr. Jesse Holmes. And your name is Apple. Excuse me. I do not believe I caught your last name."

"I did not give it. You guys have the floor, so talk," muttered Apple.

"As mentioned earlier, we are lawyers specializing in real estate, stocks, bonds, treaties, and things," explained Bobby.

"I don't care about all that. How did you kill those two, and where are your weapons? And can you teach me that stuff?" she asked.

"Slow down. Slow down now, sweetie. You see—we have been around a long time, and it won't hurt to kill a little time with the whole story since we ain't going anywhere," Bobby continued.

Apple rested her head on her hands while trying to fake listening sincerely.

"We came into this area way before the Oklahoma land run in 1889. Heck, we were here even before the Civil War. Do you know what the Civil War was?"

Apple's expression only changed by way of her mouth turning up on the edges.

"Well, let's assume you have. There were only a few Indian tribes here when we first arrived: Wichita, Quapaws, Osage, and maybe a few Comanche. We did okay for ourselves. We worked the land, but rewards were better for just teaching the tribes English and showing them new ways of doing things. About ten years later, numerous other tribes started coming here and brought slaves with them. If they did not have slaves, the Indians bought them from the white man. Having been free and escaping the Deep South, we had no intentions of being enslaved again by civilized Indians. They called them the Five Civilized Tribes, but the only reason to call them that was they acted like white men. They had their own early versions of what would eventually be called Jim Crow Laws and emulated the white man by having slaves."

Inquisitive as ever, Apple asked, "Who is Jim Crow?"

"Just a name associated with separating the races—like blacks here and whites south of the tracks—or having black, white, or Indian schools," Jesse responded.

"Is it like having to wear one of these?" She removed a white hood from underneath what was left of her clothing.

"Where did you get that?" asked Bobby.

"I pulled it from the pocket of your headless man," she said with a smug smile.

"That belongs to those calling themselves the Klan or KKK. They are big in Oklahoma right now, and I suspect they are behind this riot," explained Bobby. "Now where was I? Oh yes, how we got here. Anyway, having lived with and around various tribes, our services became more in demand as whites continued to arrive. Anyway, let's skip forward a few years. Jesse and I, like other so-called freemen, were caught in a dilemma after the Civil War. We were by all definitions already free, but many Negros were not, so the government gave the Indian tribes two choices. The tribes could either make their slaves tribal citizens or give each freed slave forty acres and a mule. Well, needless to say, creative minds were already trying to deprive blacks of this small token of the government's appreciation for having been slaves. This of course was at Indian expense. Jesse and I were teachers, travelers, men of the world, and other things like that. What did we need forty acres and a mule for? Off we went to the promised land: Kansas. Those Kansans had more of an open mind about what freemen really entailed. We were able to formalize our education, become lawyers, and make money. You know, little Apple, money and education go hand in hand and are the true measures of freedom."

"No, Bobby, money and education are freedom," Jesse corrected.

"So, you were both Exodusters?" asked Apple.

"Where did you hear that term, Apple?"

"I heard Old Tom Duke say it many times. He would say those damn Exodusters think they're hot shit, going to Kansas and the like and then coming back here thinking they better than us. He would say they ain't shit to me. I guess that includes you two, don't it?"

"You are just full of surprises, aren't you?" Jesse muttered. "Guess you know just about everything."

"I know enough to know that you have not told me how you were able to kill those two KKK men, and I know enough to know

31

you guys aren't old enough to have done all you said. Hell, you guys would be at least eighty, maybe a hundred years old, and would be looking like Tom Duke. You can't be more than thirty years. If I's right, that makes you a liar."

"Sometimes you look and sound like the little girl you are, and sometimes, well, sometimes I hear and see a grown woman," Bobby observed.

"I am whatever I want to be!"

"There now. Don't get all riled up. We ain't your enemy," Bobby said.

"I don't know that. How am I supposed to know that? I saw you kill two men. Hell, I could be next!"

"Look, we aren't going to hurt you and what we said is true."

"Then tell me the rest. I know there's more. I know something is not right with you two 'cause like Old Tom use to say, 'I can feel it in my bones.' And you know what else he used to say?" Both men slowly walked back and forth across the room in front of Apple. She studied their motions and noticed their brand-new fancy shoes that should've made some type of noise as they walked. No sound came from their shoes meeting the floor. It was as if they were not even touching the floor.

"Oh, pray tell, please tell us," Bobby and Jesse responded in sarcastic unison.

"He would say, 'There is evil in town today,' and I think this is one of them days."

Apple knew these were not your normal well-dressed Negroes. Should she run and hide or stay calm and not upset them? Would her head roll across the floor next? The allure of these men was too much. She stayed put.

"Okay, Apple, there is more. There was another tribe here in no man's land when we first arrived on our journey of freedom. There weren't very many of them left when we arrived. I am not sure where they came from, but I am fairly sure they were created from castoffs of other tribes. They were a wild-looking, dark-skinned bunch, but no two had the same skin tone—and no two dressed alike. Some had come from tribes in Louisiana and others from Texas. Some were Apache castoffs from desert regions, or at least that is what I understand because no two spoke the same language. If they did, we did not distinguish it." Jesse stared through Apple as he described their history.

"On a dark January day, an ice storm caused us to lose our way back to the Wichita tribe encampment. We found our way to Indian Territory, which would later become Oklahoma, but be damn, we sure had a hard time navigating. Three days later, we were lost, cold, hungry, and ready to meet our maker. I said to the Lord, 'Lord, take me now for I am ready; take us from this godforsaken promised land and deliver me unto you.' Suffice to say, that little part about godforsaken land probably caused my prayer to be brushed aside because God refused to take us by his side, but he sent the meanest, scariest, and ugliest men the world had ever seen to rescue us.

"They stripped our clothes off right there in the weather and dipped us in oil. Bobby yelled, 'They going to eat us, they going to eat us!'"

"Eat us alive!" interrupted Bobby.

"I said to Bobby, 'Hell, if they were going to eat us, they would not have dipped us in this stinky oil.' The next day, I changed my mind. I really did think Bobby had it right, and they were going to eat us. A guard kept watch over us as we watched them gather berries, leaves, twigs, dried bugs, and other varmints that they wrapped in leather scrolls. This castoff tribe mixed all these ingredients and added drops of their own blood to the mix. The mix was smoked and appeared to receive a blessing by one of the elders. The concoction was then mixed into a boiling brew. The pot was made from what appeared to be one giant stone. All I knew was it was large enough to throw us in it. Yes, Jesse and Bobby were about to be eaten. I had heard tales on the road about cannibals and such—about voodoo, witch doctors, medicine men, banshees, and just plain demons. Well, needless to say, this tribe or whatever it was, had all the above."

Apple's eyes grew larger. If they weren't telling the truth, they were at least great storytellers. *Maybe not as good as Old Tom*, she thought.

"They left us naked for two days while they danced, sang, prayed, and drank this potion, brew, or whatever it was. Then things got really scary—not like it wasn't already. What appeared to be the truly crazy one with the strangest dress came over to us with two dead gray rats. Upon closer review, the rats were headless with hollowed-out bodies. There was a mixture already steaming out of the rat carcasses. The crazy one cut his neck, held each rat against the wound, and bled into the carcasses. We knew what was coming next—but not without a fight. We were not well or strong enough after two days of nakedness and three days wandering the wilderness to put up much resistance, but resist we did." Jesse was growing more and more involved in the story.

"It actually did not taste that bad," Bobby added, "but we did fall to the ground in tremendous pain after drinking. I don't think we woke for at least three days. It was hard to tell, but we were asleep and still able to feel the pain."

Jesse continued, "When we awoke, we found ourselves dressed in tribal garb and smelling like them. We were no longer being watched. It was morning, and all the others had either returned to their caves or were in their windowless mud and grass huts. We could see or hear no one, but what we could hear was amazing. At first, we thought of hangovers. That's right—we were hungover. There was a ringing in my ear, but as I concentrated on the ringing, I could discern a direction and distance of it. I crawled across the frozen ground, expecting but not feeling the cold. I cut myself on jagged ice clinging from blades of grass, and I watched my blood splatter across the crystal grass. A moment later, my cut completely healed. Out of panic—but also to determine if I was dreaming—I slugged

Bobby. He was just sitting there, staring at a coyote at least a mile away. Bobby did not move, and my hand hurt only for a second. I was awake, but I wasn't sure about Bobby. I crawled across Bobby until I located the ringing. It wasn't my ear at all. It was a maggot eating and trying to stay warm in the stomach of one of our rat cups. The maggot was slowly circling a tiny rat thighbone. Maggots in the middle of winter? How could this be? Then I remembered the drink."

"I think you two are making this entire story up," Apple sternly stated. She was growing bored with the two and was sizing up her chances of grabbing some books and escaping.

Bobby interrupted her thoughts and continued his tale. "How can I see that coyote. I don't believe what I could see."

"It was dawning on both of us that our senses had changed. We should have left. But our will was controlled; we just sat there all day, testing our newfound abilities. I must have cut myself thirty times, just so I could watch myself heal. For payback, Bobby slugged me several times, so he could tell me his hand didn't hurt. Nightfall arrived as our new tribal family gathered. They spoke, and for the first time, we understood all their different languages. I was correct; they did practice a menu of different religions and spirits, including some we'd never heard of before."

"'We are the gifted ones,' the spiritual leader explained. 'We are hunted by the other tribes for our gifts. We are killed, so we don't share our gifts, but we share with you two now.'"

"As he was speaking, the tribe was preparing to leave. Desheeta, as the spiritual leader called himself, ordered an elder to stay and teach us how to live with our gift. We could never pronounce our elder's name, so we just called him Shithead because that was what he smelled like. And his hair looked like, well, you know."

Apple chuckled at the nickname the two had bestowed upon the elder. If this was real, it was better than almost any made-up story she had ever been told, she thought.

"Shithead was none too pleased to be left behind. He explained a great deal to us, but the most important was that our newfound powers were strongest at night and that if injured during daylight hours, to heal, we must live until night. So we could die from daytime injuries if we were not careful. Desheeta had told us the other tribes kept his tribe a secret and hunted them only during the day, and that was why no movement was allowed during light hours. The other critical guidelines were to maintain strength of the gift. We had to rest upon the ground our gift was created from. My dear Apple, the gift was from Mother Nature. So, we have always kept the soil and other items we were given as part of the transformation ceremony. We must take them with us and sleep close to them or face possible extinction," said Jesse in a somber tone.

"That's enough, Jesse," Bobby interrupted. "We are not certain of the power in any of the items we carry that were ceremonial and sacred to the tribe. All of nature was sacred to them. As the years go by, I have come to believe the blood was the only active ingredient in our gift."

"But who's going to take a chance that they are not?" interrupted Jesse.

"Anyway, this stuff can wait. Actually, that is enough, and there ain't anymore. You should understand who and what we are by now. Do you understand?" Bobby asked.

"You're not real, I think, and you are much older than you look," replied Apple, now somewhat shaken by a moment of reality. How could she escape these thoughts and pretend this was still the Fourth of July or New Year's Day. She had been taking the story in from the floor and pretending she was reading from one of the many books on the large bookshelf.

"So how did you kill those men? You never got around to them," Apple snapped back. She sensed frustration in their story. Are they frustrated because I don't believe them—or because Old Tom asked them to watch over me? *Maybe frustration comes from how old they are,* she thought. She had experienced the crankiness and low tolerance of old people before. "Fantasy, that's all it is. This whole story is just a fantasy," she whispered to herself.

"Apple, our little dearest, we have told you more than we probably should have, and you still do not believe. There will be no demonstrations of how to kill and no in-depth explanation of our abilities. Understand this: we are not your enemy and will not harm you. That is all you need to know," explained Bobby. He leaned back in his chair and crossed his arms to signify the chat was over.

"Where do we go from here?" she asked, feeling somewhat better about her safety.

"Jesse and I need to return to the basement bed. Our life-sustaining ingredients are under the bed: dirt, rocks, twigs, and things you found. This will keep our gift strong."

"I know that make-believe stuff from where your concoction was created or maybe the ground where your hollow rats came from," Apple responded with a smirk.

"Yes, but I will let you in on a little secret. Being naked for two days, the oil, and all the other rituals were just showmanship from old Desheeta and Shithead. We found out later, all we needed was the concoction and the elements from the ground it was cooked on and from, and of course the blood of a Deadwalker. All that other stuff was just ceremonial and created to satisfy their spiritual need. It was just a blend of various tribal ceremonies to create a new one for the Spirit Walkers."

Now they were making up scary names, she thought, trying to bring fear to the little girl in her. Who had ever heard of a Spirit Walker? Did they not understand she was not afraid of the dark or them? If they could actually see her soul or speak to her without speaking, they would know this.

Apple curled up in the chair Jesse was sitting in and watched them exit through the tunnel toward the basement and the magical strength-giving bed. She laughed out loud at the thought of a magical bed. "Strange," she whispered. "The chair should have been warm since he had been sitting in it for hours." She found it colder than the floor. Apple removed the first book she could reach, *Wuthering Heights*, and started to read.

She didn't see the weapon cutting off the head or the weapon with what appeared to be fingernails on the end, but she knew they existed. More questions would be asked in the morning—or was it morning already? That is why the two so-called Spirit Walkers were in need of rest. There was no way of telling night from day in the caverns. It was all probably a dream anyway. Tomorrow Old Tom Duke would be in his chair, dipping snuff and telling stories. Lizzy would be sweeping out the food store, and Mrs. Johnson would be telling her to stay out of the street. Focusing on the book was impossible. Analyzing the decapitation of the white man's head without a weapon kept creeping back into her mind.

CHAPTER 4

Omega

"There she goes. Get her—over here!"

Apple heard the yells as she ran faster than ever. Instinctively, a zigzag was better than a straight line. The sharp, tall johnsongrass cut her forearms, leaving a familiar sting as she used them to clear her vision.

There were more white people in the neighborhood than she had ever seen together in her whole life. The wind was blistering, and the humidity was thick as she looked to the sky to judge the time. They had started chasing her soon after she had walked onto the street. Unsure of where she had exited from the tunnels, her guard was down in the unfamiliar surroundings. At first, she ran straight down the road, and then looking back, she saw they were gaining on her. She had run into an alley, across railroad tracks, and up a small hill.

The men had fallen back some but remained in pursuit. Thinking she could hide in the grass, Apple made a quick left turn, ran a few yards, and threw herself to the ground. With dark eyes piercing, she waited on her stomach, as flat as a snake. Would they pass her by or find her?

Grasshoppers crawled across her bare legs. Red ant scouts passed by her nose and looked up at her as if to say, "You've got to be kidding me. She looks delicious but much too big for carrying back to the hill."

Hard steps shook the ground. She heard the heavy breathing moving closer and smelled the wet leather of boots. She smelled liquor, tobacco, snuff, and the staleness of sweat-drenched clothing, twice dried. Instinctively, her hand moved before it was stepped on. The two red ants were not so fortunate.

"Where in the Sam Hell did that girl go? She must have cut right through here and be on Denver Street. Go help with the others we've already caught. Kill the ones that fought back and throw them on the wagon with the other dead naggers. Let the damn national guard come and find the rest."

Apple lay motionless while the hot sun beat down. She was thirsty and more scared than ever before. Slowly, the pounding of boots on the cracked red soil faded. Without hesitation, she jumped to her feet and ran back from where she came. Her only thought was to find Jesse and Bobby. Surely, Old Tom would be there by now. She should have stayed put.

Smoke was everywhere. Every building in sight was either on fire or already burned to the ground. It was like she imagined hell might have been except there were no demons, at least not yet. Gray flakes of soot floated from the heavens and coated everything. A church on the corner burned slowly as the flames kissed the sky. In a daze, Apple twirled in the middle of this unfamiliar street. *Omega,* she thought. *This is what the end looks like.* Mrs. Johnson was the only one who had taught her Bible stuff, and Omega was all she could remember.

Apple's twirling in the street was interrupted by gunshots, followed by a car racing by and dragging the body of a black man. There was too much caked blood and dirt cocooning the body for her to determine if the man was young or old.

She twirled again as panic started to engulf her. As she spun, the black, gray, and white smoke spun with her, mixing into one hue, even though smoke was reaching for the heavens from many points.

She stood in front of another burned-out church with only a steeple rising from the ashes. Blasts of light streamed from a window below its highest point. "Angels," whispered Apple, "I see angels." As she stared to catch a glimpse of the angels, rapid gunfire came from her left. A truck with two white soldiers started firing toward the church. She had never heard such rapid firing, even on New Year's Eve when all were celebrating. Only a hundred guns could sound like that, but there were only two. A street sign read Boulder. *How did I get here? I know Boulder Street, and I know Boston Street. I have gone in a circle.*

"Get out of the street!" A black man was motioning for her to run toward him. She trusted no one and started to run again. She ran across the road, between a row of burning houses, and through a back alley. Several armed white men and several armed black men saw her, took a momentary glance, and continued to shoot at one another. Looking back at the gunfire and running as fast as she could, she tripped and crashed into the packed red dirt in the alley. Her jaw hit the ground since her arms and hands were not strong enough to take the full brunt of the fall.

"Take me to Momma. Take me to Mommy," a young boy said. He was camouflaged in the dirt. "Mommy, I want my momma," he cried.

Apple rose to her feet and took off running again. She could feel the blood from her face trickling down her neck. The young boy's cries faded as the distance became greater. Without slowing down, she abruptly made a complete circle and ran back toward the boy. Kneeling down, she dusted him off and lifted him to his feet. He appeared to be about her age, but he had blond hair and blue eyes. He was white. She had never willingly touched a white person before.

"Get the hell up and run," Apple demanded.

The boy rubbed his eyes and stared at her.

"Go that way," she pointed toward the south, downtown, the white part of Tulsa. She took off running north again.

Jesse and Bobby's law office was a smoldering heap of ashes and blackened boards. The doors to the basement had been burned. Running down the hot steps, she frantically looked around the room. She pushed on the basement wall, but it didn't move. A noise behind her made her instinctively grab a partially burned broom for a weapon. She spun around, expecting to fight the KKK, only to find the frightened white boy.

"Don't hit me," the boy cried.

"What you doing here?" Apple yelled.

"I have no place to go," he whimpered.

"You can't stay here, and you can't follow me."

"My name is—"

"I do not want to know your name," Apple interrupted like a drill instructor. "Stay here if you want. You can rest on the bed." Suddenly she noticed there was no bed and the floor had been swept clean. Against her better judgment, she grabbed the boy's hand and led him out to the war, to the Omega, to hell.

The boy must have lived south, so they ran away from the fires and toward the train tracks. No one paid attention as the fighting and killing continued while a young black girl and a small white boy ran hand in hand through the carnage and devastation. No one knew at the time that they were experiencing the worst race riot in United States history. A massacre that would remain hidden from the history books for generations.

They hid behind a tree as a flatbed truck rolled by. It was stacked so high with dead black bodies that the bodies would fall off with every bump in the road. When the way was clear, they ran across the street, taking a small detour around three charred bodies frozen in time. One had his hands reaching toward the sky, causing Apple to momentarily think he must have been retrieved by God after begging for relief. Begging was the right word; she did not believe anyone needed to pray for relief. Her prayers had failed, and begging was unacceptable. She had never begged and could not imagine circumstances causing her to beg. No one had told her not to, but she knew it was just not in her. Old Tom Duke had explained how the truth was just not in some people. She knew the truth was in her—but not the begging.

They ran to an open field, but a huddled family occupied her hiding place. They jumped through the first row of weeds, gained momentum, and crashed into a pit. As with a synchronized church choir, they cried out with fear, disgust, and a forsaken sense of humanity.

They had fallen into an open grave full of black bodies, old and young. She immediately recognized one as the father of the huddled family. They heard the growling and backfiring of a truck coming toward them. Scrambling to climb the walls of the grave, Apple threw the boy on a body and jumped on top of him.

"Quiet. Be still. Don't move. Don't say a word," she ordered.

The young boy froze. Within a few seconds, two more bodies with eyes opened came tumbling down, just missing them.

"Two less naggers in Little Africa," one of the body snatchers said.

"Little Africa ain't going to be no more," the other laughed.

As the truck engine grew distant—and they could no longer hear the gear changes—Apple summoned the boy to move again. He obeyed, and for a moment, Apple was quite pleased with herself. She was a protector, and she had someone obeying her every command. She kind of liked it.

Apple could see the way south was blocked. Hiding behind an overturned car, she peered south. Behind a line of whites in military uniforms and regular clothes, she saw a row of inquisitive white women. The women looked like they were watching everything.

They ran back to Greenwood Street and then east.

"There," the boy screamed, pointing toward the Williams Dreamland Theater. "My daddy was delivering movie reels there when I lost him."

As they crossed the street, airplanes flew low overhead. There was an explosion and gunfire; the Dreamland Theater was engulfed in flames.

Both children fell into the street, protecting their heads and covering their ears from the explosion. Holding hands and crawling on all fours, they scurried behind a weathered bench.

"Gotcha! Well, hell, we got a black one and a white one." The white man grabbed Apple and the boy by their ankles and dragged them from underneath the bench. Apple grabbed a bench leg, and the boy grabbed her leg, but they were carried upside down and thrown to the ground.

"Boy, you a damn nagger lover?" yelled one of the captors.

"No, I ain't," cried the boy. "She's my friend."

Apple felt even more protective of him. "Leave him alone, you sons-of-bitches. I'll kill you!"

One of the men kicked Apple in the side, causing sharp pain. She felt urine drip down her leg.

"Look at that, the little nagger girl done gone and pissed on herself."

It did not matter to Apple. Her clothes were almost unrecognizable from when she had jumped into Tom Duke's arms yesterday morning. If not for her hair, and her customary pigtails, she could hardly have been identified as a girl. She was covered from head to toe with dirt, dried mud, and blood.

More men were starting to gather around. Several of them were talking about which would burn to the ground first: the Dixie Theater, the Williams Theater, or the Redwing Hotel.

"Hell, we must have burned three hundred buildings today," one bragged.

"Yeah, and I bet as many if not more naggers killed," another chimed in.

"Take her to the convention center," ordered a man in police uniform who had just arrived.

"Hell, she will grow up like the rest of them. We'll end up killing her later; now is better than later."

"No. Take her to the convention center. We will sort things out later down there."

Apple was thrown into the backseat of a rusty car. She grabbed for the door handle, but there wasn't one. She grabbed for the other side, and there was not one there either. The door opened just as Apple kicked with all her might, and she kicked the little boy in his teeth. Stunned but unfazed, he grabbed at her arm and yelled, "Come with me!" Both now had bloody faces.

They were on the run again. Darkness was engulfing the day as the two raced away. The fire silhouetted one of the most bizarre sights of the hell-forged day: a white boy and a black girl, holding hands and running for their lives.

Fighting and gunfire were everywhere; no one was really paying any attention to the two young runners. Stumbling as they crossed the road, Apple recognized the corpse they had fallen over. He was one of Tom Duke's whittling buddies. She intuitively gave a quick perusal to ascertain if she recognized anyone else among the dead. If any of the other bodies were people she knew, they were unrecognizable.

Charred bodies, spent shell casings, burned-out cars, and an elderly women rocking in her chair were in the middle of the road.

"You can't just sit here and rock. You have to run," Apple said. The Negro lady just looked straight ahead, kept rocking, and did not acknowledge their presence.

"Come on. We have to run!" the boy said to the old lady.

Startling both of them, the old lady reached out with the speed of a striking rattlesnake and grabbed each one by the arm. "The devil will walk tonight, children, and I will go home. The Lord has told me this. Pay no mind to anyone; just go home if you have one. My home is gone. My son is dead, and the Spirit Walkers will clean tonight. Now go, damn you. Get off the street before it is too late," her gravelly voice shrieked in their ears.

They ran as fast as they could without looking back until they came to a partially burned church. When they crept inside, the smell of burnt flesh and smoldering cloth permeated the sanctuary. Water mixed with burnt offerings from the pews, curtains, wallpaper, and hymnals formed a thick black soup that clung to their feet. Silence controlled this environment, and with every step, echoes arose from the mush below their feet. Early stars sparkled through the gaping hole in the roof. There were jagged holes large enough to walk through on both walls. They crouched in a dry corner and waited for daylight. Within minutes, both were sound asleep.

CHAPTER 5

No Rest

"Oh, what beautiful round eyes you have. And those pigtails are so cute." Apple was dreaming and hearing voices from her short past. Mr. Hall, a former caretaker, always commented on her beautiful, round eyes. He would try to sneak into bed beside her, but Mrs. Hall always stopped him. She appeared to never sleep. Apple always wondered why Mrs. Hall would tolerate such a vile and disgusting man, but most women she observed let their men get away with just about anything and everything. Having no real role model, she had learned from a menagerie of what not to do. Even at a young age, she was committed to not repeating these social cancers.

"Apple, Apple, my girl, wake up." Too tired to be startled, she gingerly opened her eyes, rubbing them for clarity. Bobby was bending over her and touching her shoulder with a cold hand. "Who's your friend," he asked.

"I don't know, and I don't want to know. I found him—or maybe he found me. Bobby, what's happening to our town?"

"Tom Duke was right when he used to warn us that we Negroes were getting too rich and too smart. He always said the white man won't stand for it. Tom would say it was the majority's responsibility to take advantage of the minorities. If not, what is a majority good

47

for? Well, little Apple, that time has come and has only taken about two days to destroy about a hundred years of progress. Every church, house, and business has been burned. I bet you I have seen five hundred dead bodies in the streets—some of them even white."

"Where's Jesse?" She was starting to realize how tired and sore her legs were from running, falling, and jumping for survival.

"I think the Knights of Liberty have him down at the convention center if they have not killed him yet. They caught him in the daytime while we were looking for you. Remember—our strength is much less in daylight."

"Strength?" Apple checked to see if the boy was still asleep.

"Oh, maybe you didn't catch on to all this when we were in the caverns. Remember that we can heal our wounds, and if we are careful, live forever, or at least I think we can."

"Tell me how old you are?" Apple was determined to find the answer.

"You may be smart, and functioning well beyond your years, but sometimes the little girl creeps out like with this inquisitive streak you have."

"I want to know; maybe I want to be like you."

"Trust me, little one. You don't want to be like Jesse or me."

"Why not?"

"There are many reasons. For example, you get close to people—and then they die. Then there's having to move all the time because people start questioning why you don't look any older after twenty years or so. You do age, but oh so slowly, and then it kind of stops. But … the worst part is the blood."

"But how old are you?" Apple asked.

"I am 132, and Jesse is about 136 years old," Bobby proudly stated.

Apple caught a glimpse of sadness in his eye. "See, wasn't that hard?" Apple joked for the first time since meeting Bobby. "But you really aren't that old, are you?" *I am not falling for this*, she thought.

"Little girl, ask and you shall receive—and you have to live with the answer. Now, no more questions. I have to retrieve Jesse from the almighty Knights of Liberty."

"Take me with you. I mean take *us* with you," she demanded.

"Sorry, my little darling. I have told you things you do not believe, and I have no intention of showing you things for confirmation."

"What's confirmation?"

"Oh, I see. Maybe you are not as intelligent as I thought. No more talk. Stay here, and I will come back for you. There will be hell to pay if you disobey like before. Jesse would not be where he is if he had not gone out looking for you."

Apple turned to look at the boy for a moment, and when she looked back up, Bobby was gone. *He will only slow me down, and he should be safe here.* She glanced at the boy one last time.

She ran into the sultry night air with the fires still blazing all around her. The occasional gunshot crackled in the night. Bobby was nowhere in sight. How could he be gone so fast? Without hesitation, she ran south toward downtown Tulsa, away from the fires and the familiarity of Greenwood. She darted in and out of the shadows and occasionally dove for cover behind anything that could hide her ten-year-old body. She crisscrossed her way toward where she believed the convention center was located. She had never actually been there because only those Negros who worked in the area could be there without causing undo attention, but she had heard about it many times. Several times she had wanted to venture there to see the circuses when they were in town.

The sky behind her was a flaming orange, much like a sunrise after a storm when the remaining storm clouds had been left behind by their more aggressive cousins. The cloud she was viewing was actually smoke reflecting off the blazes against the backdrop of the beginning of the Osage Hills. The hills appeared black. The thick covering of trees and blanket of dark green leaves created a canopy over the land. She had not forgotten the boy; it was just time to part

49

ways. She figured he would be all right in the morning. Someone would find him and take him home, and everything would be normal again for him in his world.

Cautiously, she waited before running with all her speed across the train tracks that divided the Negro world from the white world in Tulsa. Later in life, she would realize this was not unique to Tulsa and was common practice in many American cities. *Why train tracks? Why not a fence or a wall or some other impenetrable barrier?* Once across the tracks, she was surprised to find relative calm. Running from tree to tree, she crossed the street in front of the county courthouse. Sheriff's deputies were standing guard as several Negro jail trustees were mopping blood off the sidewalks and street.

"Little Africa ain't no more," one of the men said.

"Damn right. Them bastards got what was coming to them. They should have known better than to come down here to save little Johnny from a lynching. If the damn sheriff would have just let the KKK have him, hell, we would have saved a lot of killin', but all those damn naggers would still be alive. Damn sheriff just like them a little too much," grumbled the potbellied white man.

"Guess you're right. He tried to save the life of one nagger for the right to kill thousands," another deputy said.

Apple could hear their laughter, and for the first time, she started to understand the magnitude of the hatred and violence she had witnessed. For the first time, she felt the need and determination to take a life, to kill, to inflict harm. This level of hatred was new to her. Catching her breath and waiting for the trustees to move on, Apple realized she was no longer creating explanations or making believe to cover reality. She had not thought about this being the Fourth of July or New Year's Eve for a while. She knew yesterday was May 31, and today was either June 1 or June 2. She wasn't sure which. She knew it was 1921. As the trustees walked back up the courthouse steps, the deputies turned to watch them. Once again, Apple moved swiftly from shadow to shadow under the starry night sky.

She stopped dead in her tracks and dove behind a bush. Bobby stood in the middle of the street, looking at the park across from the convention center. Hanging totally still from a small oak tree was a Negro man with his feet only inches from the ground. The rope around his neck appeared to have almost cut all the way through his neck. Or maybe his neck was just broken. Either way, the man was dead.

Apple cautiously walked up and whispered, "Bobby, that is you, ain't it?"

There was no sound, but she knew it was Bobby from his striped suit and fancy shoes. The silence seemed to last an eternity, but she was willing to wait for an answer. She had nowhere to go. She had already violated Bobby's instructions, and if he killed her, so be it.

"They cut off his fingers, his ears, and his toes." Bobby stuck his hands into a gaping wound in Jesse's side. A piece of his liver fell out and made a squashing sound as it splattered in a pool of blood beneath Jesse's feet.

"Those fuckin' bastards most have got him while he was weak, and it was still daylight." Bobby cut Jesse down even though she never saw a knife. He had yet to acknowledge her presence. Bobby held Jesse like a baby in his arms. Jesse was almost unrecognizable, but there was no doubt it was him. Bobby drew him close and gently kissed each cheek. He took a small glass bottle from his pocket, cut open Jesse's foot or what remained of it, and filled the bottle with blood. Again, even though she tried to see, there was no knife in sight.

"Apple, darling, do you see this?"

"Yes, Bobby. I see it," she whispered.

"Spirit Walkers can be killed but only in a weakened state. Jesse was caught in the day and did not have the benefits of enough rest, blood, and makings to renew his gifts."

"Makings?" asked Apple.

"Yes, makings—stuff like what was under our bed," he clarified.

He turned for the first time and faced her. His eyes were bright yellow, and every vein in his body bulged to the surface of his skin. He tore his shirt off, revealing a multitude of scars and a muscled body a god would die for. He picked Apple up by her arms, held her up to the light of the sky, growled, and showed his teeth, which were as bright yellow as his eyes. Each tooth appeared lengthened and sharp as a razor.

"I ain't scared of you, Bobby Beene!" Apple screamed.

"Good, because there is no need to be scared, my little darling," he responded with a growl.

"There's another nagger right there!" Both turned to see a group of white men walking swiftly toward them. Once they saw Bobby staring at them, they stopped in the street.

"Well, what do ya know? Hang a nagger, and it's like a mousetrap with bait. They come a runnin', lookin' for their kind. Well, guess what, boy; you goin' to die tonight just like your swingin' friend. The question is how you want to die. We good guys and will give you a choice," the tall, white man spouted while placing his stubby hands on his hips.

"Careful, Stan," one of the others said. "He may have a gun."

"It don't make a fat rat's ass if he got a gun or not. Hell, there's, let see, one … two … three … four … five … well, hell … damn, there's enough of us."

Bobby gently placed Apple on the ground. She needed no further instructions. She ran and climbed the nearest tree, faster than a squirrel with his tail on fire. Bobby faced the men and motioned with both hands for them to proceed in his direction.

"Hell. I think, well, damn. Damn nagger wants to fight us with his bare hands," Stan said.

"Careful, Stan. It could be a trick," the man behind him warned.

"Hell, Gary. What do you think? You think that little girl up there in that tree goin' to save him? Hell, ain't nothing goin' to save his black ass. The rest of you guys put your guns on him, and me an'

Gary goin' to beat this buck down, down to the ground. If we can't kill him with our bare hands, shoot him."

They walked cautiously toward Bobby as if their brave rhetoric was somehow not equal to the swagger. Bobby just stood there with his head tilted slightly toward the ground. Shadows covered most of his face. Apple wondered what the men would think when they saw the yellow eyes and large sharp teeth.

The larger of the two men, who was wearing a steel helmet common to oil field workers, quickened his pace and slugged Bobby's jaw with all his might. Bobby did not flinch or move an inch. The next man stepped forward and hit Bobby with the same might, and still no movement. The second man then quickly brandished a knife from his overalls and stabbed Bobby in the chest. Both men stepped back in unison, waiting for Bobby to fall.

Bobby gripped the knife in his chest and slowly removed it while raising his head to look at the two assailants. Apple could see his eyes were even more yellow than before. She was surprised the two men were not startled by what they should have seen. *Maybe they are drunk or partially blind,* she thought.

She saw them for the first time, if only for a flash or a second. Fingernails a foot long shot out of Bobby's hands. Just as quickly, both men's heads fell to the ground before their bodies relaxed for death. Some of the other men, having witnessed this, turned and ran, and others started firing. The deadening noise forced Apple to cover her ears and hide her face in the tree branches. She heard tearing of flesh and crackling of bones, then silence. Afraid to look, Apple remained motionless for minutes. The smell of gun powder was the dominant fragrance in the night air. It covered the stench from the night before.

Finding her bravery, she slowly looked down and saw bodies mangled and thrown about the street. "Bobby must be one of the bodies," she murmured to herself. After climbing down from the tree, she went from body to body, looking for him. The carnage was incomprehensible, especially for a ten-year-old—no matter how street-smart she was or how old she was beyond her years. One man's heart was in his hand, and another's head was turned around backward. Several had their innards on the outside, and some had no eyes.

"This is a dream. This is a nightmare," she quietly repeated. She pinched her arm until blood surfaced and ran down to her hand. Suddenly she crumpled to the ground, rocking back and forth. Her pigtails were no more. She was pulling them out from the ribbons and holding them along with wads of hair.

"Stop that!' She looked up to see a normal-eyed but bloody Bobby. He had several bullet wounds on his chest, stomach, and forehead.

"Don't stare. It is not polite to stare. I know I don't look too good right about now. Those Knights of Liberty fools ran faster than I thought, and the catching and killing took longer than anticipated." She felt relief that normal Bobby had returned. She pulled all her strength together; even Bobby should not see any weakness in her. No one had ever seen weaknesses in her, and they never would. She had weak moments, but they were hers to share with no one.

Pulling herself together, she finally said, "Yeah, you're right, Bobby. You look like a sack of shit, an old sack of shit." Bobby looked much older than he had before the fight.

"I've lost a lot of blood, so if you will excuse me for a second." Bobby picked up each mangled body, holding each one by the feet, enabling the remaining blood to drain into his mouth. "Damn. I hate it when I get so angry. I waste so much blood, and it's hard to replenish when bodies are all drained out like this."

Apple stared in disbelief, and she was amazed when Bobby started to look like his old self. Even though the wounds were healing, she knew the source of his scars.

"I am much better now," said Bobby, taking her hand and heading back to the north.

"Aren't we going to give Jesse a burial?" she asked.

"Not to worry, Apple. The sun will take care of things. Once the body of a Spirit Walker is dead, the sun will return it to the tribal spirit. His blood will carry on, and I have some of it right here." He removed the small glass bottle and showed it to her.

"What will you do with that?" she asked.

"In due time, my little friend. In due time."

Gunshots still echoed in the distance, and an occasional explosion interrupted the night. They walked without incident back to the church where the little white boy had been left.

"He's not here," Apple cried as if she was actually disappointed by his vacancy. For some reason unbeknown to her, she frantically looked about the destroyed church for him.

Bobby could see she was in distress and assisted with the search. Bobby dropped on all fours to the ground and started sniffing like a hound on the hunt. Apple could see a glow his eyes as they started to turn bright yellow again. In a growling voice, Bobby declared, "At least three men took him with no fight or struggle. I guess he will be all right. He is with his kind."

"How do you know?" asked Apple, showing much confusion with Bobby's matter-of-fact confidence.

"Trust me, Apple. I can smell them, and it wasn't long ago. They were white, and they smelled of gunpowder and moonshine. They probably haven't bathed in a week."

"You can tell all that just by sniffing the ground?"

"As a matter of fact, I can. Being a Spirit Walker gives one many advantages over normal humans; it just takes time to develop such skills. I suspect all humans have potential to develop such skills but not the capacity or desire to focus. Living for more than a hundred years—with the potential to live who knows how long—will create the need for such focus."

They sat across from each other, both thinking the same thing. *What do we do now?*

"It will be light in a few hours, and I have expended a great

55

amount of energy and have taken in less blood than I lost. Rest and more blood will be my priority. To do this, I must leave you."

"Bobby, I have nowhere to go. What will I do? What if they come for me?"

"Apple, have I misjudged you? Where's the little grown-up girl who was so obstinate and strong when Jesse and I came to your unwanted and unneeded rescue. If Old Tom had told us how difficult you were going to be, we would have passed on the assignment."

"Do you blame me for Jesse's death? If had stayed put, he would still be alive."

"You should not believe that. Things happen for a reason. Desheeta told us this many times when we were with the tribe. Anyway, Jesse was tired of our type of life. He wanted to be pure again, to be human again, but we never learned the secret."

"You could be like me again?"

"I'm afraid no one could be like you, but we could be human and age and die at your rate, just like you, but the tribe was destroyed before we learned all their secrets."

"Tell me what you know. I want to learn."

"You are much too young, and besides, you do not want to live the life you have witnessed Jesse and me living."

"Yes, I do. I want to be able to run, smell, and see like you. I mean not smell like you—but have the sense of smell like you. You do stink like something dead," she said, wrinkling her nose.

"I know what you speak of, and I only smell because of all this dried blood on the outside and undigested blood on the inside."

"I want to kill like you, kill all these mean men who have done all this." Apple waved her arm to show Bobby all the destruction just outside the church door.

"I am sorry, Apple. Killing is the wrong reason to be like us. We only kill when we need to for survival."

"Then why did you chase those men down and kill them? They were running from you—not after you."

"Okay, sometimes we kill for revenge. Plus I didn't want any witnesses who could attest to my powers. As far as I know, there are only ghost tales and rumors that Spirit Walkers even exist."

"I have never heard of anything like you, and I've been around."

"Okay, maybe it is all in my head or an overactive ego. Who knows?"

The sun was starting to rise, and Bobby could feel himself weakening. He had performed too much carnage on his victims and was unable to retrieve enough usable blood to maximize his strength. His cavern was several blocks away. Normally, this would not pose a threat during the night, but he was taking no chances today. He would have to leave Apple within the next few minutes and was not sure what to do with her except take her with him. He sat in silence, thinking about Jesse. They had been together for what seemed an eternity. To a pure human, it would have been an eternity. They had spent more than a century together, and even though they appeared as young men, wisdom of the ages was their blessing. He would miss Jesse, and he truly did love him. The thought of eternity without him was almost incomprehensible.

Apple watched the red sun rise, fighting for space through the smoked-filled Tulsa sky. Birds chirped, and a morning breeze was awakening anything that could move. Even the charred body outside the church door had a sense of calmness. The singing birds caused Apple to pause and remember the doves. It seemed so long ago when she witnessed their murder.

"Let's go, Apple. You will need to stay with me today and tonight. I will help you find Mrs. Johnson. After we find her, I must go. Leaving this town will be critical for my survival. It has not always been like this. It was not that many years ago when we only had to move a few miles or just go to another town. Now with the requirement to provide Negro citizen identification and all that, we have to change our names and everything. You don't want to be like me. When people you are close to notice you are not aging like they are, suspicion becomes the enemy."

She wasn't sure exactly what he was talking about or why he was going back to that conversation. She wanted to be like him and Jesse. Who wouldn't? Somehow she knew this desire was not because she was a child with an imagination and very few inhibitions. She always knew she was meant for something different.

Suddenly, multiple gunshots rang out, breaking the morning's tranquility. Apple saw Bobby standing in the church door, looking from side to side to see if it was safe to venture toward the caverns. There were more gunshots, but Bobby continued to stand in the doorway while she wiped the sweat from her face.

"My God!" she cried out loud, "Bobby, my sweat is bleeding!" Bobby did not say a word or turn to check on her. He stumbled backward but did not fall.

"I think we got the young buck!" someone shouted.

"Be careful, the son of a bitch is still alive!"

"Motherfucker got a gun!"

Bobby stepped backward from the door. He pulled a pistol from his pants and fired two rounds. Blood was oozing out of his back, and Apple realized the blood on her face was Bobby's.

"Bobby! Bobby!" She screamed at the top of her lungs. Bobby just stood there as in a trance and occasionally fired a shot.

Apple could hear men running by outside the church. Bobby fell onto her. His eyes were going from brown to yellow and back again. She saw his fingernails grow and recess into his fingers. She counted twenty holes in his chest. Some were starting to heal.

"Bobby, Bobby, don't die," she cried.

Bobby reached up and softly touched her face. "Do you feel that, Apple? Does my hand feel warm?"

"Yes, Bobby. It feels real warm."

"That's a sign, my darling Apple. I am near death."

"Don't die. Please don't die. Don't leave me here," she cried.

"My death is for the best. I will be with the tribe soon." He pulled the small bottle of Jesse's blood from his pocket. "Do you still want to be like us?"

"Yes," she replied while trying to regain composure.

"I can't make you exactly like us because I don't have time. I have one dose of blood. I am fading fast. I have only heard stories from Desheeta about those who were only partially given the gift. I believe some who were not fully provided the gift walk among us, even though I am not sure I ever met up with one. For some reason, Jesse was stronger than I am. Here. Drink this blood." He held the bottle close to her face.

Apple held the bottle and removed the lid. "What will this do?"

"I am not sure, but I think it will heighten your senses and maybe allow you to live longer and be stronger than most people. Remember—Jesse and I were chosen by the tribe and given the gift. We were not original members, so we were always weaker than them. I never knew the origins or how the first tribal members became pure. I assume each time the gift is passed to another, it becomes weaker."

Another shot rang out, and Bobby's head exploded in her lap. She backed up like a crawfish, faster than most people could run. More shots rang out, and with each one, Bobby's body jerked upward.

"Don't waste any more ammunition. The nagger's dead."

Apple crawled on top of Bobby, hoping they would not shoot him anymore. "Come back. Come back," she whispered in his ear. She heard more footsteps entering the church. She hid her face close to Bobby's and drank the bottle in one large swallow.

For some reason—and in later years, she would never be able to explain why—she took the empty bottle, held it to one of his wounds, and squeezed his blood into it. She then drank it. Maybe Bobby's blood would help her be like them, and Jesse's would make her even stronger.

What could it hurt? I know what Bobby was trying to say. He was saying even though they did not have all the ingredients, many of the ingredients would still be in his blood. Now I have both of their bloods and ingredients in me.

She licked the last noticeable drop of blood off her lips.

CHAPTER 6

Enslaved

The sun was relentless, beating down on anyone and anything not shaded. The crowd was growing larger as more and more refugees, hostages, rioters, war criminals, and misfortunates streamed into the ball field. Some Negros walked freely, and others were tied, handcuffed, or dragged in. Many were walking wounded, and several appeared as walking dead, but they were all here.

Apple did not go peacefully. She had fought Bobby's killers with all her might. The blood she drank had made her sick but not strong. The more she thought about the gift and all Bobby and Jesse had explained to her, the more she was starting to believe it was all a hoax, even if she had witnessed astonishing events.

She and every other Negro who could be found had been rounded up like cattle and taken to a local white man's baseball field. Upon arrival, she wandered about the crowd, looking for any familiar faces. Seeing none, she resolved to just sit. Apple would find out later that there were more than six thousand in the detention area. She did see the old lady with the rocking chair, but she could not be counted as a friendly face. The old lady appeared as crazy as ever. She kept telling everyone how glad she was to have so many Negroes gathered for a ball game. Apple thought the woman was crazy.

The Oklahoma National Guard had been called in to regain control of the city. Apple didn't understand why the soldiers needed to point guns at them. Nobody was fool enough to fight them. Besides, everyone was searched before being placed there. They had even taken her empty blood bottle. Several soldiers asked her what it was for. Utilizing silence as her best form of protest, they eventually left her alone. She felt no difference and could not determine if her senses were enhanced or if she was any stronger. Did she have any of the gifts displayed by Bobby and Jesse? She tried to get mad at a group of teenagers who were making fun of her hair and dress. Her hair was matted with dried blood and samplings of everywhere she had been in the last few days. Without a mirror, there was no way of telling if her eyes were yellow, but she knew her fingernails hadn't grown. She asked a young mother of twins if her eyes were yellow, and the woman just shook her head.

"You got a name?" a soldier asked.

Apple stared at him and started to walk away.

"I said, 'Do you have a name?'"

Apple kept walking.

"It's okay with me if you don't answer; you will just be here that much longer."

"My name is Apple Lewis, and what do you need to know for anyhow?"

"Well, you can't leave here until someone claims you or we can determine where you belong."

"I don't belong anywhere," she snapped.

"I just guess you don't." The soldier handed her a white ribbon to write her name on. He then told her to pin it to her clothes. She had not seen her name in writing since going to school several years earlier. Mrs. Johnson was good to her but did not make her go to school, and Apple did not have a profusion of scholarly motivation. Mrs. Johnson believed a young lady should learn how to keep a good house, please her man, and stay at home. Apple never agreed with this, but she figured going along with it kept her out of school.

Everyone enslaved in the ball field was receiving ribbons. Some were actually allowed to leave when whites came to claim they worked for them. Others were allowed to leave if enough Negroes claimed they knew them. She overheard several of what looked to be sheriff deputies complaining about the white rich oilmen in town.

"They think they are better than everyone else, saying they can't live without their Negros to clean their houses and cut their lawns and do the laundry," one of the deputies grumbled while his cigar flicked up and down between his lips.

In response, his partner said, "I ain't releasing any Negro to a white family just to get them out of here."

The day passed with no water, and the humid weather was unmerciful. Relief came when the sun surrendered to the night.

Apple awoke early the next day to the sound of trucks entering the ball field. A group of well-dressed white women entered the ball field and started identifying their maids, butlers, and servants. Apple guessed the two soldiers were wrong about people picking up their Negros.

The day faded, and the captives were dwindling. One by one, they were released to employers, families, and relatives. No one came for Apple.

"You were the one with that crazy nagger who killed twenty or more men with his bare hands!" Apple stood frozen while a large, fat white man pointed at her.

"That girl knows something about those killin's 'cause it weren't right the way he killed those men."

Apple ran as fast as she could from his grimy hands. She was amazed by her speed. She ran circles around the ball field, zinging and darting about with no fatigue. She looked back, and no one was giving chase. She kept running, overjoyed with her newfound ability.

Others watched her in amazement. Everyone soon lost interest in her—or they didn't have the energy to chase her down.

Apple awoke on the third day of chaos in the compound. Apple had slept on the ground again.

"Get in line, you all. Eat now or go hungry," the cook yelled.

"No need to yell," Apple responded. "It ain't like we are hard of hearing or we have a choice to eat somewhere else."

"Hey, you little smart-ass. You're lucky to be fed at all. Lord, someone come get this girl today; she is driving us all crazy," the chow line supervisor said. She had become fond of Apple but had a strange way of showing it. The sarcasm and yelling was just her way of endearing herself to the unclaimed children.

"Why, if it isn't little Apple Lewis?" Apple looked up from eating runny scrambled eggs and hominy grits. Lizzy Raines was the food store owner.

"You been in here all his time, Miss Raines?" she asked.

"No, but I heard you were here, and I thought I would come by to let you know Mrs. Johnson died in the riot."

"My God, lady, why don't you just come out and tell her?" the chow supervisor said angrily.

"She can take it; this little girl is tough, aren't you?" Lizzy continued. "Besides, she should know there is no one to come claim her, and you people will need to do something."

"Why don't you take her?"

"I'm leaving town like most everyone else. No use in rebuilding just to be burned out again. I am headed to Kansas," said Mrs. Raines.

Apple stood and listened as the adults talked about her as though she wasn't standing there. *I don't need Mrs. Raines or anyone else. I have Bobby and Jesse's spirits in me, and I will survive.*

Lizzy was led away after delivering the short news. Apple awaited other news, but none came. She kept expecting Old Tom Duke to show up. By the third day, no one came to claim her, and it was soon apparent she would be the last to leave—if she was allowed to leave at all.

There was much commotion later that day when Mrs. Mabel Ramsey arrived at the compound with several of her servants, a chauffeur, and a bodyguard. Apple watched her speak first to the head soldier and then to other workers. Sitting in the dugout had become her favorite pastime. She could see and hear most from this location without being noticed. From the visitor's dugout, Apple saw Mrs. Ramsey pointing toward her.

Mrs. Ramsey and her entourage walked toward Apple. Moving back into the shadows, Apple tried to hide by paralleling herself with the bat rack.

"Miss Apple Lewis, I presume." Mrs. Ramsey wore a gray shirt, matching slacks, and a white and gray cowboy hat. To Apple, she was quite the sight. Apple had not noticed any women the age of Mrs. Ramsey in slacks before, and she certainly had never seen a lady wearing a cowboy hat. She knew Mrs. Ramsey from seeing her picture in the newspapers. She also had read several articles concerning her donations to charity and other good intentions. Apple often pulled old newspapers from the trashcans to fill her voracious appetite for reading.

"I say there, are you Miss Lewis?" Only one of her schoolteachers had ever called her Miss Lewis, and it wasn't liked then or now. "Step out here. Let us take a look at you."

Apple slowly moved from shadow to light. A barefoot girl in a homemade flower sack dress—covered with mud and blood—was in plain view for all to see. She also had small scabbed-over scratches and cuts. Her eyes were encased in bags of puffiness.

"How could they let her stay here looking like this?" Mrs. Ramsey demanded.

"Who in the hell is she talking to? What does she mean, looking like what?" whispered Apple while looking down at the dirt she was kicking.

"Come closer. Let us look at you. We are not here to harm you. I understand no one has come to claim you, and I might just want to take you home." Mrs. Ramsey kneeled down to examine Apple.

Apple stepped from the shadows. She was angry and frustrated.

Mrs. Ramsey and the entourage stared at her, and she returned the stare with a vengeance. She would not speak or blink first. Surely, they would soon realize this little one could not be trained and certainly not domesticated.

"I don't think you are going to get much—if any—response from her," offered a young soldier who had been guarding the compound from day one. "She keeps to herself and doesn't appear to require much of anything. You best not waste your time with this one."

"I have never backed down from a challenge, and I suspect Apple here hasn't either."

Again, they were speaking about her in front of her and acting as if she weren't present. Infuriated and enraged, she decided to speak. "He's right, you know. I do keep to myself, and I don't need no charity or anything from you." The words sounded strange since she had fantasized about being like Mrs. Ramsey and living her lifestyle.

"I haven't offered you anything yet, and I am not sure I ever will. Settle down. No one is going to force you to do anything you don't want to," replied Mrs. Ramsey in a calming voice.

"Then go and leave me alone. Mr. Tom Duke will come get me soon enough." Apple used the most sophisticated tone she could muster. She wasn't sure she had ever called him Mr. Tom Duke before, especially to strangers.

"She asks every day if Tom Duke has come to fetch her," explained the young soldier.

"Is he a relative of yours?" asked Mrs. Ramsey

"No, he is not. He is the wizard of, well, never mind." She decided these people would not understand, and she did not have the mind to have to explain it to them. She looked at the two servant women who were young, attractive, and a lighter shade of black than her. They looked back at Mrs. Ramsey, and she felt a strange sensation like she could read their minds.

You little dumb-ass Negro. Don't you know a good thing when you see it? Surely you are not as stupid as you sound. You are about to blow probably the only chance you have to get out of here or at least off the streets of Little Africa.

Apple used her own thought process to say, "What the hell would you know about anything, dressed in your matching black dresses with your white headscarves; you ain't anything but slaves and we were freed long ago."

I know who you are and what you are, responded the tall one without moving her lips. Tom Duke told me about this little orphan girl named Apple—and don't think I don't know about Bobby and Jesse. I suggest you shut your overgrown mouth and accept whatever is offered to you.

"Apple, dear, are you all right?" asked Mrs. Ramsey, startling Apple. "I am not offering anything free or providing charity, but what I do offer is a job, a place to live, and an education. Do any of these sound good to you?"

"How much does it pay?" Apple quickly responded.

"My, my, aren't we the little businesswoman," Mrs. Ramsey replied. "Your pay is the roof over your head, food in your stomach, and the knowledge in your brain."

"Freedom is money," Apple responded. She had been unable to finish the thought argument with the tall one, but maybe she could win this real one with Mrs. Ramsey.

"No, freedom is education, and education can provide the world to you. If the world for you is money, so be it," Mrs. Ramsey replied.

CHAPTER 7

First Blood

Seven years had passed since Apple accepted Mrs. Ramsey's offer. There were times she regretted living with her, but the years went by quickly. At first, she missed the freedom of the streets, her hiding places, and Mrs. Johnson. Mrs. Ramsey had confirmed to her what Lizzy Raines said had been true. Mrs. Johnson's death was listed as an accident: *Burned to death refusing to leave her house.* Clarrisa Downs, who was now a maid, was the tall servant who read her thoughts. She called the death "collateral damage."

Mrs. Ramsey's home was a large, two-story rock home on a hill southwest of downtown, overlooking the Arkansas River. It was contained within a high rock fence with black iron gates imported from Paris. There were so many trees in the yard, grass had to find somewhere else to grow. Apple lived in a carriage house in back of the main house. She occupied one room downstairs; Clarrisa and the other maid, Shelby Barnes, lived upstairs.

Apple had refused to wear the black uniform with white apron and headscarf like Clarrisa and Shelby. Mrs. Ramsey had conceded the victory to Apple by allowing her to wear long, baggy dresses. She had only enough clothes to wear one set per week. Mrs. Ramsey spent several years convincing her it was acceptable to change clothes more often.

She was not allowed to attend the local school system because of her color, and it was too far to travel to attend a Negro school. Plus, Mrs. Ramsey was afraid Apple would run away if left unattended. Mrs. Ramsey had educated the maids, and they, along with Mrs. Ramsey, educated her.

Apple was seventeen and was also receiving an alternative education, sometimes self-taught and sometimes with the help of others. Being one with nature was an education within itself. Even after seven years, she was still attempting to determine how blood— and whatever else from Jesse and Bobby—affected her. Sometimes she felt some of her senses and thought processes were just imagination and a type of slow metamorphosis. She often thought her experiences were typical of all women, but they simply did not speak of it. She identified more with animals and other aspects of nature than with people. Sometimes, when sitting very still and concentrating on a beautiful flower, she could hear petals closing. She could hear blades of grass rubbing each other in the wind.

Gardening was one of her favorite chores. She discovered the ability to locate worms while preparing garden soil. She simply had to lightly touch the ground with her fingertips and concentrate on nothing else but the soil. She could feel the worms burrowing and could determine to a fraction of an inch where they were under the earth. Apple believed these types of experiences and developments were far better than class work. Besides, no one allowed her any credit for being well-read. She told Mrs. Ramsey about the books hidden around Greenwood, but no one believed her, and if they had, she was not going to be allowed to return to search for them.

Mrs. Ramsey had many books to read, but several were off limits, which of course made them more desirable to Apple. Often, she would sneak out of the carriage house, and crawl through a window in the main house to gain access to the books. She would find a secluded place along the river's edge and read by candlelight or moonlight. Eventually, she discovered no light was required. Reading in the dark was another benefit passed on by Bobby and Jesse's blood. On one of those nights, she made a major discovery.

She was resting on her back with her knees bent and feet flat on the ground. This was her favorite position for reading. She held *The Scarlet Letter* between her knees. It was dark, and only the occasional boat or passing car interrupted her solitude. She longed for a certain pristine feeling and was close to achieving it.

"Apple Ramsey, what are you doing out so late this night?"

She looked up to see Edward Henson, a tall, muscular, young man. He lived several streets over and was said to be the heir to a great oil fortune if his daddy ever died.

Apple had heard him walking toward her direction a quarter of a mile before he arrived. She had hoped he would turn around and go home as he always did. He had no clue Apple had heard and seen him approach her many times on evenings such as this, but he would always turn and go home. She did not question his bravery and believed he had none.

"Apple Ramsey, don't we look cute tonight?"

She had yet to acknowledge him and certainly felt no requirement to correct the fact her last name was not Ramsey.

"We don't look anything," Apple answered without the will or strength to stop. It was as if someone took over her mouth and forced words in and out of it and gave her a stronger attitude than she would have chosen under such circumstances.

"Aren't we a little smart for our age!"

"As I said before, we ain't shit. Understand?"

"No need to get all huffy. I just wanted to get to know you a little better. Know what I mean?"

Obvious to Apple—and obviously not to Mr. Henson—there was going to be no improving on anything between them. She had never been with a man before, but she had read about them in Mrs.

Ramsey's forbidden books. Actually, she had never had a sexual attraction to anyone, but that is not to say she wasn't somewhat curious. She believed curiosity kept her in control, and desire diminished control; therefore, she would always choose curiosity. She would choose neither tonight, especially with a white rich man. Apple gave him her best *get the hell out of here or I will rip your head off stare*, but it did not seem to be working. He reeked of liquor, adding to his nauseating demeanor.

Edward Henson bent down on one knee and sluggishly nudged Apple. She lost her bookmark and almost fell over.

"Get the hell out of here and leave me alone!" Apple demanded.

"Well, look at you, you little bitch. I was trying to be nice."

He grabbed at her and tore her shirt. His tearing motion momentarily stopped as he glimpsed her crossing her arms to cover the flesh he had exposed. Mesmerized, he stared at her dark skin in the moonlight.

She did not require his fascination with her exposed skin to make her move. With one motion, her fingers penetrated his neck. She felt her fingertips touching his spine. Realizing the lethal blow, she quickly removed her hand. Then, the uncontrollable urge returned. Once more—twice, three times, and then four—she allowed her hands to penetrate his body and squeeze his insides. Her arm passed all the way through him on the last hit. Her assault was so quick and furious that Edward Henson was alive to experience every blow. With blood quickly draining, he stared in disbelief.

Apple kneeled down, looked him in the eye, and said, "Take that!"

Paralyzed from the very first blow, he stared at her torn shirt, which was close to his face. He made a vile attempt to smile, and then he died with his eyes open. Looking down at her body, she realized it was covered with a spattering of blood that had started to pool around her feet. His body was void of all blood except for his small veins, which refused to deliver their last precious drops. She wiped the blood splatters across her chest and drew an unfamiliar symbol. She licked the blood from her fingers, dipped them in the pool of blood, and licked them again. The blood was exquisite. She felt pulsations and twitching throughout her body.

Now what to do? She had just brutalized a white man. He was dead. She could run for help and explain how she had simply defended herself from his attempted rape. No one would believe her. She was a Negro, and he was rich and white; they would hang her.

She expended little effort in dragging the body to the Arkansas River and throwing it in. She was surprised when it landed thirty yards into the main river current. Slowly, his mutilated body floated and twirled with the current. Standing perfectly still with eyes closed, Apple believed she could hear the curious river fish nibbling and tasting human flesh.

CHAPTER 8

Lust Hurts

You know I know, right? Shelby asked without saying a word.

Apple responded in the same manner. *So what are you going to do about it?*

You should try some first before you kill. You might like it. A man might tame some of that attitude and wildness. You know you won't survive going around killing like that unless you don't want to survive.

How did you know?

Girl, I could smell that white man's blood on you a mile away. Do you actually believe soap and river water can erase the scent of a fresh kill? Like I said, next time, let him have you for a while; it kind of allows the smell to come out in his sweat, then you kill him.

Are you like me?

Hell no, girl. There is no one like you. I have abilities but nothing compared to what you will have someday.

A week later, the police came around to ask questions. Edward Henson may have been young, but he had a reputation for frequenting whorehouses and living the wild life. Therefore, searching for him or declaring him a missing person was not hastily initiated.

Apple overheard the police officer speaking to Mrs. Ramsey. The officer was asking about her girls: Apple, Clarrisa, and the clairvoyant Shelby.

"My girls never leave the property without supervision. Besides, I hear Edward likes the more wayward women; my girls are properly trained. He never came around here. If he did, I would have ran him off myself," Mrs. Ramsey stated in a manner that caused Apple to smile and the police officer to cringe.

"What about the young one? The neighbors say she's sometimes seen down at the river by herself?"

"Oh, I know she sneaks off down there; I have known it for a long time. She just reads and keeps to herself. There is no harm in it."

"I know she is only hired help, but she is too young to be down there by herself at night. With all the hobos and undesirables following the river, she could get hurt."

"She is seventeen and more than capable of taking care of herself. She can run like the wind and is strong as an ox."

"That little skinny thing is seventeen? She doesn't look a day over ten," the policeman stated.

"Thank you for your concern and interest, but I assure you my girls know nothing. He will show up someday, and everyone will want to kill him," Mrs. Ramsey said.

"Thank you, ma'am, but if I were you, I would keep a close eye on that Apple one. She's cute for a Negro, and that can cause problems," he said.

Staring into a mirror after the police departed, Apple wondered if she actually appeared to be ten. At seventeen, she was growing taller, developing breasts, and becoming stronger. *What the hell was he talking about?*

Did she enjoy killing this man? Surely he deserved it. She probably saved someone else from the humiliation of him touching them. What had come over her? Would whatever it was come back, and was it part of the gift? Was drinking Jesse and Bobby's blood mixed without the other unknown ingredients the answer to her uncontrolled behavior? She did not like being out of control—or did she? All these questions were circling in her mind, and she was determined to find answers.

More questions than answers came when she met Marcus Brown. He was several years older than she was. He worked at a lumberyard frequented by handymen on behalf of Mrs. Ramsey. It was spring, and Mrs. Ramsey had decided to build a new wood fence to replace the iron one from Paris. Shelby and Apple were asked to go with the handymen to the lumberyard to assist with holding down the lumber load by riding in the back of the truck.

"Damn. He's just mighty fine. Look at that broad chest and strong arms," Shelby said while grabbing Apple's arm and pointing toward a young man stacking fence posts. Sweat streamed down his arms and chest as he struggled to lift a corner post and throw it in the truck. Apple took particular notice of every crease and line in his bulging muscles. She started feeling a warm, tingling sensation, similar to what she felt after killing Edward Henson.

"He has potential," replied Apple.

"We are women of few words, but I can tell you like what I like. Look good. He's coming our way." Shelby hiked her skirt a few inches higher and unbuttoned two buttons from the top of her blouse.

Apple looked at her in disgust.

"Good afternoon, ladies. It's mighty hot today, ain't it?" Marcus flashed his white teeth.

"Sure is. And my name is Shelby, Miss Shelby Barnes." She smiled while offering her hand.

"I am Marcus Brown and am pleased to meet both of you fine ladies." He smiled, wiped his hand on his pant leg, and offered it for a shake. Shelby reached out both hands, cupping his, shaking it, and looking into his eyes as if to devour him right there on the back of this truck. Somewhat ignoring Shelby, his eyes fixed on Apple. "Your name would be?"

Apple only replied to counter Shelby's jezebel introduction. "Apple Lewis."

He waited for her to continue but soon determined nothing was forthcoming.

"She's always like that, kind of touched, you know," interjected Shelby.

Apple felt that other Apple burn inside of her; the killing Apple was itching for action. *How dare that bitch talk about me with me right here? This is like being back at the ball field after the riot; everyone talking like I ain't here.*

"I can speak for myself, and if I need any help from you, I will ask," Apple retorted.

"Well, excuse me, all high and mighty. Who knew you had anything else to say? We all know you don't talk much anyway," Shelby said.

Apple burned within. She had not seen this side of Shelby and did not understand her behavior.

Marcus Brown continued to look at Apple while listening to Shelby, and then he extended his hand to her. Apple shook his hand and felt a warm sensation spread from her hand to her arm and her chest. She observed his strong, large hand with veins lifting the skin. She knew this was a symbol of physical strength, as she had begun developing smaller versions in her own hands.

He cupped her hand in the same manner Shelby had cupped his hand. This didn't go unnoticed by Shelby, and she inched her skirt up higher.

"Excuse me, ladies. It was my pleasure to have met you all." With that farewell, he turned and slowly walked away.

Both ladies admired his strut.

"Surely, you will excuse me for a moment, sweet Apple. Obviously, you are not the apple of his eye, and I have unfinished business." Shelby slid off the truck bed and followed Marcus around to the side of the lumber shed. In a few moments, she returned.

"Son of a bitch. He ain't nothing but a stupid son of a bitch. What's wrong with men who won't take what's offered to them?" She sputtered with anger and frustration.

"I am so sorry, Shelby dear. Was the meal not hot enough—or does he not appreciate leftovers?" Apple grinned.

"I don't need that kind of back talk right now, Apple. Shut the hell up before I slap you silly." Shelby crawled into the back of the truck.

Apple sighed. "Oh well."

They did not speak on the way home.

Apple dropped the incident and decided it was only worthy of her diary and not much else.

"I don't want you in my room anymore!" Shelby yelled once they returned to the carriage house.

"What's the matter with you anyhow?"

"You know damn well what the matter is. I could have had me a fine man if you would have stayed out of it! You and your big round eyes and baby face. Next time, stay out of my damn business—or you will be sorry!" Shelly yelled while shaking her finger at Apple.

Apple didn't like or believe in arguing. It had never gotten her anywhere before. Prior to the Tulsa race riot, she had learned it was best not to argue; action was much better. She had witnessed many a street brawl, and arguing was only a delay tactic for the weak. Strike first, fast, and hard; that had been her motto. Now that she had experienced newfound strength, she thought her motto might require changing. She certainly did not want to take another life. She continued to be confused from the pleasure and strength derived from tasting Edward Henson's blood, but her old Greenwood coping skills of masking reality with fantasy were put to good use with issues like desire and anger.

Sorry? I will be sorry? I am sorry now for even knowing a whore like you. Apple responded with words read but never used. These were words read from Mrs. Ramsey's forbidden books. It seemed appropriate to call Shelby a whore because she was acting just like a woman in one of the books.

Shelby stormed away without saying another word. Apple finished the day's chores, found a quiet, cool spot under a backyard tree, and started writing the day's events in her diary. She had learned much that day. She experienced warm feelings for a man and learned men could cause strife between women just by showing favoritism.

Two weeks later, the lumberyard made a large delivery to the Ramsey home. Apple saw Marcus watching her as she cleaned the front windows of the house. She peered back at him with a broad smile. He waved and motioned for her to come outside. Checking for witnesses and seeing none, she strolled toward the front gate to meet him.

"I wanted to see you again, so I volunteered for this delivery."

She looked down at the ground and then back up at him several times before he spoke again.

"You really are shy, aren't you? I have been waiting to see you again. I thought you might come back to the lumberyard. How have you been?" His large grin and flashing dark eyes captivated Apple.

"Look—I should not be talking to you. Mrs. Ramsey thinks I am too young to be entertaining men. She constantly reminds me."

"Just looking at you entertains me."

"Guess you are easily entertained," she shot back in her most flirtatious manner.

"Guess I am, but there are different levels of entertainment. Why don't I come pick you up this evening, and we'll go for a ride? It took me a long time to save up for an automobile, and I would like to show it to you."

"How long have you had this hearing problem? I told you Mrs. Ramsey ain't going to let me go off with some man."

"I ain't some man; I could be your future."

"If I went with you, neither of us would have a future. So scat." Apple walked slowly toward the house, knowing he was watching her every step. She felt her senses intensify; his sweat hitting the ground sounded like a hard rain on a tin roof. She took pleasure in knowing she caused some of that sweat.

"I will be by tonight!" he yelled when she reached the door.

"Won't do you any good," she shyly replied.

Marcus Brown was on her mind the remainder of the day. When he left, she had no doubt if he were to come by tonight, she would not go with him. However, as the day passed, curiosity, desire, and maybe revenge against Shelby played in her head. By evening, she was consumed with indecision.

Shelby and Clarrisa were behind the carriage house, hiding their cigarette smoking when Apple noticed a car drive by with its lights off and park across the street. She was sitting on the lowest limb of a large blackjack tree close to the corner fence.

She had no trouble seeing Marcus in the car even though night had arrived. She saw the glow of a cigarette and heard ashes hit the floorboard of the car. Had she been perched in this tree waiting on his arrival, or was it just the need for solitude? She had convinced herself of the latter.

He scanned the grounds for her. She was not well hidden by the tree, but she guessed he was not accustomed to calling on women in trees. Her heart raced and pounded. She soon found herself walking toward the car.

Marcus leaped from the car and opened the door for her. She entered without saying a word. He started the car and drove away from the house. The car was old and smelled of gasoline and dirt, but her senses were more in tune with something else.

"I was thinking you were not going to show. I am glad you did." He placed his hand on her knee. She did not move. His hand felt like fire on her cool skin. She studied the sensation. He drove along Riverside Drive until entering a small park, where he turned the engine off. Apple stared straight ahead and watched the river flow, not once looking at him. "For a warm summer night, you sure have cool skin," he commented.

In the last few years, her skin stayed cooler than previous years, and she believed it contributed to her having more energy at night.

He moved toward her and placed his arm across the back of her shoulders. She immediately opened the door and stepped outside.

"Sure. Let's go for a walk. Good idea," he said. Frustrated, he threw his arms in the air and exited the car too. Apple took off, leading him at a fast pace.

She was frightened but wanted to know more about this man. She had been reading books since she was an orphan on the streets of Little Africa. She wished for the same experiences she read about. She thought about Shakespeare's *Othello* and the power of attraction, desire, and love. She knew Marcus Brown was different from Edward Henson, and no matter what happened, she would control herself. Yes, she would show self-control.

She walked for several hundred yards, circled back to the front of the car, and stopped. Marcus followed after her, bewildered by this strange and beautiful girl. She did not wish to go any farther away from the car in case she was wrong and all men were alike. Leaning on the car grill, she tossed her head back and gazed at the stars, forgetting for a moment she was not alone.

His lips felt similar to a moist warm sponge as he moved them up and down her neck. She did not move. She closed her eyes and engaged her heightened senses. His fingertips crossed her lips, calling for her head to turn. She turned and met his lips with hers. Her first kiss was wonderful, and he continued to kiss her even though her curiosity had been fulfilled. *I must be patient,* she thought.

He felt her shoulders, moved up against her, and attempted to investigate other parts of her body.

"I don't want to do that," she whispered.

"How do you know? Have you tried before?"

"I have not been with a man before. I just wanted to kiss."

"I don't believe this. Looking like you do with that body and baby face. You're lying."

"No. No, I am not," she responded, changing from a whisper to normal volume.

"I believe you, honey; sure I do." He continued to attempt to explore her body until her hand restrained his progress. He was surprised by the strength in such a soft hand.

She thought she had kept control and had passed the point of difficulty. She liked his touch, his kiss, and his smell. Maybe next time she would act on her other desires.

"Come on, baby. Just a little indulgence, please."

The sound of a man begging pleased her. She kissed him in an effort to distract him from his single focused destination. Kissing worked for a while but soon lost effect.

"Come on, Apple. Don't leave me like this."

"Like what?"

He took her hand and let her touch explain what he was talking about. She quickly moved her hand away. He grabbed her hand and put it back. She instinctively pulled back, and with the other hand, she punched him in the stomach. She kept her hand in a fist, not knowing exactly what had happened when she first struck Edward Henson. She did not want to destroy Marcus, so the hand stayed in a fist.

"Yes, baby. Man, that's some rough play there. Give some more, please. Please."

This was enough begging. She got the kiss she came for, and he could wait on anything else. She needed to regroup and think this over. Mrs. Ramsey had kept a close eye on her for seven years. She accepted naiveté as her shackle. Would Marcus Brown?

She attempted to pull away and could have easily done so against his resistance. He held her shoulders and attempted to keep her up against him. "Come on, baby. Give me something for my efforts." He attempted to place her hand back in that unwanted area. "See, baby? I ain't going to push it with you. Just give me some attention in certain areas, and everything will be all right. You'll see."

She was fascinated but angry that he was not paying any attention to her. The fascination had more to do with anatomy than anything else. Even Mrs. Ramsey's books did not come close to describing this scenario. Marcus leaned back on the car hood, ensuring she did not turn loose by keeping both of his hands wrapped around hers.

"Come on, baby. Put your hands right here, and I will show you what to do."

Her muscles tensed, and her heart pounded. She glimpsed her yellow eyes reflecting off the chrome bumper. *My eyes are like Bobby's before he killed.* She felt herself growing stronger and stronger.

"Almost there, baby. Now let's move them right here," he moaned. He was not even acknowledging that she was resisting all efforts to cooperate in whatever he was trying to get her to do.

The scream pierced the night and echoed through the pecan trees and across the river waters. Marcus crumpled to the ground. He rolled over and over from the damp grass to the gritty river sand. He was crying and screaming. She smelled blood, which only made her more intense.

"Marcus, are you all right?"

He continued to scream and moan as he staggered to his feet. "My god, what have you done? I am bleeding to death," he screamed.

"I don't think I did anything," she said while walking toward him.

Marcus clumsily ran away from her. Every few steps, he fell to the ground and tried to run again.

She realized there was blood and flesh in her hand. She sat on the ground and wiped her hands in the dirt. Her yellow eyes created a reflected glow off her hands.

Try as she might, the gift from Bobby and Jesse controlled her. She heard Bobby's voice in her head: *No one must know what you are. If found out, you must eliminate their knowledge.*

"It was an accident!" she exclaimed.

Hesitation and confliction passed as she followed the trail of blood. Marcus had not gone far. He was curled in a ball like a puppy trying to keep warm; he was whimpering and crying. He looked at her while holding his wound. "Your eyes, your eyes," he muttered. He rolled over several times. "Yellow, yellow. What have you done to me?" He fell down in the weeds.

"Sorry, Marcus," she said while lifting him off his feet. With one strike, his heart was pierced. He died instantly. She wanted to cause him no more pain. Having no control, she drank and licked as much blood as possible. His blood was tastier than Henson's blood. He was healthy and strong. Upon consuming his blood, a new strength emerged. She threw the body in the river and gave her second water burial.

She had never driven a car, so her idea of driving it into the river failed. She could not even start it and practically tore off the hand crank. She ran through the woods and back to the house.

Lying in bed, she wondered if she had known she would kill him. She had no choice. It was an accident, and he caused it to happen. How dare he make her do that? She had only wanted a kiss. It was his fault she had to kill him. She would write this in her diary; she had learned several valuable lessons that night.

I smell the blood on you. You little whore! You killed Marcus Brown, didn't you? Just like you killed Edward Henson! You would not let me have him, so you had him for yourself. Shelby stormed into the bedroom, pulling the covers from Apple. "They should have never shared the gift with a whore like you; you're not worthy!" Shelby was screaming at the top of her lungs.

"Leave me alone, Shelby—and get out!"

"You're the one getting out, bitch!" Shelby grabbed Apple's feet, dragged her onto the floor, and started kicking her. Apple sprung to her feet but not before Shelby caught her with a fist to the jaw. Apple felt her jaw break. She fell against the wall, experiencing the sting and breaking of ribs as Shelby kicked her. Apple's muscles grew three times their normal size in a matter of seconds. Her yellow glaring eyes were no match for Shelby's glowing eyes. Their eyes illuminated the room like a hundred candles flickering in the wind.

Apple struck Shelby's arm, breaking it. Shelby, lunging forward, grabbed Apple's neck, and they rolled to the floor. Apple landed on top and hit her with all her might, tearing her head from her body.

Shelby's head rolled away from her body. Rolling, the head cried, "You can't do this. I am like you, a Spirit Walker." Suddenly her eyes closed, and she whispered, "Impossible. This can't happen. This can't be happening."

"That's how the head came off in the basement when I first met Bobby and Jesse," Apple said to herself.

"Go, Apple. Just go."

Apple swirled to see Clarrisa standing in the doorway.

"Your gift is too strong. Shelby didn't understand, but I do. You can't stay here."

"I have nowhere to go. Help me, Clarrisa."

"There's a good life for me here. Many years will pass before I have to start over somewhere," Clarrisa continued.

"Why leave at all?" asked Apple.

"Apple, others grow old, unlike us. Oh, we grow old, but each one of us at different rates based upon the strength of our gift. My gift is weak, but I still have to leave before people start wondering why I am aging so slowly."

Lights came on in the main house.

"How will you explain all this?" asked Apple, surveying the destroyed room.

"Oh, that's the easy part." Clarrisa threw a lit oil lamp on the bed, and it burst into flames. "I will simply tell them we were attacked by the Klan, and you were kidnapped. So go!" Clarrisa waved her hand toward the door.

Apple ran as fast as she could down the stairs, across the backyard, and jumped the fence like an antelope. Tulsa was left behind.

CHAPTER 9

1969

"What is this shit? Gomer Pyle needs to go to Vietnam. This shit ain't funny," Apple said as she and Treasure Freeze watched television.

"Well, it's better than that damn new show you've been watching. What's it called, *Grady Lunch*?" Treasure asked.

"*Brady Bunch! The Brady Bunch*, and for your information, it is a sign of our times. You know: divorced families, half-brothers, half-sisters, and shit like that."

"Apple, dearest, I believe Carol and Mike Brady are surviving spouses from previous marriages, meaning their better halves died. They probably killed them so they could legally screw each other. You're an orphan. What do you know about family life? There's nothing good to watch since *Peyton Place* went off the air."

"They're the way families should be or can be," replied Apple.

"You want an ideal family? You should pay attention to *Leave It to Beaver*. Now there's an American family." Treasure grinned while taunting Apple with pop culture knowledge.

It was December 1969, and Apple and Treasure had had a tumultuous, exciting, exhausting, and experimental year. They were still writing Woodstock stories in their diaries, or as Treasure referred to it, Penelope Ashe's *Naked Came a Stranger*, part two. She never believed a group of journalists wrote the book as a gag—and there was no real Penelope. She would argue the social merits of her favorite book, *Portnoy's Complaint*, compared to Apple's favorite for the year, *One Flew over the Cuckoo's Nest*. They did agree on the pure entertainment value of Jacqueline Susann's *Valley of the Dolls*.

"Hey, Treasure, besides placing men on the moon, what do you think the highlight of the year was?"

"It depends if we mix the good with the bad. Sirhan Sirhan's dastardly deed and Frank Zappa naming his son Dweezil are on the bad side, but they are certainly in my top ten highlights. On the positive side, meeting Jimi Hendrix and securing a signed copy of *The Electric Kool-Aid Acid Test* from Tom Wolfe was so cool."

"I can live with *cool,* and I'm glad you're broke from using *groovy,*" joked Apple.

"So, what was your cool number one happening from 1969?" asked Treasure.

"You mean besides the one from Richard Nixon and his tricky dick?"

"I believe you mean Tricky Dicky, sweetie, my little soul sister."

"Then I would have to say Bob Marley, Sly Stone, Richie Havens, and that Wisconsin chick, Golda Meir, becoming the Israeli prime minister. We'll see how she stacks up against the new guy of the PLO, Yasser Arafat."

"You're so damn prodigious, Apple. You should have been born in a different generation."

Apple had met Treasure in 1963 while working in the Peace Corps. Her name was Betty Gates then, but through the hippie movement and other influencing circumstances, she had her name officially changed—but illegally documented—to Treasure Freeze. They met at an American-sponsored orphanage in Mexico City. Treasure's father was a Mexican diplomat who lusted after the young, blonde, freedom-seeking hippie women who migrated through

Mexico on journeys of discovery. Most of them continued on to South America from where Apple had just returned.

Her mother, allegedly seeking treasures of the human kind, met one. Through free love, she created a love child. The mother tried to raise her child, but the father never claimed her. The result was a ten-year-old homeless child. The orphanage had no knowledge concerning the whereabouts of her mother. She had dropped her off claiming to have found her, but she had too much knowledge about the child to be totally believable. Treasure claimed to be part of the scam. She was instructed by the mother to play along so they could get food and clothing. The mother never returned.

Apple had been visiting orphanages throughout South America even though her Peace Corps assignments were not related. She joined as part of the first Peace Corps group after President Kennedy created it in 1961. She decided not to accept the flight back after her tour of duty, opting to hitchhike instead. What home, she wasn't sure of.

Life is what happens when you are making plans, Apple would often remind herself. Helping people was the goal—a voice and a helping hand for the disenfranchised—but nothing ever went smoothly. Treasure must be part of the plan. A plan that wasn't fully developed and might never be. Life is the journey, not the ending to one.

Offering services for a warm meal and bed, Apple was allowed to temporarily work and stay at the orphanage. Believing she saw characteristics of herself in Treasure, they bonded and decided to continue the journey together.

Purchasing a new identity was not difficult, especially in Mexico. Treasure's Mexican citizenship made the process even easier. However, if needed, Apple had developed many connections in the underworld who could quickly and cheaply produce the necessary identification. They did argue about the name. Treasure was chosen because her mother was somewhat searching for such. *And Freeze? Who the hell knows why a ten-year-old would choose such a name?*

Treasure was being ten years old when they met, and she reminded Apple of her Tulsa days. She was almost as independent as Apple had been at that age. She certainly had the right attitude. Treasure had intelligence and independence.

They were living in a small two-bedroom, wood-framed house on a hillside overlooking Los Angeles. With two palm trees and no grass in the front yard, the home looked like a thousand others in their sprawling neighborhood. Apple liked the anonymity of her current home. Not wishing to bring too much attention to herself, she struggled with Treasure's propensity toward loud music, psychedelic lights, and hanging glass beads. Apple appreciated the current youth culture but not to extremes. The only extreme for Apple was hair. She enjoyed the freedom of the Afro; in fact, larger was better. Treasure loved picking at the Afro and sometimes spraying it different colors.

The two orphans may have been intellectually and spiritually connected, but their appearances held an extreme contrast. Apple was five-foot-eight, muscular, and darker than most blacks. Treasure was barely five feet with long blonde hair and blue eyes. Her father's Mexican brown skin gave her a terminal tanned appearance. Of course there was a huge difference in age. Apple was now fifty-eight but did not appear a day over twenty. Treasure was sixteen but could be mistaken for twenty.

When they first met and made their journey to California, Apple carefully chose her words and evaded any dialogue about her own history. Explaining to Treasure about surviving a race riot, being a hobo, attending college, and having killed was not something Apple cherished. She did explain her Peace Corps years—but not the dark side of those adventurous years. She didn't explain her reason for joining the Peace Corps and volunteering for assignments to South America. She had held hopes of finding more Spirit Walkers.

Having studied ancient Indian tribes at the University of Chicago and acquiring degrees in history and American literature,

Apple concentrated her efforts on uncovering the secret tribe or society Bobby and Jesse spoke of. She had settled in Chicago after leaving Tulsa, however, she did make a few stops along her journey. She spent some time in Saint Louis before being detained on suspicion of murder. However, despite the evidence, the authorities didn't believe a young girl could have mutilated the deceased. A few weeks later while, rummaging through the trash in Kansas City, she read about the police making a connection between the Saint Louis killing and two similar cases in Tulsa. Apple knew the cases were not similar. The Tulsa killings were accidents when she still did not know or understand her strength. The last killing was purposely committed.

She had just arrived in Saint Louis after hitching rides on trains and walking when no other form of transportation was forthcoming. He was recruiting workers from dock stations along the Mississippi River when they met.

"With a good scrubbing, cutting those pigtails and a little makeup, you will be just right. You see—I find workers for the docks, railroad, mines, farms, but you have potential to make some real money." This is what the fat-bellied white man with a straw hat and red, white, and blue suspenders said to Apple when she was caught as a stowaway and dragged, screaming, off the boxcar.

Her departure with Mr. Clump, as he called himself, was both voluntary and coerced. Mr. Clump was well read and had understood Oklahoma authorities might be looking for a young, strapping black girl like her. Many blacks left Tulsa after the riot, so it was not unusual to see orphaned boys and girls heading north and east. However, since he suggested she might be the one they were looking for, she took his inference as buying his silence if she went with him.

Her job was to stand on the street and solicit attendance at selected speakeasies that specialized in blues music. It was an easy job once she learned how to deflect all the men's advances toward her. *Momma says I have one of them venereal diseases too. And tuberculosis runs in my family.* Of course, there was always that stupid or crazy man who just did not give a damn and kept trying.

Apple lived above one of the bars owned by Mr. Clump. Two other women lived in the same one-bedroom apartment. The other two satisfied customers when they wanted to do more than live the blues vicariously through music. Apple learned to sleep during the day and work at night. Mr. Clump actually became somewhat of a friend. He was demanding but would bring her books he had traded for other worthy items. He was a scavenger and player about the east end of Saint Louis. Apple had to provide a sampling of her physical strength to her two roommates only once. After that, they no longer complained about her books taking up too much space. Mr. Clump did dock her pay for a week because one of the roommates was unable to provide her services with a broken nose and arm. Apple said she was sorry but figured a lesson had been learned for all involved. At least she could differentiate between lethal and nonlethal strikes.

Apple became restless after six months in Saint Louis. She had saved enough money to avoid having to relive the life of a hobo—even if it was just for a one-way ticket to the next large city. She had already decided being able to get lost and blend into a large city was to her advantage. She also made friends with her roommates and several other women in the area who would pay her for teaching them to read. Some would also bring their children by for a quick reading lesson. During one of these lessons, the police ended her stay in Saint Louis.

Apple had been feeling sick for the first time in her life. She was throwing up everything she tried to eat and feeling weak. Maybe her gifts had an expiration date. Her hearing was no longer acute, and she could not read in the dark. She figured the illness was sapping her strength or the gift was expiring. She thought the gift would eventually fade since she didn't go through the ritual or drink the same concoction as Bobby and Jesse.

Ruby, a mixed-blood waitress from the corner bar, had brought her child for a reading lesson when one of the roommates had a customer show up. Tina was not present, and the intoxicated customer demanded his usual quick satisfaction. At first, he attempted to induce Apple to provide services, but her sickness and flash of yellow eyes quickly deterred him. She figured he was too drunk to question why her brown eyes turned yellow. He then tried to convince Ruby by offering an advance fee for possible additional encounters, assuming Ruby would enjoy the experience. He became agitated and belligerent when she declined his most unworthy offer.

Apple could sense the situation was deteriorating quickly and tried to ensure the frustrated customer he could come back later when Tina got home. He would not take no for an answer and grabbed Ruby's daughter. Mary was no more than eight years old. He backhanded Ruby, knocking her across the room, while holding Mary by a handful of her black hair. Apple reacted quickly by striking him in the chest with a closed fist. Startled, he glared at Apple, and then struck her in the nose with the full force of his flying fist. Apple bounced off the wall and fell to the hardwood floor.

Two things surprised her: her punch had not fazed him, and his punch had broken her nose and almost knocked her unconscious. It had been the first injury since her jaw was broken down by the Arkansas River in Tulsa, and her gift had healed it quickly. She attempted to lift herself off the floor when she felt his foot kick her in the ribs.

"Forget this little bitch. I will just take you!" He threw Mary toward her mother in the corner. He reached down, picked up Apple, and flung her like a rag doll onto the rickety bed. His weight was almost unbearable as he jumped on top of her. Apple could not move the massive man. He slapped her again and again until she surmised that being still would stop the assault. Kissing her neck, he attempted to tear off her clothes. Apple took the abuse because she did not wish to get lethal in front of them. She believed she could resolve the situation without force.

"Get out of here now!" Apple screamed at Ruby and Mary. They scrambled out the door.

Apple didn't discover until much later why she did what she did next. She bit down on the assailant's neck with all her strength. He screamed and started punching her in the ribs with both fists. She locked her legs around his waist and pulled him back down on her when he tried to rise, never letting go of his neck. His blood dripped in her mouth and slid down her throat. A flashback to the exhilaration she received from tasting the human blood in Tulsa overwhelmed her. She started sucking to draw his blood in quicker. She was consumed with sucking and drinking the man's blood. His arms flailed about, striking all portions of her body, but she felt nothing.

The polished blade shimmered from what little sunlight escaped through the window. She saw the knife appear from his waistband but was helpless to block it. Her focus was on sucking the blood out of this man. She sensed his weakness under her teeth. Maybe this was his last desperate attempt to free himself. With a last gasp of effort to survive, he struck. Once, twice and then a third knife struck her left side, but she felt nothing.

His face had turned from beet red to clam white. Apple rolled from under her assailant and viewed the mouth-sized wound on his neck. She bent over and took a closer look. The wound appeared as if an animal had chewed its way through his skin and tore his jugular vein away from the neck. The vein resembled a water hose hanging over a fence. Looking down at herself, she noticed her entire body was covered with blood, and there were three gaping wounds in her side. She stuck a finger in the lowest wound and was surprised to see she was not bleeding.

"Surprising," she whispered to herself. "I am not feeling sick anymore. As a matter of fact, I never felt better."

Apple walked to the bathroom mirror, and with just a little pressure, bent her nose enough to make it appear straight for a while.

The room was a mess; blood was everywhere, including hers and probably some of Ruby's and Mary's. She stripped off her clothes, washed the blood from her body, and started to dress in clean clothes. She discovered her knife wounds were gone. All that remained was scar tissue, slightly lighter than her normal skin.

Apple grabbed a bag and started packing. There were few possessions: some clothes, her diary, and several unread books. She ran down the street, hoping to make it to the train yards before anyone found the body. She traveled about three blocks before police, accompanied by Ruby and Mary, met her. Apple created a story consisting of an attempted rape and an unknown hero who had rescued her. The police would not allow her to proceed down the road. They accompanied her back to the scene of the crime. One of the police officers puked wildly upon seeing the crime scene. Apple laughed while thinking how the officer was in the wrong business.

Dishonesty, lying, and deceit must have been part of her gift. Obviously, the police had doubts concerning her entire story, but they appeared to believe her on the key issue: her claim of innocence. She knew the ranking officer could not comprehend the possibility that this young girl could have done so much damage to a human body.

Apple explained how she had packed quickly, fearing the killer would return for her. Her description of the killer was based on a hobo she had met on one of her train rides. The police advised her not to leave town, but as soon as dark arrived, she was on the next train north.

Chicago was the largest city she had ever experienced. Cars and people were everywhere, scurrying about with no apparent rhyme or reason. She knew it was the place for her as soon as she departed the train. The train yard made the one in Saint Louis appear miniature. The train ride allowed her to forget what she had left behind. She felt invincible; a new life would start there. Based upon what she had learned from her previous employer, locating employment would be a snap.

Her looks and her ability to be so expressive with her eyes easily landed her a job at a speakeasy just south of the intersection of Wacker Street and Michigan Avenue. She worked there for several years, tending bar, waiting tables, and running errands for local mobsters. Because she was black, she and her bosses knew she would never be given more responsibility than she already had within the organization.

The mobsters and so-called legitimate businessmen who ran and invested in a cluster of speakeasies were quickly impressed with her. She was impressed with how open these clubs were. In Saint Louis, speakeasies were more hush-hush, and customers had to know someone to gain entrance. Here, anything and everything went.

They recognized her strength and determination, but there was always something else they just could not put their fingers on. They used her attractiveness to attract black and white men into their clubs. Apple would work several nights in the black end of town and then work several days where all the white mobsters hung out. She truly immersed herself in the role of eye candy for the patrons. Tips alone allowed her to buy the finest clothing and jewelry on Michigan Avenue. She upgraded her apartment location three times in one year.

She learned a lot from her mobster friends, employers, and regular patrons. She learned how to make fake identifications, which would become extremely helpful in years to follow. She learned how to gamble and invest. She learned the law of supply and demand. Booze, sex, gambling, and murder were the hot consumer items of the day.

The books made Chicago appear to be heaven. Books and libraries were everywhere. In addition to books, she could go to school. With some assistance, she created a high school diploma and a partial college transcript. Also, with documentation she was Catholic, she enrolled in DePaul University. She found with the correct blood-feeding schedule, she could operate with only two or three hours sleep for every forty-eight hours. This allowed her to attend college and continue her club employment.

Feeding is what she came to call her hunger for blood, which became insatiable after six weeks. She would have no choice but to kill to renew her gifts. If an opportunity availed itself, she would certainly take full advantage of it. One of the reasons she stayed in the speakeasy business was the availability of fresh blood. She rarely had to kill on her own and even more rarely had to wait the full six weeks. At a minimum of once per month, some poor fool would say the wrong thing or be unable to pay his bar debts. He would find himself beaten unconscious in the back alley. Apple observed these beatings and waited until everyone departed. If they were still alive, she finished them off by tearing into their necks and quenching her hunger. She realized very quickly how blood from those already dead for a while was unacceptable. She would become deathly ill if one drop entered her stomach. If this had not been the case, she could have fed daily as murders happened daily in the neighborhoods she worked in. She followed her senses because there were those few unfortunate victims she could not feed from. Their blood carried sickness. Why take a chance? There wouldn't be this ability to detect diseases if it weren't for a good reason.

John Torrio became the new owner of the speakeasies where Apple worked. He took a quick liking to her. He would always leave her huge tips and eventually promoted her to club manager of one of his all-black speakeasies. It was at this club where she was introduced to one of Mr. Torrio's lieutenants. His name was Al Capone.

Apple did not care for Capone, and the feeling was mutual. Capone complained to Torrio how he should not trust this black witch. Apple had made a mistake one night when Capone was drunk at the club and running off good-paying customers. She calmly placed a hand on his shoulder and asked him to calm down. He turned and slapped her with the back of his hand. He was surprised when his hardest slap did not cause her to step backward or even flinch. Apple did, however, lose control for a second and flashed her yellow eyes at him. Her eyes flashed off his sweaty, polished forehead.

"Shit!" Apple screamed, knowing the inability to control her eyes would someday cause trouble.

Capone stood as if he had seen a ghost. "I knew it. I knew it, you fucking witch!" Capone grabbed his hat off the bar and stormed out the back door.

Several of Apple's coworkers warned her to leave town immediately, but she wouldn't entertain the thought. Chicago was perfect for her. Books, money, and blood availability without really having to kill anyone who wasn't going to die anyway were enough reasons to stay. Besides, Mr. Torrio would not allow one of his lieutenants to snuff her out.

Apple was correct. Weeks passed, and every time she would cross Capone's path, he would not even look at her. Mr. Torrio had only spoken to her once about the Capone incident. He said she should stay away from Capone because he was crazy, but Capone required crazy people do certain things in his business.

"Darling Apple," Torrio said. "Capone ain't right in the head. That scar on his head under his hat messed him up."

She understood two things from what Torrio had told her. The first and most important was Capone certainly was more valuable than she was; secondly, Capone was crazy. Everyone already knew he was crazy, but Apple had a difficult time labeling someone as crazy, considering the life she was living.

One day the news became very unpleasant for Apple. Al Capone was now the new boss, having replaced John Torrio. Apple decided not to leave town and to take her chances. She had the gift to protect herself; besides, Capone surely had forgotten her yellow eyes. They could both live in this town. It was plenty big for both of them. Capone would be too busy running the business to find time to fuck with a little Negro girl from Oklahoma.

Wrong. The killings started quickly after Capone's takeover. Anyone who had ever had a harsh word with Capone was being killed. Apple did not go to work for several days and stayed locked in her eighth-floor apartment. She had been studying atlases and facts about other cities. Not sure where she would go next, she found the studying entertaining and distracting. She felt comfortable Capone wouldn't come looking for her, but danger would be present if she met him or his goons on the street or at work. Having recently quenched her hunger, Apple stayed locked in her apartment. This allowed her to read many books. Besides, she had stuffed her mattress with enough money to last her for many years.

On a windy, snowy night, her gift allowed footsteps coming up the fire escape to resonate in her ears. She heard whispers as she sat quietly with legs crossed, naked in the middle of her bed. Her room was kept toasty warm in the winter. The enjoyment of being naked for days while locked in her apartment was consummate pleasure. She heard footsteps walking the stairs two flights down. *Why send so many to kill me? Does he know what I am?* She glanced out the window toward the fire escape. Huge snowflakes reminded her of ashes and soot raining down on her when she and the little white boy ran through the riot-torn streets of Tulsa.

Her muscles tensed and hardened as she quickly slipped on a shirt and skirt. She reached under the bed and brandished a Thompson machine gun given to her by Torrio. She had had only one firing lesson, but she remembered all the details. She had a few rounds loaded and never thought of having to shoot anyone.

Bullets pierced the door and embedded in her dresser. Firing back through the door, she heard a man scream and another fall hard to the hall floor.

"The bitch got a gun!" one of the men yelled.

"Roberto is hit!" cried another.

The smell of blood quickly flared her nostrils. Turning toward the window overlooking the fire escape, she blindly fired again. She only succeeded in shattering the window and bouncing a few rounds off the metal fire escape railing.

One bullet entered her thigh, and another slammed into her right shoulder. Two men on the fire escape were returning her fire. They had arrived unnoticed. She squeezed the trigger again, but nothing happened. *Damn. I am out of ammo.* She threw the Thompson at the two, striking one of them in the chest. He fell over the rail and landed in the deep snow below. The second assailant on the fire escape, having momentarily hesitated, raised his weapon to fire. His hesitation killed him.

Apple swiftly moved across the room and was standing on the fire escape, just a few feet away from him. She grabbed him and tore out his throat. *What a waste. I am not hungry.* A bullet entered her back. One of the men at the front door had successfully broken through the door. Without turning, she jumped down eight stories to the ground.

Three more men entered her room and ran down the fire escape. Apple buried herself in the snow, and the men ran past, firing randomly up and down the alley.

"Did you see that shit?" one of the assailants yelled.

"Hell, yes. Motherfucker dropped eight stories and kept running. She should be fucking dead."

"Capone said she was a goddamn witch or something like that," responded another.

At the bottom of the stairs, they discovered their dead associate. Another associate hung from the third-story railing. His fall had been caught by someone's makeshift clothesline. His head was barely connected to his torso by bits of muscle and vertebrae.

The three men backed up against one another to form a tight circle. None wanted to show their true fear. A cat ran down the alley, and all three immediately shot, sending it to cat heaven.

"Dumbass, stop firing! Listen for her. She is here somewhere," one of the men said.

They were shooting into the snow. Apple could feel her wounds healing, but she did not want to take the chance of being shot too many times so quickly. She remembered how Bobby and Jesse did not have enough time to use the full strength of their gift.

When Apple vacated her hiding place, the men fired in her direction, but they were too slow. With fingernails growing and arms striking, Apple tore into the three. Their weapons fired into the ground, sky, and walls; no rounds struck her. Her left hand struck one man's throat, and the other hand tore the heart from another. They fell to the soft white snow without a sound. The third stood shaking and began pissing himself. Apple was ready to strike him dead, but she stopped.

The man's teeth were chattering, and Apple started to laugh. "What a big, bad, strong gangster you are," she chuckled. She poked him in the chest, causing him to fall backward.

"Don't kill me. Please don't kill me," he cried.

Apple straddled her assailant. "How old are you?" she asked.

In a stutter that kept snowflakes from landing on his lips, he said, "I am seventeen, ma'am."

"What the hell do you think you are doing? You're just a kid with a gun." She placed her bare foot on his chest. Fearing for his life but still being a young man, he looked up Apple's dress.

"Like what you see?" she asked. The young assailant nodded.

"You want to live? You think I should spare your life?" Again he nodded.

"Get it up," Apple said.

"What?"

"I said get it up, and I will allow you to live another day."

The young man turned his head to the right and saw his fellow gangster with his heart beside him. He turned to his left and saw the throatless corpse in a pool of blood. The snow around them was speckled with red.

"Get what up?" he asked.

"Your manhood, my little gangster. Your manhood of course."

"I don't think I can," he stuttered.

"Too bad." Apple drew her hands back to deliver his death.

"Wait! Wait! Wait!" he screamed.

Apple stopped and stared down at her prey. *What a pitiful sight,* she thought. Here was a man with yellow snow between his legs—splattered blood all over his body—and thinking he could call his manhood from the dead.

"You have one minute to rise or you're dead."

"I need some help," he replied.

"What kind of help?"

"Anything. I can't concentrate with all this around me—plus it's cold as hell."

"I have given you as much help as you are going to get."

In a few seconds, his member rose from the dead. Apple was amazed by the rising and accepted full responsibility for it. Was this part of her gift or just a newfound talent?

She grabbed the young man, threw him into the snowbank, and commanded him not to move for one hour. She then ran back up to her apartment, packed her money and some belongings, and fled toward the docks. "Hell, prohibition is over anyway; it's probably time to leave town," Apple muttered to herself while walking away.

The young gangster counted down the minutes until he believed an hour passed. He was almost frozen when he crawled from the snow. A single gunshot struck him between the eyes.

"Nobody fails to follow my orders—not even you, you little fuck. Sons of bitches can't even kill one black witch." Al Capone kicked the other bodies that were now partially covered with snow.

"Check the train station. That's where she will be headed," he barked to his thugs.

Apple spent the next thirty years or so moving from one city to the next. Most of these years were spent in the north and on the East

Coast. She had to change identification and change names many times.

She chronicled all her escapades in her diaries and was careful not to allow Treasure the opportunity to find them. Besides, even if she did, it was 1969—and "everything goes" in 1969.

CHAPTER 10

Book Man

"Beware. Don't trust your eyes, for they are the whores of your senses," a beggar said to Apple and Treasure as they crossed the street.

"What did you say?" asked Apple.

"I've said it, and I ain't going to say it again," the beggar stoically replied.

Apple continued to be uncomfortable with the times. Flower children, hippies, and druggies dominated the scene. She much preferred the thirties. The fifties were too bland. She and Treasure were in San Francisco for a few days to attend a free concert by the Rolling Stones. The concert had been moved to the Altamont Speedway, and they had missed it. It was December 1969, and she had promised Treasure one last concert for the year. They voted for Big Brother and the Holding Company, but they quickly changed their minds in hopes of catching a free Stones concert.

Treasure and Apple did almost everything together. They appreciated good rock and pop music, and they dressed in bell-bottoms, tie-dyed shirts, love beads, sandals, and flowers in their hair. Even though Apple was sixty-two, she appeared no older than twenty-five. In fact, several of their friends believed Apple was even younger. Treasure, on the other hand, looked older than her age. She was sixteen but easily passed for being in her twenties. With Apple's black skin and Treasure's light skin and blonde hair, they could have been poster children for the decade.

Apple walked down the street in her tight bell-bottoms and a plaid halter top tied high enough to expose her muscular stomach, and low enough from the top to give any man brave enough a glimpse of heaven. Apple had realized several years ago that even though she aged very slowly, her body continued to develop and become stronger. She was not overly muscular like a bodybuilder, but she possessed enough muscular definition to attract attention from those who admired her animal magnetism. She walked with an aura of confidence, taking note of all who stole a moment to watch her; however, she always kept one eye on Treasure.

Apple didn't know how a sixty-two-year-old should feel or act, but she felt young and full of energy. She would forget Treasure didn't have a lifetime of experiences in her sixteen years. At times, Treasure was mature, trustworthy, and sophisticated, but at other times, she would be naïve, immature, and adolescent. No matter how hard Apple tried to mold Treasure into a sophisticated, educated young woman, nature would regain control. The result would sometimes be utter chaos.

Treasure crossed the street to sample aromas from a vendor selling the latest incense. Vendors sold everything from headbands to survival kits and marijuana cookbooks. Pushers on every corner offered LSD, mescaline, mushrooms, and other illicit items to broaden the mind. Apple had tried marijuana a few times but with no noticeable effect, but LSD was a different story. It made her eyes yellow for three days and made her skin sensitive to the light. The nastiest part was apologizing to the neighbors for running naked through their yards. One neighbor thanked her for eating all the bugs on his tomato plants.

Treasure had gained Apple's trust in being able to take care of herself, and being aware of her environment, especially when they went concert tripping. She was grounded from concerts on at least two occasions for failing astuteness tests. Apple would allow her enough rope to determine how she would cope. Such situations included getting high, saying no to a boy, and fighting a jealous girlfriend. Apple quickly surveyed the vendors and determined there were no immediate threats to Treasure. Therefore, she ducked into an antique bookstore she had been eyeing. Actually, one of the reasons she agreed to the trip was an advertisement in *Rolling Stone*. The Book Daze specialized in antique books covering the occult, witchcraft, vampires, zombies, and unexplained phenomenon.

The Book Daze was old and dusty on the outside. She entered through a broken stained glass door depicting Satan fighting angels dressed in traditional Native American garb. The floor was made of wood with seams that allowed a close view of the ground beneath it. Some of the boards in the floor were worn to the point where shoe-sized imprints had created smooth dimples. *This place has potential,* she thought.

A tall white man dressed like a cross between Jesus Christ and Sly Stone greeted her. He wore bright yellow hip-hugging, sequined bell-bottoms. An unbuttoned pink leather vest exposed a forest of chest hair. His shoulder-length hair was parted in the middle and held in place with a beaded Indian headband. A medieval medallion hung down to his belly button, and five layers of love beads hung tightly around his neck. He wore American flag tennis shoes and carried a rawhide leather satchel over his left shoulder.

"Damn, you one fine groovy chick," crooned the man.

"I'm not from the *Brady Bunch*. Give me a break and cut the lame pickup lines."

"Stop, baby. You're turning me on like a radio."

Apple turned her head toward the man and gave him a look.

He walked behind the checkout counter, lit a cigarette, and blew smoke rings toward her.

Apple followed her senses, and they told her this man was harmless and full of himself. She walked through the cluttered, dusty trails and around book stacks from the floor to almost the ceiling. The only reason the books stopped just short of the ceiling was to allow room for a massive system of worn black rubber belts and rope pulleys that turned six large ceiling fans. Mounds of dust rode on the fans as they turned just enough to move the stale air. Other walking trails went through stacks of discolored *Look* and *Life* magazines. Touching them would probably cause their destruction.

She lost herself in the books. She bagged up a couple of early American tribal histories, and every book she could find referencing Oklahoma history, spiritual leaders, and medicine men.

"Hey, not-so-groovy chick, is there anything I can help you find?"

"My God, Jesus Stone has a sense of humor," answered Apple.

"Jesus Stone? What kind of name is that all about? My name is—"

"Stop! I am not into names, especially from people I will never see again," Apple interrupted.

"Just thought I could help. I know every title in this store—and every title ever sold out of here."

"Sure, I will try you. Have you ever had anything on an ancient Indian tribe consisting of outcasts from other tribes, who were last sighted in Oklahoma? They were believed to have mystical powers to prolong life," Apple asked.

"Sure, I've heard of the Spirit Walkers," he replied.

Apple turned to face the man so quickly, a miniature tornado of dust swirled around her ankles. She was shocked and startled by his answer. She had not heard those words since the riot days. *Stunned is the word I will use in my diary tonight*, she thought. "What did you say?" she asked.

"I said Spirit Walkers. Sounded like you were describing Spirit Walkers. Yeah, that's what it sounded like."

With stern eyes and a serious expression, Apple asked, "Which book, and how much do you know?"

"Whoa. Slow down there. I only said it sounded like you were describing Spirit Walkers. I didn't say I had a book on them or anything else."

"I am not in the mood for games. I will buy any and all the books you have on this subject. Name your price."

"You know, you are very cute when you become so intense. I bet you're good in the sack," he teased.

Apple thought about just grabbing him and shaking the information out of him, and if he refused, she could always feed her gift. However, she had been trying to be more peaceful to match the generation she was living with, plus she needed to be a good example for Treasure. Additionally, she wore a sterling silver peace medallion Treasure had given her for her birthday. Apple wasn't sure when her birthday was, and it really did not matter anymore, so she just made up a date. She couldn't kill while promoting peace.

"Hey, look, I don't mean to be rude or to imply I didn't require your assistance. I have just been looking for information on myths or stories about Spirit Walkers for many years. The thought of maybe having found something, no matter how insignificant, is a great find for me."

"Yeah, we got off on the wrong foot. My humor gets me in more trouble than it should. But honestly, when you walked through that door, my heart skipped a beat. I am really in touch with myself, and I know when something is right for me, and you are right, baby."

How wrong can this guy be? Maybe with a little haircut, some decent clothes, and a better pickup line, he could have potential. *He is kind of cute,* she mused. Lost in thought of how to continue with this conversation and socialization, a check on Treasure had been forgotten. Developed gifts included abilities to accurately calculate time passage and tell time without a timepiece. Thirty-two minutes had passed since entering Book Daze. She walked past the book man—who was still waiting for her reply—but Treasure was no longer across the street. Apple concentrated on her ability to hear. Normally, she could detect and follow Treasure's voice from a mile away. There were no sounds from Treasure.

"Hey, sweet momma. Don't leave. We were just starting to thaw."

Apple extended her arm backward, palm up. The book man initially accepted this universal sign of shut up. Listening for any sound of Treasure, Apple had to maneuver her keen sense of hearing through a bombardment of sound-wave traffic. She stood motionless with her stop sign still holding off the talkative book man. He was amazed at her remarkable frozen statuette pose. *How beautiful,* he thought. *This is the most beautiful woman I have ever seen. Who cares if she is black? This is love at first sight.*

"Hey, beautiful, do you want to look a little longer, 'cause if you don't, it's time to lock up," he inquired softly. Book Daze had no set hours. It opened and closed when the book man felt like it. Today he felt like closing right about now. This would provide an opportunity to maybe hang out with this beautiful angel who had graced the steps of his store.

"Oh, you are going to do a great deal more than just allow me to look at your books. You're going to tell me all you know about Spirit Walkers, which could lead to fulfilling both of our fantasies," Apple demurely responded. *There,* she thought, *that should keep him interested.*

Wow, he thought, *this chick is warm for my form.*

"Wait for me please. I will be back," requested Apple seductively.

"Let it be said, let it be done," he responded, attempting to quote a line from *The King and I.* "Hey, some wacky dude dressed like a G-man came by about a year or so ago and just gave me a book with references to Spirit Walkers. He said to let him know if anyone ever bought it or asked about such a topic. I'm supposed to call him ... anyway, I have his number somewhere on a card he left."

Apple hurried down the street, focusing on her hearing and sense of smell. For the first time, she was glad Treasure preferred that damn awful-smelling Tabu perfume. She had complained about its strong odor to Treasure before. "Treasure," she would say, "moderation and subtleties are the keys to coolness, and Tabu violates both." She located a faint trail of Tabu and followed it as it wrapped around street vendors, across two streets, past a dozen bars, and through a back alley to a parking lot. There, among a hundred motorcycles and corresponding men with Hell's Angels scrolled across the backs of their leather jackets, she sensed Treasure.

Apple couldn't see or hear Treasure through the crowd and dreadful noise of idling Harley Davidsons, but she knew she was somewhere in this crowd. She cautiously approached the crowd, hoping she could extract Treasure without making a scene. This hope was quickly dashed. A drunken Angel grabbed her by the arm and attempted to kiss her with a beer-soaked mouth. Survival instincts demanded something much less than lethal force. It wouldn't be cool to take out a few of these gangsters—certainly not in broad daylight with so many witnesses. Besides, Treasure might get hurt.

"Sorry, man. I am already spoken for. My big daddy is around here somewhere," responded Apple.

"Hey, that's cool. But if it don't work for you, you are one hot black fox. I will be waiting."

"Sure, I will keep you in mind," she coyly responded.

Batting her eyes, and acting as timid and sweet as possible, Apple meandered her way through the crowd. There was the occasional grope and grab at her ass and breasts, but nothing serious enough to delay her mission. She pushed her way through a circle of Hell's Angels. Treasure was standing on a bumper of an old Volkswagen bus. As Apple worked her way closer, she saw that Treasure was actually pinned against the Volkswagen hood. She appeared to have been backing up to create a safer distance from her pursuers. Apple detected a frightened and panicked look in Treasure's eyes. Treasure was shuffling her feet and trying to push the bus.

"Oops, got to go. There's my mom," Treasure eagerly advised her admirers. Treasure scooted off the bus hood but was quickly hoisted back up by a burly, leather-clad Angel. He had "Hells Angels Frisco" tattooed across both biceps.

"You ain't goin' anywhere, little lady. Hell, this soul sister is your momma? She looks more like your fuckin' evil twin." He laughed while heads turned to survey Apple.

"No need for trouble, man. I just want to get my girl and go about our business. So if you will pretty please, step aside, we will be on our way," Apple said.

"Pretty please, really. You girls must be an item, 'cause you damn sure aren't mom and child, and surely not sisters. Come on over here and show us some of that girly action love you types like to do. Now, if you're not homos, then prove it." The comments excited the crowd. They started chanting, "Show us, show us, show us!"

Apple struggled with her desire to kill this self-appointed leader and make an example out of him in the worst way. She had no doubt the carnage and bodily destruction she was thinking of would turn the others into fleeing cowards. However, she knew she could not expect to kill and get away with it like she did in Tulsa, Chicago, and other cities. This was a different age. Criminal investigations were more sophisticated. However, if this situation were at night with few witnesses, she would not have hesitated to kill them all.

"Like I said, I don't want any trouble here. I just want to take my girl and leave," Apple reiterated.

"I don't think you understand. We found the little bitch first, and we aren't through with her. So fuck the hell off!"

"Excuse me, Mr. Dipshit. I can call you Mr. Dipshit, can't I? We have not formally been introduced. I have tried to be respectful of this situation, but you, my friend, are being difficult. I am going to take my girl and peacefully walk out of here. Okay?" Apple walked around the large, mouthy Angel and stood beside Treasure. She could feel the gifts inside her, beseeching for playtime. She had felt these aches before, but years of practice and experience had taught her that with patience, they would subside.

"Look, you fucking black bitch whore. You just talked yourself into a good little whipping. You had your chance to leave but blew it, babe. Now, me and the boys are just going to have a little fun with you and your little white sister, right here and right now."

Apple heard the sound of leather rubbing leather as the gang eased forward, forming a tight circle. She saw some of the women on the shoulders of their men, encouraging the proposed action. Apple had learned from the Chicago mobsters that a good defense is a *hesitation-absence offense.* She had already hesitated too much by not killing the son of a bitch when she was called a black bitch. No one had called her that in decades. Such language brought back harsh memories from Tulsa. The gift was imploring her to kill and kill now. Her mind was racing as the circle of leather moved closer. They were taunting her. She grabbed Treasure's hand, which was wet and shaking. She could feel Treasure's young hand racing with blood. *Kill,* she thought. *I will have to kill all of them. Leave no witnesses.*

"Hey, soul sister, come get some of this," an Angel said.

Mr. Dipshit stepped forward. With a moment that was only witnessed as a blur, Apple struck. He grabbed for his throat, but it was too late. Apple's hand had already been there and departed. He grabbed where the front of his throat used to be. Blood splattered those closest to him. He fell to his knees. Then his head fell forward. Then a thud as face kissed asphalt. The others quickly brandished knives, guns, chains, and other weapons. Apple reached for the one who was yelling nagger but missed his throat. An ear in her hand was a consolation prize. The gifts were in complete control of her.

"This nagger got your ear, motherfucker," a female Angel screamed.

"She's a fucking demon!" cried one of the crowd's bravest.

"Kill the fucking whore!" screamed another.

What a fool I am. I might survive now, but Treasure will certainly be killed. In defiance, she threw skin left from Dipshit's throat at the crowd. She knew their fate would be arriving in a few seconds. She heard the cocking of shotguns and saw the flashing of knife metal reflecting her yellow eyes.

A roar started from the back of the crowd, then screaming. She heard honking and felt the vibrations of a powerful engine roaring through the crowd. Weapons turned away from her and started firing toward a faded, three-tone green convertible Chevy Camaro. It tore through the crowd, running over anyone in its path. The driver was fishtailing and cutting donuts through the crowd. The car slid to a stop after running over Dipshit's corpse.

"Get in now! Now!" yelled book man.

Apple could not believe her eyes. It was the hippie bookstore owner. Without hesitation, Apple grabbed Treasure, lifted her off her feet, and slammed her into the backseat. The car sped away, slinging loose gravel at those brave enough to give chase. The book man shifted to second from third gear, then back to third as they spun onto the street. He shifted again, and the pistol grip of his Hurst Competition shifter broke off. He shifted again, causing the jagged shifter to cut into his hand. Within seconds, they were going 120 miles per hour, leaving their assailants in a wake of air.

No one spoke as they raced over the hills. They were soon miles away from the city. Apple knew they were damn lucky the police had not stopped them as they fled the scene of the crime. Turning onto a sandy country road lined by a heavy overgrowth of trees and scrubs, they sped over the first hill and parked behind a dilapidated barn. Time froze as all three of them waited to see who was going to speak first.

"It wasn't my fault, Apple. I just wanted to get a closer look at the choppers, and they would not let me leave," Treasure exclaimed.

"Shit, man, you killed him, didn't you?" The book man was shaking.

Apple did not respond to either of them. A cavalcade of thought was invading her consciousness. There were witnesses this time. Forensics would be much better than in past decades. She had never made a mistake like that in front of so many witnesses in daylight hours. Sure, she had replenished her gift with blood as necessary over the years, but she had always been careful to create the illusion of accidental deaths so they could never be attributed to her. *Damn … Treasure had witnessed this kill.*

"Hey, gorgeous, what do we do now? And what about those crazy yellow cat eyes? What's that all about? Man, are those real? Now that's cool, man. Can you teach me that?"

"We are not going to do anything. I thank you for the ride, but Treasure and I are leaving." Apple didn't take the time to open the car door. She simply leaped out of the car followed by Treasure.

"Where do you think you are going? You never answered my question, but I do believe you just a killed a man. How far do you think you will get? A beautiful black sister looking like the model who just stepped out of my black light poster of Foxy Brown, and a blonde Hollywood starlet look-alike. How far do you think you will get before the cops catch up to you?" Sweat drizzled down his face. "Man, look at my hand."

"Apple, you did kill that man, didn't you?" Treasure whispered.

"I'm sure I did. His life or ours, and I made a choice for our lives to continue." Apple sat on the car hood and stared down the road.

"Apple, thank you," offered Treasure.

Apple did not know how to respond. Treasure now knew her capabilities. Would she start asking questions related to the manner of the killing—or did she possess coping skills that I used as a child in Tulsa? All I really wanted to do was raise this child, experience the relationship, and move on before my lack of aging caused unanswerable questions. *Shit, now I have ruined it.*

Staring at the ground, and without looking at him, Apple asked, "Where in the hell did you come from, book man?"

"I was born and raised in Santa Fe, how about you?"

"No, not where you were born. I mean, how did you know we were in trouble, and why get involved?"

"Baby, it was love at first sight. When I saw you walk out of the store, I locked up and followed you, hoping to convince you to have dinner with me. You ended up in that parking lot where my Z was parked. Then I saw the shit coming down and thought you might need some help. Guess you did, huh?"

"As a matter of fact, I did have the situation under control."

"Yeah, sure, whatever you say." The book man pointed at Apple's stomach.

Noticing thick, dried blood encrusted around her belly button and upper chest, she tried to cover it. She wasn't sure all the blood was hers. Her body could have been cut or stabbed when reaching to tear the assailant's neck. She wasn't sure because there had been other confrontations where she realized later she had been injured. She had determined her ability to heal was dependent on the time from her last gift replenishing. Therefore, there was a distinct possibility she had been wounded and already healed.

Treasure gazed upward. "Apple, I have rewound this in my head again, and it does not make any sense. How could you do that? I don't mean kill but how you killed. I didn't even see your hands move, but I felt the blood splatter across my face. If I learn karate or something like that, could I do it too?"

"Yeah, love of my life. Give us your usual succinctness on this one." The book man was trying to get a 4-track out of his stereo. "Damn, Grateful Dead would sound good right about now."

"It was just a martial arts move I learned. How was I supposed to know the man had a weak throat? He should have taken better care of himself. Must have been his sinful lifestyle." Treasure and the book man looked at Apple, trying to ascertain if she was serious or just displaying some rare nervous humor.

"I did what I did, and that's it. Enough already," commanded Apple.

"Okay, we need a plan. Like it or not, we are all in this together—or at least two of us are. Treasure was a victim, and you and I are what they call codefendants. I am sure every cop in town is looking for a Camaro Z with a 'Hook 'Em, Hippies' bumper sticker," the book man said.

"It's not the cops you should be worried about," Apple said. "The Hell's Angels will do much worse to you. You were just my savior coming to rescue me—not in a shield of armor, but more of a white knight in a very recognizable car." Apple took his hand in hers and licked the blood off his gear-shifting hand. *Not bad,* she thought.

"Yes, and I would do it again. Here I am, Sabin Brown, at your service. However, for now, I suggest we sneak back to my place, gather up some stuff, and hide out until things cool down."

"Sounds like you watch a lot of television cop shows," interjected Treasure.

"Never watch television. So many books in my store, and such a short life to read them all."

Similar, Apple thought. She had remembered thinking the same thing about all books and life. With her gift, she would have more time to read than normal humans.

"Don't forget, Sabin, we have that little subject matter of Spirit Walkers to discuss. I did hear what you were shouting as I left the store, and I may be more concerned about a G-man than the Hell's Angels."

"Sure, love of my life, no problem, whatever you say," cooed Sabin.

They proceeded back to the bookstore. Sabin resided in a loft above the store; however, the store was in flames. Firemen were making sure the flames did not spread to adjacent buildings. Sabin slammed the brakes, stopping the car in the middle of the road. Leaving Apple and Treasure, he ran to his store and was immediately wrestled to the ground by two police officers.

"Man, that's my bookstore that's on fire!" Sabin yelled.

The officers assured him everything that could be done had been done. The store was totally engulfed in flames when they arrived, and nothing could be done to save anything. They also informed him foul play was suspected. One officer explained how the broken bottles and smell of gasoline on the sidewalk were dead giveaways to arson.

Sabin watched in disbelief as the roof crashed in. Apple moved the car across the street and concentrated on her listening gift. The police were questioning Sabin about any enemies who would wish to do him harm. When the police were through with their questioning, Apple was surprised and pleased to hear Sabin asking a few questions of the police.

Sabin asked if there had been any other crimes reported in the neighborhood today. The police said no, but they had increased their visibility in the area due to complaints of Hell's Angels and a large-scale fight at a parking lot down the street. Sabin inquired if anyone had been hurt in the fight. A large amount of blood was found in the area, but there were no reports of injuries. Hell's Angels usually took care of their own, and this time would be no different.

"I would not want to be in anyone's shoes who fought with them today," one officer commented.

"Being in prison might be slightly safer than being on the street with a Hell's Angel contract out on you. At least you might receive protection from your cellmate. Of course you have to pay. Get my drift, hippie?" joked another officer.

Apple was cautiously optimistic. Maybe those damn Angels didn't have any intention of reporting her kill. When Sabin was allowed to leave and return to the car, she breathed a sigh of relief.

Sabin started to explain what the police had said, but Apple assured him she had heard the conversation. Sabin started to question how that was possible but retreated back to his hippie attitude. "Oh, to hell with it all. I did it once. I can start over again, but somewhere else this time. Of course, insurance would have been nice, but premiums are just a way to feed the man."

Treasure enjoyed Sabin's hippie's attitude, but Apple had little use for it. She did, however, think Sabin could be cute in the proper place and time. She would have to clean him up a bit. She would try to keep him around for a while to see just how much he knew about Spirit Walkers, and she needed information on the G-man who brought the book to Sabin's store.

CHAPTER 11

Mystery Man

Time passed very slowly after the killing in San Francisco. Sabin, as agreed, stayed in San Francisco just long enough to tie up loose ends related to the fire. He also confirmed no reports of a killing by a beautiful black woman on the date in question. However, he did confirm through his network of hippie bookworms that the Hell's Angels were looking for two chicks: one black and dangerous, one blonde and skinny. They were also looking for a drugged-out, crazy hippie in a Camaro. The Angels had been sidetracked by a killing at the Rolling Stones concert where they were allegedly providing security for Mick and the boys. The police were hauling all Angels in for questioning. This distraction allowed Sabin to achieve what required accomplishing, with only a small amount of hide-and-seek with local Angels. He did have enough sense to sell the getaway car.

Thirty days after their first meeting, Sabin arrived at the home of Apple and Treasure, driving his new Malibu Super Sport 396 that Apple had loaned him the money for. It was dark green with a pistol-grip shifter to go with the four-on-the-floor gearbox. No air conditioner, for who in their right mind would allow such a thing to drain the power of a muscle car. Where she came up with the $3,700 was an unsolved mystery to him, but he just accepted it for what it was, a mystery. They had invited him to stay with them. Treasure suggested they offer him a place to live and an opportunity to start over in the Los Angeles area. Apple, out of a need to show gratitude and set an example for Treasure, agreed. Apple agreed to the offer even though she was still unconvinced Sabin's rescue had been necessary.

Apple sought to feed her gift before Sabin arrived, but the opportunity did not avail itself. She had learned many unique ways to replenish the gift in the last few years. Her favorite was to locate the unlucky few who could not control their drug intake at local concert venues or clubs. Finding such conditioned persons, if they were not already unconscious, she would assist them to unconsciousness through additional drug usage encouragement or a stiff jolt to the chin, whichever was easiest. The goal was for them to find the sandman. She would cut their wrists or use some other method of easy vein access to drink their blood while being careful not to kill them. If everything went well, her victims would wake up weak, a little pale, and in the need of a stitch or two. Also, if everything went smoothly, she would not experience a high from the drugs in their blood. That's not to say there was not a sporadic kill every now and then. Kills always involved circumstantial issues.

Her last kill was almost two years ago. One evening she witnessed a man beating a woman while she was driving home. She could not tolerate a man hitting a woman. She had stopped several previous incidents without resorting to extreme violence; however, this instance went south in a hurry. She instructed the man to cease and move on—or pick on someone his own size. He turned and caught Apple by surprise with a tire tool to the head. She fell to the ground. She determined later that such an unexpected blow could actually knock her out. Without time for the gift to prepare the body, she was momentarily mortal. The dizziness from the blow lasted only a second. However, a second was only what the gift required to respond with extreme prejudice. He was dead in an instant, introduced to death with one powerful blow. She had drunk blood from a partier just a few days previously, so she did not require blood from this kill. However, she drank from vengeance, and his blood tasted the sweetest. After this kill, Apple made a promise to herself not to become a blood-drinking vigilante.

Apple felt a twinge of obligation to Sabin but not enough to willingly donate her bedroom for his temporary usage. Treasure believed compromise was the art of giving, so she moved into Apple's room.

Buffalo Springfield and Jefferson Airplane posters loosely tacked to the wall caused the first major disagreement. Surprisingly, Treasure had the issue when Sabin replaced two of her concert posters with these two. She explained the bedroom was his to use, but she forbid him the option of redecorating. There was really nothing to redecorate. A room has to be decorated first before it can be redecorated. This room was a blank canvas for creating if only Apple would allow.

Sabin understood Apple's need for privacy and aloneness. He and Treasure would sometimes go for long drives or eat out in an effort to allow Apple time alone. He assured Apple that she should not confuse his assistance with her need to have alone time. He did have a need and a desire to make love to her. She was actually thankful he was pursuing her. This kept her from worrying about his time alone with Treasure. Being protective of Treasure was an understatement. She would kill anyone who would bring harm to her.

Two months passed without any indication of Hell's Angels locating them. Still, no one in the household took any chances. They even joked about how looking over their shoulders had become second nature—and how driving with one eye affixed on the rearview mirror was mandatory. However, no one was going to become too relaxed for a long time.

Apple quit her job at a restaurant when part-time work as a librarian at UCLA became full-time. She handled her UCLA interview so well that no one cared to verify her credentials. Skills she learned from the 1930s mobsters and documents she created during that era continued to be of value, particularly the fake degrees. Of course irrefutable knowledge concerning the job one is applying for doesn't hurt. The world was becoming more sophisticated, and false documents would have to be created to match the times she lived in. Apple retained everything she ever read or studied; therefore, every profession was attainable. She also volunteered to provide reading and writing tutoring to illiterate adults and children in Los Angeles.

With a low-interest loan from Apple, and a limited partnership with an antique-store operator, Sabin was again in the collectable and used book business. Apple had invested much of the money she saved from Chicago, so loaning him money was not a hardship. She recently had invested more than $10,000 in a new company called Walmart. This investment was the last one she made to end the decade.

Treasure begged to be educated at home, but Apple insisted on a public school education. A lack of proper socialization concerned Apple. Someday, she would have to leave Treasure. Her goal was to produce the most independent, self-sufficient, intelligent daughter possible. Success would be measured by Treasure's ability to leave her. She had often thought adopting Treasure was going to more trouble than beneficial. Her motives for adoption were very self-serving and therapeutic. Now she realized Treasure was receiving immense benefits also. Both dutifully approached the relationship.

"I don't remember everything about him, Apple. He waltzed into the store one day back in San Francisco and perused the store all afternoon. He kind of looked at the same books you were looking at when we first met. Besides, you have asked me the same questions about the dude every day since I moved in, and I always give you the same answers," exclaimed Sabin.

"Yes, I know, but this is important to me. Besides, you sometimes remember details previously unmentioned. Oh yes, have you had much luck in locating another copy of the book?"

"Look, Apple, that book was in the store. I am not convinced it was even published by a publisher. Some churches used to publish their own books. The type of manuscript appearance it had would tend to make me believe it was some type of subsidy publisher or homemade."

"What kind of storekeeper are you? You didn't have all your inventory recorded, and you can't recall who published a damn book!"

"Now be cool, my soul sister. You know you get all worked up when we talk about this. Now tell me again why this book is so important."

"It's the man and the book. I told you I am a history buff, and I needed that book to complete some research."

"History buff? Is that why you sometimes say things that sound like they came from a different generation? And another thing, I don't ask you about seeing those yellow eyes on the day I rescued you, and I don't ask how you were able to kill that man. So give it up and stop asking me the same questions over and over again."

"You need to learn to listen. The best part of communication is listening," insisted Apple.

"I know, I know. And every now and then, a person needs a good listening to. Or at least that's what you have told me every day since I've been here."

"There may be hope for you yet," Apple said.

"Well, the man was kind of like you. Guess I remember that now. Something new, huh, just like you predicted. Yeah, he also used a few words that sounded past generational."

"The book, Sabin. I need that book! And what do you mean he sounded like me?"

"I don't know. You know. He just sounded like he didn't belong in the sixties. That's all."

"Damn you, Sabin! I swear you are driving me crazy!"

"Sorry, dear. I just didn't think anyone would ever come along as beautiful as you. I think it was called something like *Tribe of the Dead.* You rip out a man's throat and keep me as arm candy. This shit has all been so surreal."

"You were doing all right until that arm candy comment, smartass," joked Apple. "Anyway, find the damn book. There has to be another one. Who knows? I might present you with a reward."

"I can only hope. Guess I don't have a chance of choosing the reward?"

Treasure sat on her beanbag chair, reading the current edition of *Rolling Stone.* Her Beatles hat concealed her eyes. Treasure wondered if the adults might really like each other. She was becoming quite fond of Sabin and sometimes had mixed emotions about her feelings for him. *Here was a man who did not pursue her like others did.* Maybe he should act like a father. Maybe he did, and she did not know it. What did she have to compare father acting to? She had never known her father. Maybe he was just a kid like her who didn't have a sex drive. Maybe he was cute but gay. *Anyway, it feels right for him to be here. Why didn't he try harder to make out with Apple? He should be crazed for her by now.*

"Apple, wake up." Sabin shook her gently.

Apple slowly opened her eyes as the soft, buoyant rays of morning light danced through the window. Sabin's long hair gently brushed her face as he bent closer to her with his finger pressed against his lips. Dust particles capriciously darted through the sunlight being propelled by a mystical cul-de-sac wind. Apple experienced all of this pristine state of being. Then she realized this was not a dream, and Sabin was in her bed.

"You have one second to explain yourself," Apple whispered between her grinding teeth. Sabin moved slightly backward with his hands out. "Talk, buster!"

"Okay, okay, okay. See that car across the street? It has been there all night," Sabin whispered while pointing in the direction of a vehicle.

"So, are you getting a little too paranoid or crazy? Cars stay on the street overnight all the time."

"Yes, but not with a man in it who could be an identical twin to the man who brought your book," said Sabin.

"What are you talking about? My book?" Apple rolled over on her side, looking toward the window. "Oh, that book."

Sabin momentarily lost his train of thought when Apple inadvertently exposed parts of her that Sabin had only fantasized about. *What a magnificent work of art,* he thought. His mouth froze, and butterflies dive-bombed his stomach.

Apple wasted no time jumping out of bed. She completed the peep show by slinging off her nightgown and sliding into a pair of jeans. Sabin ogled as she wiggled tight jeans through the final stages over her hips. He paid scrupulous attention to her firm but bouncing breasts. He eyed her amorously.

Turning toward Sabin while buttoning up her shirt, she demanded, "Come on. Get your shoes on. Let's go check this out."

"Wait a minute. You just can't go barging across the street and demand a book."

"Yes, I can!" barked Apple.

"Think about this, Apple. If it is him, why would he be watching our house? What would he want with us? Maybe he's a scout for the Hell's Angels. Maybe I'm wrong. Maybe I'm confused!"

"Just shut up, Sabin. I can handle myself. I will go check this out, and you cover me."

"Cover you? Cover you with what? We don't have any weapons around here."

"Just use your damn imagination, Sabin!"

Without hesitation, Apple scurried out the front door.

Sabin watched from the living room window, clutching Treasure's miniature softball bat.

Apple showed no signs of caution as she approached the car.

"I was wondering when you would visit me," said the man in the car upon Apple's arrival. He didn't turn to face Apple but stared straight ahead.

Apple stopped a few feet from the driver's side and said, "Say what?"

"Are you what I think you are?" the man asked, again without turning toward her.

Apple shifted her stance and ensured a safe distance between her and the car door in case it flew open. She didn't immediately respond to him. She never had the patience for long pauses and said, "Who do you think I am?"

"I am not sure, but I may have an intelligent guess or two. By the way, that was an impressive kill back in San Francisco," the mysterious stranger said in a deep raspy tone. The man had yet to turn and face her. He sat with both hands on the steering wheel and continued to stare straight ahead.

Apple focused her eyes on him. His short, black hair barely touched his collar. She was curious—but not enough to walk closer or to attempt a frontal view.

"Yes, an impressive kill indeed, but messy, so messy. Too much carnage and too many witnesses. You give Spirit Walkers a bad name."

"Spirit Walkers? Man, you on dope. I think you have mistaken me for someone else. I just want to know why you are watching my house."

"You should thank me, Apple. I found you before that mourning brood of overgrown motorcycle enthusiasts found you. You know, those misunderstood Hell's Angels respond extremely violently during periods of bereavement."

"What are you talking about? I think this conversation is over." Apple wondered how he knew her name. She wanted to inquire about the book. The man was playing some sort of game, and she was not going to play along. While standing next to his car, she had already initiated a plan to assail this man. They would talk again, but next time, it would be on her terms.

"Step a little closer and take a gander in the backseat. You might see what I am talking about and have an improved understanding of this situation."

Apple moved closer to the back of the car, and tiptoed while balancing her body by placing a hand on the trunk. Leaning forward, she peeked into the backseat. There, restrained in duct tape, were two leather-clad Hell's Angels. Another few feet of duct tape, and they would have had the appearance of total mummification. An intravenous tube was embedded in each one's neck. The clear plastic intravenous tubes snaked across their bodies and disappeared into an ice chest on the floorboard. The tubes were flowing with deep red, almost black blood.

"Interesting, is it not? Normally, I would have just killed the bastards, drank a little blood, dumped the bodies, and been done with it. But hey, a guy has to have a little fun every now and then, doesn't he? I know you understand fun. Remember Tulsa and your first kills? Besides, with all this new technology and a little ice, I can have a fresh Bloody Mary every day." The man laughed hideously.

Gifts were awakening. Her ears detected all surrounding sounds, including a sparrow's flapping wings. Smell separated the fresh blood from the dried blood that must have been on the man's clothing, and her eyes saw the oxygen bubbles escaping blood as it methodically dripped through the tubes. Her body tensed, her muscles hardened, and her heart raced.

"Let me guess. Your heart is racing, and your gifts desire to rumble? For shame, for shame. Here I am offering you my morning catch of Angels, and what thanks do I receive? Oh, how I enjoy hunting and gathering similar to how my ancestors used to do. Not your ancestors, but mine."

Apple watched the two angels. They were still alive; their eyes darted back and forth, expressing pure, unadulterated fright. The mystery man turned around in the seat and studied his two captives for a moment.

"Enough. Guess I have enough now," he said. He produced a two-foot metallic spear and stabbed them through their ears. He licked the blood off the spear and focused on Apple.

He was of Native American descent with a downward hooked nose and high cheekbones. He was darker than most Indians she had met. He wore black-framed sunglasses. *Strange,* she thought. *How did I miss those glasses before?* She thought about fleeing, but Treasure was in the house asleep, and her hippie cohabitant was hiding somewhere too. There was no choice. She would have to stand here and deal with whatever happened.

"See," he said, "you should thank me. These two bastards were appointed to hunt you down and kill you. I anointed myself your savior." While saying this, he sprinkled a few drops of blood from the spear onto his head.

Apple stepped back and said, "You don't scare me."

"It was never my intention to scare you. I believe you have witnessed plenty of deaths in your short life, relatively speaking, of course."

"Then what do you want from me?"

"Oh, I really don't expect much of anything from you: just your life, your hippie boyfriend, and that little blonde sweetie you have. Now, control those eyes. The sooner they turn completely yellow, the sooner I will be inclined to kill you."

She sensed her eyes were turning. "I've always been ready to die, but that is not to say I am ready today. Leave the others out of this." Apple noticed a glare coming from behind his sunglasses. At any moment, the fight would commence.

"You're going to die, but aren't you curious about why?" he asked.

Apple stared, saying nothing.

The man stepped from the car. He was wearing a cheap, dark gray suit with a thin black tie. He removed his glasses and gingerly placed them inside his coat.

"Finding you was difficult. I thought you would be looking for anything related to Spirit Walkers so I planted that silly book at various stores all up and down the West Coast. What the hell? Maybe she will show up. Just when I was about to lose patience, you and your little groupies appeared in a parking lot full of the devil's misfits. Guess it was my lucky day. You see—it was my idea to put that book back in circulation. The elders said no, but I convinced them. I said those two Afro lawyers should have never written their accounts of Spirit Walkers. But, it just might lead us to their only known surviving convert. Yes, we took care of your mess at Ramsey's place and a few others we found in the Tulsa area. So they agreed, and here we are at journey's end."

"Afro lawyers?" Apple inquired, attempting to restrain the shock in her face. Surely he was not speaking of Jesse and Bobby.

"Look, cut the shit, okay? We both know what I am—and what you think you are. I am a true Spirit Walker, and you, little darling, are one some kind of Spirit Walker wannabe. I guess in today's terms, you are a half-breed, a mix, or something like that. I have been appointed by the elders as your savior, to deliver you from imprisonment. Yes, my dear, I am going to parole you from this hell. What's the matter? Devil got your tongue?"

"Elders? What elders?" Apple asked.

"As I said, we planted copies, and if we didn't hook our fish, we would pick them up and try again. Don't you remember in Chicago, it was checked out but never returned? I was just about to catch up with you, and then you had to go and replicate your own version of the Saint Valentine Day's massacre. Messy, very messy. Yes, that was just more evidence you were not a pure Spirit Walker. Such gruesome and repugnant slaughter would never have been allowed by a true specimen. Yes, my dear, you have provided a trail of revolting amateurisms, envied by no elders. Therefore, you are a liability, and you must die."

Apple weighted her options. She had already squandered the option of surprise attack. She should have attacked once his identity was discovered. How did she know he was going to be a Spirit Walker? She had killed Shelby in Tulsa, and she was a Spirit Walker. But that was many years ago, and what if she was a mix like her? Does being a mix indicative of a weaker subspecies? Had Bobby and Jesse given her the gift also? Was this man stronger than she was?

"Such thoughts, Apple. Yes, don't look so surprised. I can read what you're thinking. Now, Shelby allowed you to read her thoughts, but she too was weak. You actually never had an opportunity to perfect those mind-reading skills, did you? Too late. It is futile to attempt to read mine. Oh, by the way, if those KKK had not killed your boys back in Tulsa, we would have. You see—they violated the covenant of the gifts several years before you met them. They should have taken the forty acres and a mule. Sure, they would have died of old age and never met the tribal elders, but that's the chance you take for being mortal. Then they wrote that damn book. There was enough money flowing in Black Wall Street. They did not have to make more."

"How do you know about me? Jesse and Bobby were dead. I turned myself into a Spirit Walker."

"Unexplained deaths, theories of immortal humans, and folklore have followed your escapades of carnage. Granted, you learned to survive, and I guess you have improved your mode of operations in recent years, but it's too little, too late. Besides, I have strong bias against women, especially black women, being one of us. They are scars to our race." The mystery man grinned again.

She had not blinked, and was staring straight at him, but she still didn't see the spear in time to completely avoid its point. It pierced her shoulder with such velocity that it exited through her back and hit a tree thirty yards away. She must have instinctively flinched enough to avoid a direct hit to the heart. She broke the radio antenna off the car and struck him across the face. His eyes glared a deep, dark yellow. He flew toward her as if he had wings. His hands gripped her neck as she fell backward with him on top of her. Grabbing his forearms, she found them hard as steel and immoveable. He growled like a rabid animal. His saliva dripped across her face. Her eyes were beginning to release from their sockets. Her breath was expiring. Holding and squeezing her throat with one hand, he removed his other hand and produced a wooden arrow with a sharpened stone tip.

"Sorry, Apple. You weren't meant to be this way, and now we have to make things right; it's nature's way. This artifact from my ancestors will ensure death with no healing. A piercing blow to the heart will set you free."

Apple closed her eyes and awaited her fate. He was much too strong and overpowering. Suddenly she heard a dull thud and felt his grip loosen. She took immediate advantage by producing a hard punch to his throat and rolled him off her.

Sabin stood over them, holding a splintered baseball bat. The man quickly leaped to his feet, but Apple grabbed a piece of bat from Sabin and forced the sharp wood into his heart with a force that propelled him backward. He fell to the ground. She placed the bat butt against her sternum and forced it through his body, pinning him to the ground. Blood ran from both corners of his mouth and his ears.

"Man, Apple, I think you killed him," Sabin said with shock on his face.

Apple wasn't sure about anything and had no intentions of backing away from the bat.

Sabin jumped backward. "Fuck, Apple. There's two dead Angels in the car!"

The mystery man opened his eyes and said, "There will be others. You got lucky this time, but the elders will send more like me. You will never be safe." He struggled for a last gulp of air, raised his arms, and died. The remaining blood escaped from his body and raced down the road, disappearing around the first turn. The blood appeared to have a life of its own.

Apple and Sabin looked toward each other as if they were having hallucinations.

"Wow, Apple. What are we going to do?"

"I don't know! Give me a damn moment to think! You're raking my nerves, Sabin. Please shut up!"

"Guess that's the thanks I get for helping you. Shit, wait a minute. This ain't right. You saw it. The blood ran away, and he looks like a dried prune. Fuck. This is bad."

"Sabin, please go to the house and stay with Treasure. I will be back."

"But you're bleeding. I saw that spear go through you."

"Shut up! I'll explain when I get back."

Apple drove the mystery man's car as far into desert toward Las Vegas as the amount of gas would allow. She drove it off a canyon after setting it on fire by stuffing a lit rag in the gas tank. However, before burning the car, she searched the car for the book. She only found an FBI badge and identification belonging to the mystery man. He was agent Mark White—or at least the identification indicated so. *Shit. He was a Spirit Walker and an FBI agent? What the hell is that all about?* She pondered this and many more questions while hitching back to Los Angeles.

Treasure and Sabin were waiting for her in the front yard. She was not absolutely sure what to say. Fourteen hours had passed since she had left. *I should have stayed a loner. I don't need people.* She walked past them without saying a word. They hastily followed her into the house.

"Take off your shirt. I sent Treasure to the pharmacy to buy what we need to patch you up—if we can. I knew you wouldn't go to the hospital," Sabin continued to rattle.

"Does it hurt?" Treasure curled up in the security of her beanbag chair.

"Does what hurt?" Apple replied.

Sabin, being rather brave, felt Apple's shoulders.

"I swear it was this shoulder, or maybe it was this other one. Damn it. I know it's here somewhere."

"Stop it, Sabin. Just stop it!" Apple pushed his hands away. "You're just trying to get a cheap thrill."

"I'm serious. I can't find your wound."

"Look, I've healed." Apple pulled her shirt down both shoulders to reveal a discolored round scar.

"I see … another idiosyncratic process of yours. What the hell is going on here, Apple?"

"You wouldn't understand."

"Try me."

"No! Leave me alone!"

"She's a Spirit Walker—or at least thinks she is," interrupted Treasure.

Apple and Sabin ceased their bickering and stared at Treasure.

"She's a fifty-nine-year-old Spirit Walker. Isn't that right?" Treasure continued.

"Treasure, what have you done?" Apple asked. "Have you read my diary?"

"Sorry, I was so concerned, and you made us wait all day for you. I had to know what was going on. It's not like I didn't know something was not right around here. You never get sick, you read in the dark, and—"

"All right, I get your point. You can stop now."

"What point? Is there a damn point around here … anywhere?" added Sabin.

"Yes, damn it. The point is I am different!" exclaimed Apple. "Treasure, I can't believe you violated my trust and read the diary."

"I trusted you. I can't believe you kept secrets from me!" Treasure wiped the tears from her eyes.

"I'm sorry, baby. I did not think anyone would understand. I was going to tell you eventually."

"When were you going to tell me? When I looked twice as old as you—or when you traded me in on a younger model? Tell me, Apple. Damn it, tell me."

"Treasure, be cool," interrupted Sabin.

"Fuck you, Sabin. This has nothing to do with you!" cried Treasure.

"Okay, okay, okay ... I give up. What do you need to know?"

Treasure asked most of the questions as Apple explained what she knew about her gifts.

Sabin referred to the gifts as Apple's condition.

She presented a limited history, but it was enough to satisfy their natural curiosity. She omitted many of the killings and drinking of gift-sustaining blood. She explained her self-healing powers and their origin. She admitted to being older than she appeared, but as a lady, she reserved the right not to divulge her true age. Any other information they desired concerning her so-called condition would have to come from their vivid imaginations. After all the explanations and disclosure, the three were fatigued.

"The blood in the diary, the blood—what about the blood?" Treasure asked.

"Not now. I do not wish to speak about the blood tonight. Give me that, okay?"

Apple contemplated what to do now and what the future would hold. To describe what she was feeling as anxiety would be a gross understatement. She read magazines, books, and watched television, but sleep eluded her all night. At three o'clock in the morning, she woke Sabin.

"Sabin, wake up."

He sat up in bed, rubbing his eyes and scratching his tangled hair. "Oh, wow, man. I was having some type of incubus dream. Some female demon was harassing me. It was real shitty, shitty, and then shitty some more. You all right, Apple?"

"Couldn't sleep. I was resenting the fact you were asleep, and I was walking the floor." She softly placed the palm of her hand on his chest.

He responded by cupping her hand in his. "Look, I know you didn't tell us everything tonight, but that's all right. We're with you."

"You don't understand. There are three burned bodies in a government car out in the desert. Eventually, the police will be coming our way. We are not lucky enough for no one to have seen anything today."

"I'd say those damn Hell's Angels will almost certainly get us first." Sabin started to rub Apple's neck. "Tell you what—convert me to a Spirit Walker, and we will kick all their asses."

"Don't joke. Do you even believe what I say I am?" asked Apple. "Don't even joke about what you think you know. Besides, I don't exactly know how to share my gift. You heard the man, and obviously I did not receive the gift correctly."

Sabin playfully pushed her backward while explaining how he was only joking. He had no desire to be any kind of spirit, and he continued to make small talk.

"Rub my shoulders some more." Apple was on her stomach beside him. "You know, I appreciate your lighthearted approach to the world, especially these last twenty-four hours. Don't get me wrong—I am grateful for your bat-swinging abilities, but just being you has helped me."

"My God, are we showing some emotions, my dear? Is that suit of armor now not so impregnable? Can this woman be conquered?"

Apple reached and squeezed his face, forming a perfect pucker with his lips. She laughed and stared at the faces she created with her squeezing.

He chuckled and presented her with a serious gaze.

She gently kissed his lips.

He hungrily reciprocated with a passionate kiss, creating the slightest of openings between her lips. Pulling his long hair, she silently beckoned him to her. Sabin rose from the bed, resting on his knees as they sunk into the mattress. Warm, moist kisses raced across his chest as Apple hugged his waist and rubbed her face from one side of his chest to the other.

Sabin encouraged her to lie back on the bed by gently attempting to nudge her in that direction. This mode of persuasion was unsuccessful. Apple obviously desired to control this endeavor they were embarking upon. He found his hands held together above his head by only one of Apple's hands.

"You're scaring me," he whispered. "Please be gentle with me. It's … it's my first time."

"I see, my little victim. It's my first time also. If I make a few mistakes, neither of us will know the difference. Of course this could be lethal for you."

Apple had experience. Usually, her hunger for sex came in waves of basic physical needs. She called it her need to be scratched. Sometimes she would have sex frequently, and then the need would dissipate, lying dormant for years. She learned to appreciate the dormant years, realizing true intellectual freedom could only be achieved through absence of a sex drive. Over the years, several satisfiers, as she called them, had been conditioned to respond when she called and advised them she had an itch. They knew scratching time had arrived.

"My, my, Mr. Sabin Brown. You sleep in the nude. I would have never guessed. Now slow down. What's the hurry? Oh my, aren't you glad to see me." *Don't bite or scratch him. Have discipline. You can do it, girl. Easy does it.* A few sexual encounters had experienced a mishap or two, but for a decade or so, nobody had been seriously injured during Apple sex.

"Heaven help me," cooed Sabin.

"Do you always talk during sex?" Apple positioned herself for the final destination.

"Only when I have just experienced the firmest, smoothest, most exquisite body on earth. Do I thank heaven? Trust me, that has never happened before." These were the last words he spoke for the next hour.

Apple began scratching her itch with an unsurpassed, methodical intensity no man could resist surrender to.

⊰ ⊱

"I never liked the idea of Mark becoming an FBI agent. That's getting too close to the wrong authorities for my comfort level," Phil Parks said in a high-rise in downtown Oklahoma City. "Ingenious. I believed this was an inventive way to locate and eradicate undesirables of our kind. Now, I am not so sure. Are you sure no one has heard from Mr. White since he last reported finding the mixed woman? I think he called her Apple."

"Faith, you have to have faith. Mr. Mark White has always been our best cleanser. He has always been able to eradicate and cleanse all assignments without criminal justice involvement. He is our best. Relax." Teddy Riley attempted to calm the reigning elder, who reported only to Desheeta.

"I still don't like it. He should have reported back by now."

"Look, everything will be all right. Besides, White is a pureblood. If anything had happened to him, his blood would have returned," Phil explained, attempting to reassure his fellow elder.

"I know, but the FBI may have wised up to him. I know we changed his identity and took all precautions, but authorities are becoming smarter all the time. Hell, they will be as smart as us someday."

⊰ ⊱

The sun invaded the room, casting its illumination across the naked bodies of Sabin and Apple. Sabin awoke first and peered at

Apple's perfect skin. That is of course where the skin had no scars. The sunlight glistened across her ebony back. She felt his stare, smiled, and wrapped him in her arms. An hour later, the encore was concluded.

PART TWO

CHAPTER 12

Chicago Revisited

"Triple grande soy caramel macchiato, please. Give me a blueberry scone also."

"So you're having the usual, Mr. Jones," Apple replied.

Apple had been working at Starbucks for almost six months. She enjoyed working there, and she loved the aroma of fresh coffee. What was most enjoyable were the sundry characters who frequented the Chicago location. There was a Starbucks on every block along Michigan Avenue. Being able to work at multiple stores was a great benefit. She started by working relief shifts for four stores in a five-block area of downtown. To her, Starbucks was reminiscent of a type of nonalcoholic speakeasy. Coffee had replaced alcohol, and gangsters were replaced with yuppies, Generation X, and Generation Y. Gangsters still remained, but there were more young ones than old ones. Now they were called gangbangers. *What self-respecting gangster would frequent a Starbucks?*

Working at Starbucks kept Apple young and current. She didn't need to work because of investments, but work kept her entertained. There was Max, the ex-city manager with an engineering degree who succumbed to a deviation of Alzheimer's mixed with manic depression. He was harmless, even though the local terrorism task force initially took seriously his practice of free speech about the "Train Conspiracy." They stormed into Starbucks one cold, rainy Sunday morning and ushered him into a waiting, dark-tinted sedan. The sedan was a modern symbol of a "G" car, as Sabin would have described it.

Apple had run after them in an attempt to explain his illness. Nevertheless, he was taken away and returned two days later. Apparently Max's theory that terrorists had been working for decades to eradicate America's reliance on trains, thereby creating a Middle East dependency on oil, didn't hold merit with the authorities. Apple always thought Max had some good points though.

Roger Merit was another regular customer. He always wore dark sunglasses, faded denim jeans, and a corduroy blazer. He was at Starbucks for a minimum of five hours per day. He would order six shots of espresso in a venti-sized cup and fill the rest with a combination of tea and chocolate. He retired from teaching too early and was bored with life. Apple was on to him. The glasses were for the extensive girl-watching he did. Many men hung out at Starbucks to watch the women, and Apple suspected the women returned the privilege. He would have to settle for his own narcissism; he was the most unattractive man Apple had encountered in her eighty-four years.

Another notable character was Abduhla Kahn. He was from Iran but had been an American citizen for twenty years. He paraded around with a perpetual broken nose. The nose was broken less frequently now that several years had passed since 9/11. Nonetheless, he continued to proudly respond to anyone criticizing his origin or blaming him for terrorism. Apple believed Abba, as she referred to him, never made the connection between his compulsion to engage his critics with dialogue and the broken noses. Jokingly, she would refer him to the Dear Abby section of the newspaper whenever he asked her an unrelated Starbucks question. He would roll his eyes when Apple would say, "Abby for Abba." Apple felt some sort of kinship with these three distinctive vagabonds.

Her favorite customer, Cornelius Cox referred to himself as "CC de Fox." Apple just called him CC. He was a small, young black man who worked as a bellhop for two Michigan Avenue hotels. He would explain how Apple was not actually black. She just looked black. He would continue by attempting to engage her in Ebonics. He said, "To be black, you have to sound black."

Apple would counter by detailing history and explaining how education was the key to true freedom—not how someone spoke. On slow days, the regulars would gather around for the entertainment their weekly debate would offer. He and Apple looked the same age, maybe late twenties, which added to his confusion concerning her intellect. He would conclude every exchange by asking her how she knew so much. Apple was equally curious about where he came from. Neither answered questions. She would respond by explaining the need to feed one's intellect and the power of books. She would end every debate by concluding his inability to secure improved employment was directly correlated to his speech.

Apple wrote Sabin and Treasure about all her regular coffee hounds. She would describe them in excruciating detail. Sabin would write back and provide his opinion on whether or not he believed them to be FBI. Apple was afraid of the FBI ever since she disposed of the FBI Spirit Walker in 1970. At first, Sabin believed the FBI had blown up their house three months after she killed Agent Mark White. She didn't believe Spirit Walkers had done it, even though that was Treasure's best guess. Eventually, all the inconclusive evidence indicated Hell's Angels. They spent the next few years moving up and down the West Coast.

Apple stayed with Sabin until 1977, the longest she had stayed anywhere with anyone. Sabin was not pleased with her departure. He intellectually understood why she needed to leave, but emotionally, denial prevailed. The first year or so after departure, she frequently called and wrote him. Her altruism was in full bloom. Then realizing Sabin was continually clinging to her for stability, she created more distance, quit calling, and wrote only the occasional letter. The past few years found her writing and calling Sabin again. She wasn't sure why she needed more contact with him and quit analyzing it.

Distance had been created with Treasure after Apple refused to attempt Treasure's proposed conversion to a Deadwalker. Treasure wouldn't accept Apple's explanations, especially her lack of conversion knowledge. They rarely spoke these days—even after ten years without speaking. Sabin finally intervened and mediated an understanding of differences. Apple was thankful and rewarded Sabin with a night of gratuitous affection.

Treasure, now at the age of fifty-one, was twice a grandparent. Apple saw her children when they were very young, but she had never seen the grandchildren. Apple was too difficult to explain for Treasure, especially when the children were older and asked too many questions. Treasure lived in Dallas and was leading a productive life. *Why bring all my baggage and trouble to her?* Apple had weak moments of wanting to see her. *Besides, I am probably still being hunted.* She frequently reminded herself it was time to move on, and it was too risky to be around people she cared for.

Sabin would be arriving at O'Hare Airport the next afternoon. Apple was excited to see her old soul mate. Sabin stepped off the L platform. He had not changed much over the years. He still had a full head of hair at the age of fifty-eight. He wore his silver-streaked hair in a long, braided, off-center ponytail. Wisdom wrinkles surrounded his eyes, and a cute little sagging chin topped off his aura. He smiled from ear to ear when his eyes connected with Apple's. "Woman, I say woman, over here." His speech continued to be reminiscent of a decade of free love, hippies, and protests. She had broken him from using *groovy* even though a comeback could be on the horizon. Apple had lived long enough to understand how history had a tendency to repeat itself. What else could explain Dickies jeans, lava lamps, bell-bottoms, Converse All-Stars, and Rod Stewart singing the crooner classics?

At first, she thought Sabin was joking, but then she realized he was serious. He had called last week and attempted to convince Apple he had located another Spirit Walker. He was convinced Tina Turner was a Spirit Walker.

Apple said, "If that is so, then Dick Clark must be one too."

"But he's not," Sabin said, "because he is dead now."

They eventually agreed it was all nonsense. Then they would start over, not knowing who was serious.

Sabin said, "Dick Clark looked old as dirt and wore wigs. Tina hasn't aged in thirty years." He accused Apple of sharing the gift with Tina. He concluded the call by warning her to stay away from Oprah. "Oprah doesn't need your help. She can buy her immortality."

Sabin had made one request—or two if sex was counted. He had heard about an antique store that had unopened bottles of Hai Karate aftershave, and he wanted some. This was his favorite, and he had spent years since its extinction searching for a formula to recreate the pungent aroma. He thought it would awaken his bravado.

Apple considered it a mistake to have given him thousands of Walmart shares when she moved on. She had also given Treasure thousands of shares of various stocks, but even though this gift made her rich, Treasure continued with a productive life. Apple didn't consider Sabin's life very productive. He had invested poorly and often, but due to some unknown miracle, he remained wealthy by Apple's standards. Reincarnation of the old, cheap Hai Karate aftershave would be another poor investment.

Now she was going to present him with Starbucks stock she had purchased in the 1980s. She cared for him, and he had been an incredible asset over the years. One of his investments was in a private plasma center. Apple had to feed her gift by any resource necessary. A blood addiction was more difficult to conceal, and obtaining donors had become more complicated. Sabin held controlling interest in Total Life, which bought and sold plasma and whole blood. He actually got the idea while watching *The Simpsons* when Bart sold his blood to a private company. *This may be the only good investment he ever made.*

Apple remembered it like it was yesterday when Sabin called and yelled into the phone, "Hey, Sugar, let the good blood flow. Let it flow all night long!" He did his best impression of Ray Charles. Even though they were not the actual lyrics, the beat was correct. Since then, almost without fail, a courier delivered cold, fresh blood to her doorstep on schedule. Apple had to get over drinking blood from a straw.

Total Life was shut down for a month while being investigated for accepting blood from underage donors. She never asked how the arrangements were made or who knew what. She was absolutely grateful not to have to roam the streets in search of blood; she would have sex with Sabin even when he was ninety.

Apple couldn't get off work the day Sabin was to arrive for his next visit. She didn't like to drive, and he could just as easily take a cab. He did not wish to take the L again after being harassed by juvenile delinquents. He would need thirty-five dollars for the cab fare, but he seldom carried cash.

With the exception of a few regulars, the afternoon crowd had dispersed. Among them were Max and Abba. Sunrays peered through the storefront window when Apple let the blinds down.

Sabin stuck his face to the window and licked the glass, startling Apple and Max. There he was in all his grandeur: a splendor of a man in a Levi's 501 jean jacket he had worn since 1965, a 1974 Rolling Stones T-shirt, and tire-soled Jesus sandals. He kissed his love beads and blew a kiss to Apple.

Apple raced to the front door and embraced Sabin, lifting him off his feet and spinning him in circles.

"Stop, you damn bully," he said with a laugh. "You're going to kill this old man."

He grabbed her ass. She gave him a soft, playful slap across the face.

"You are still one groovy chick."

"Only for you, my doll. Only for you," she responded.

"Sit down here. Sit down." Apple pointed to a table covered with the day's newspapers.

"Viagra, Apple. It's a miracle drug. Can you take off now because I took some in the cab?"

She reached across the table, cupping his hands in hers. She cautiously turned around after feeling a hand tap her on the shoulder. She sensed danger and instantly knew evil was present. Two yellow-eyed men brandished nine-millimeter semiautomatic handguns, and each motioned to chamber a shell. She dove across the table, knocking Sabin to the floor. Shots rang out, and one of the men fell forward with a gaping wound in the back of his head. Apple scrambled to her feet while Sabin scurried under the table. The other yellow-eyed man turned away from them and fired in the direction of the shot that had struck his partner.

Cornelius Cox stood in the doorway and continued to fire at the remaining standing assailant. The assailant fired, striking Cornelius in the chest. As he fell, he yelled out to Apple, "Get the motherfuckin' cracker!"

Apple attacked with all her might by ramming her fist through the man's back and extracting his heart. The other assailant who had been shot in the head rose and grabbed her from behind, flinging her to the floor.

"Son of a bitch, here we go again!" Sabin ran behind the counter in search of a weapon, preferably a sharp object to use as a spear or stake.

Mitzy, the other Starbucks employee on duty, ran out the back door, screaming for help. Abba and Max watched, frozen in their chairs.

The attacker and Apple's fight resembled a superhero cartoon altercation. They flew about the store, crashing into shelves and product displays, destroying the place. The two fighters were equally matched. No one had the upper hand.

Sabin ran from a utility closet and struck the attacker with a mop, but it didn't affect his ability to fight Apple.

"Break him in half, you stupid motherfucker!" Cornelius bellowed at Sabin.

Sabin tried twice to break the mop over his knee.

"Throw it to me!" Cornelius ran toward the two fighters.

He caught the mop in one hand, and chopped it in half with the other. Then, with a terrific force, he slung the makeshift stake through the back of the attacker, right through his heart. He crashed to the floor, and all the blood ran from the man and slithered under a crease at the base of the wall.

"Shit! I've seen that before," Sabin said.

Cornelius grabbed Sabin and carried him out the back door just as a dozen of Chicago's finest entered the front door. The officers pointed weapons at Apple, and she got down in her own blood.

"What the hell happened here?" asked an officer, not directing his question at any particular person.

Max said "I think they were filming *Crouching Tiger, Hidden Dragon Part II* or something like that."

Abba chimed in by declaring his American citizenship and saying Bin Laden followers had arrived in the Windy City.

One of the two officers vomited when he noticed the huge hole in a blood-drained body under a table. He vomited more upon finding the man's heart in the coffee grinder.

"Okay, smart-asses, you two outside now!" an officer said.

"May I stand now?" Apple asked.

"As soon as we get some answers," the officer replied.

"I don't know any answers. All I know is there was a fight, and I got caught in the middle. You should be going after the others," explained Apple.

The officer walked over to Apple, and using his baton, he separated her hands, which were stretched out in front of her on the floor.

"If you are an innocent bystander, then why do you have pieces of human flesh stuck under your fingernails? And why does it appear you dipped your arms all the way up to the elbows in blood?"

Apple thought, I knew I should have cut those damn long nails.

Mitzy watched in horror as Apple was led out of Starbucks in handcuffs.

"Hell. I guess I will have to find another Starbucks." Roger Merit arrived just as Apple was being escorted out. "Hey, Apple, what happened?"

Apple gave him a quick flash of yellow eyes as his asinine question evoked the gifts.

"Oh, sorry, Apple. I guess that was an idiotic question. Can I get a tall coffee around here?"

Apple couldn't help but smile at her dear regular customers as she attempted to nod good-bye from the patrol car.

Sabin and CC escaped from Starbucks and ran to a bookstore, which was across from the old water tower museum. They ran upstairs and hid in the men's restroom.

"Get your own damn stall," directed CC.

"Cool it, man. Don't think for one minute I want to spend any quality time with you and your weenie," replied Sabin.

They sat quietly in adjoining stalls, intensely listening for sounds of anyone who might have pursued them. After about thirty minutes, and several flushes just to keep the occasional passing patron disinterested, they emerged from hiding.

"I am Sabin Brown from LA. Sorry we had to meet this way. Oh, by the way, I assume you are a Spirit Walker. I saw you come back from that shot you took, and I see you are uninjured now." Sabin offered his hand for a shake.

"My friends call me CC Cox de Fox, but you can call be Cornelius. You can cut the Spirit Walker bullshit. I don't know what you're talking about."

Sabin shot him a peace sign while CC attempted a modern soul shake. Sabin backed up in a defensive mode.

"Ain't nobody goin' to hurt you, fool. Shit, you act like you're afraid of black people. Shit, dawg. It's all straight, so quit trippin'. I know who you are. You're that old dude Apple talks about. She got you sprung, man. I don't know what she sees in you. Man, you're old." CC shook his head.

"Dog or dawg, I may be old, but if you are a Spirit Walker, then you're older than me. Besides, what difference does it make? It's all cool, you know. So, my vilified friend, why do you show yourself as a Spirit Walker?"

"You know, it's like this. The posse tapped me to eye the girl— in case she run into the purebloods or some shit like that. She da bomb, you know, and the man and his homies like sent me to watch over her."

"And a fine job you were doing," interrupted Sabin.

"Hey, man, don't start trippin' on me. You couldn't even break that little witch ride."

"Witch ride?"

"You know, the broom, fool."

"Guess we were a good team, CC?" responded Sabin.

"Damn straight. We kicked some ass," CC said with a hint of sarcasm.

CC and Sabin smiled at each other and shook hands. Both noticed they were splattered with blood, in addition to CC's bullet-holed shirt.

"Damn … shit … fuck. This was my only Phat Farm shirt. Motherfucker got blood on my Sean Johns too."

"What the hell are Sean Johns?" asked Sabin.

"My pants man, my pants. You been living in a cave for the last thirty years or what?"

The two went downstairs and stood by the checkout counter while everyone else stared at them.

"Stand to the left. Now turn right. Face straight ahead. Next."

Apple complied with all instructions as the camera flashed. Escape possibilities and lost opportunities were playing in her head. She could've run away from a few bullets and escaped out the back door when the police arrived, but she was trying to give Sabin and the big black man with a gun more time to escape. *I saw him come back from a fatal wound, didn't I?*

"Over here, Foxy Brown, Coffee, or whatever you call yourself." The female jailer resembled the Terminator's ugly twin sister.

Apple presented her with an evil eye and her best smirk, but the lady wouldn't be intimidated. *Escape will be difficult at best and will focus too much attention on the gifts required to escape.*

"Take 'em off."

"Excuse me?"

"Show us some skin, lady. Get your damn clothes off and pile them over there," Terminator's sister said.

Apple did as she was told. She shivered on the cold concrete floor.

"All of it, Lady Jane. Get the bra and panties off."

Apple stripped bare and awaited further instructions. Terminator walked in circles around her, staring at her from bottom to top. Apple was thinking how no one should be treated like that, and how easy it would be to teach the bitch a lesson. Not a serious lesson—just an ear ripped off or a broken arm or leg.

"Damn, Lady Jane, you got a hundred scars on that tight body of yours. Where'd you get all those scars?"

Apple wasn't sure if the question was rhetorical or if a response was required. "You do a lot of living, you pick up a few scars—inside and out," Apple finally responded.

"Guess you're right. Now bend over and spread 'em." After a quick body cavity perusal, she was led into a shower, hosed down, and powdered with a delousing solution of some type.

"Put this on, stand behind that yellow line, and wait to be called." Terminator did not seem to be as annoyed as earlier. "You know that scar bit, girl. We all have scars—and women have more than our share." Terminator walked away while singing the chorus of Alice Cooper's "Only Women Bleed."

Apple slipped into the one-piece, zip-up-the-front, orange jumpsuit stenciled with "Cook County Jail" on the back.

※ ※

"Keep it real, peckerhead. Keep it real," CC said.

"I am about as real as it gets, CC, my man," retorted Sabin.

"No barb intended, my friend. Just quit looking so suspicious," quipped CC.

"It's just that I have never burglarized before."

"Peckerwood, we ain't burglarizing. We breakin' and enterin'. We ain't goin' to steal nothin', so chill, my brother."

CC, flashing his yellow eyes, and allowing the gift of strength to take over, broke the deadbolt on Apple's apartment door.

※ ※

"Miss Apple Lewis, you're next … front and center," directed her new handler, Sergeant Bob Abernathy. "Miss Lewis, we will be booking you into our hotel tonight. I see we have a luxury room available, so this is your lucky day. Right hand, please," he said while rolling her fingers across a pad of dry powdered ink. "Left hand, please."

Sergeant Abernathy completed a personal history summary on Apple. She answered the questions, trying to remember to match her answers with what she remembered was on her driver's license and other forms of identification. Her name was the only thing that had remained the same. Pride kept her from changing her name. She changed social security numbers and birth date every decade. She was handcuffed and positioned in a holding cell adjacent to jail central control.

She gazed at the sterile, white-enameled cement block walls.

The room looked as if it had been painted weekly if not daily. She felt the walls close in on her while wondering how many coats of paint before the room became a Rubik's Cube. She studied her blue canvas tennis shoes, minus shoestrings, and pondered her existence. Was it time to surrender life by fighting and forcing Cook County to kill her in the process? Spirit Walker's version of immortality may not be so special anymore.

"Miss Lewis, coffee, cigarette, coke, anything?" asked one of two detectives who entered the room.

Apple evaluated the two men who entered. One wore jeans, a hooded sweatshirt, running shoes, and a Boston Red Sox cap. The other was in an expensive charcoal-gray suit, polished high-top Johnston Murphy dress shoes, and monogrammed cuffs. Both smiling, muscular men appeared to be in their forties.

"This is Detective Joe Dean, and I am Detective Teddy Dunn. We need to ask you a few questions."

"What am I charged with, and don't I need a lawyer?" asked Apple.

"You haven't officially been charged with anything … yet. So, a lawyer may not be necessary, but if you are requesting one, we will stop and come back later," Detective Dean responded.

"Of course that might take a day or so, and we can hold you for seventy-two hours, so you may just want to rethink that lawyer thing," added Detective Dunn.

⊣ ⊢

"Pimp my apartment, I guess," CC said upon seeing Apple's apartment.

"No surprises here," added Sabin. "I knew she was a pack rat and didn't care if anything matched."

Stacks of books in all heights and sizes were everywhere. There were televisions, mounted on brackets, suspended from the ceiling. Posters of everyone from Muddy Waters, Otis Redding, and Louis

Armstrong to Frank Sinatra, Buddy Holly, Black Sabbath, Pearl Jam, and Green Day adorned every available wall space.

"She does like her music," Sabin said. "Now tell me again why we are here?"

"Bro, you should know why we are here. We gots to ravage this place and destroy or hide anything pointing to Apple's immortality."

"She's not like totally immortal, is she?" Sabin asked.

"I wouldn't know about that. We all different," replied CC.

CC opened the refrigerator and held out a pint of blood. "Hey, cracker, you don't look surprised at this. You her hookup, ain't you? When I gots my assignment, they said Apple had a provider—and you it."

"Guess that's me."

They continued to search the apartment for evidence that might link Apple to Spirit Walkers. Sabin explained his current role with Apple, but he also expounded on his earlier years and how he would always love her and could never be with another woman.

"That is some sick shit, Sabin. You should play the field because men need to do that, and that is just the way it is. Men are supposed to spread the seed."

They collected what might have been valuable and or sentimental to Apple, along with several thousand dollars found on her dresser. They discussed retaining an attorney, but CC insisted they do nothing until he rapped with the posse. Sabin could only assume the posse was some sort of Spirit Walker syndicate or governing body. CC convinced him Apple had no knowledge of being under this posse's surveillance. CC determined that the purebloods must have been staking out Sabin on the West Coast and followed him here. Sabin was distraught over the possibility he had caused the day's events.

⊨ ⊭

"Let's start from the beginning, shall we, Miss Lewis?" asked Detective Joe Dean, the Red Sox fan.

"The beginning?" asked Apple.

"You know, the beginning: when it all came down today."
Detective Teddy Dunn pulled up a chair and sat across from Apple.

"Why am I here? I was working, minding my own business,
and apparently a robbery came down. I, like everyone else,
defended myself. I shouldn't be here dressed like some garbage
man fashion show." Apple gripped the table edge and pushed back
in her chair.

"Like I said—or maybe I didn't—it has been a long day. Allow
me to reiterate or expand, if you will, on the situation we have here.
Some would call you a person of interest, and others might call you
a victim, but then again, you could be labeled a perpetrator. Our job
is to determine what you are in this situation," explained Detective
Dean.

"Oh, yes, Miss Lewis, my partner here forgot a possible category.
You might even be tagged as a material witness. So, the sooner
you start answering questions, the sooner we know what you are.
Understand?" Detective Dunn interjected.

"You gentlemen sure I don't require a lawyer?" Apple again
asked.

"Look … it's your call. You haven't been charged with a crime.
Now, you will be the first to know if we do decide to charge you.
Then, I would strongly suggest an attorney. Matter of fact, I would
insist upon it," suggested Detective Dunn.

"All right, let's see where this goes," offered Apple.

"Here's the deal. Run us through what you recall of the robbery—
or whatever you know—and we will interrupt you if clarification
is needed."

"That's fair," Apple said. "I was cleaning tables, doing my usual
routine, and the next thing I know, I was attacked from behind by
a man with a gun. I was knocked to the floor, then customers got
involved, and the next thing I know, we have two dead robbers.
That's about it."

"That's a good start, Miss Lewis, and we thank you for that valuable information," Dunn said.

"Now, let me get this straight," said Dean. "Since you didn't mention you knew your attackers, I will assume you did not. Now, I realize that in our business, that's police business, we should never assume anything, but you seem like an extremely intelligent young woman. So let's give it a try. Shall we? Now, this may be the first armed robbery of a Starbucks we have ever encountered. Let's see, two robbers dressed in $2,500 suits, no identification, untraceable weapons? It seems they really needed money, so obviously a Starbucks would be their first choice to get rich on a hit. But their bad luck was this Starbucks was full of badasses, you know, kind of like the old Tombstone shootout or something like that. Am I basically getting the gist of the situation?"

Apple realized the game had begun. These detectives were no different from the Klan, mobsters, Hell's Angels, or anyone else she had dealt with who wanted something from her—even her life. At least the Spirit Walker assassins went straight to the point: no bullshit, dialogue, or games. She studied their mannerisms, expressions, body language, and anything else that might give her a clue. "Yes, we shall," she responded.

"Shall what?" asked Dunn.

"As you said, give it a try," Apple responded.

"Now, let's see what we might have neglected to mention," Dean continued.

Dunn chimed in, "We can start with witness statements that you, Miss Lewis, forcibly removed corpse number one's heart. Let me see. Yes, it says right here on this written statement, that in fact, the man was alive when this withdrawal was made. Now, Miss Lewis, do you have a comment for us on this issue?"

"Are you some kind of martial arts champ?" Dean asked.

"No. I don't know anything about that."

"I see … next question. Both of the deceased apparently lost all their blood, and oddly enough, all that remains of their blood was what was found on you and splattered on our witnesses. What say you about that?"

"I don't know anything about that."

"Didn't think you would."

"These deceased had no forms of identification, and their fingertips had no prints."

"I wouldn't know about that," Apple again replied.

"Let's make this easy," interjected Dean. "What do you know?"

"I've already told you what I know, sirs."

Both detectives exhibited fake sighs, and glanced at each other. Dean got up and walked behind Apple, and Dunn walked to a corner of the room, lit a cigarette, took two drags, and put it out on the floor.

"Look here, Miss Lewis. We know—and you know—there is more to this soap opera. Nobody robs a goddamn Starbucks on Michigan Avenue with a million fucking people standing around. These men were dressed well, and except for being dead, they could be categorized as professionals. Now, someone wanted you dead, really bad. We can help you. Don't you understand we can hold you for seventy-two hours without charging you? And do you not understand that unless someone of reputable character corroborates your story, we will more than likely charge you with murder?" Dunn said.

"That's it, and there ain't no more," Apple said.

The two detectives believed Apple was an assassin, possibly contracted with a branch of government, but for some reason, she had become unsupported by her contractors.

Dunn motioned toward the large two-way, mirror behind them, and immediately two female jail matrons appeared. *No fashion sense,* thought Apple. Their uniforms were at least two sizes too small, and as they walked, their thighs created a whooshing sound. *Those thighs are too large to part,* she thought.

—⧓ ⧗—

Alicia Overstreet reached for another Republic of Tea passion fruit tea bag, placed it in her favorite mug with, "I'm Not Deaf, I'm Ignoring You," inscribed on it, filled it with water, and placed it in the microwave for two minutes. This was her third cup in the last hour; another one of her excessive compulsive disorders which she accepted as harmless. As a matter of fact, compulsions, perfectionism, attention to detail, and being a geek landed her the job.

Alicia had applied for employment with the FBI while a senior at a small college in western Oklahoma where she double majored in biology and accounting. The college placement office told her that unless she was approved for medical school or became a CPA, there were no jobs for her in their database. Her friends, parents, and relatives could never understand her choice of majors. She never offered an explanation.

Alicia was a bookworm and could have passed any course offered in school just by reading the books. She was often offended when school officials wouldn't allow her to self-study a course or simply test out. They explained how she had done it too often and thought she would benefit from social interaction with other students. The school offered limited online courses.

Social skills had never been her forte, and she redefined the word *loner. College is all about money and the need to pay professors more money for less work.* Every semester she wrote letters of protest to the college president to complain about the unavailability of professors in the classroom. She believed this type of protest resulted in the FBI declining her employment after a thorough background investigation. She was adamant, though she had no evidence, that the college president had derailed her FBI opportunity. Unyielding and defiant, she wrote to the college president prior to being hired by the CIA.

Dear President Skaggs,

> *I commend your presidential bravado. For without your unsolicited assistance, you have inadvertently and successfully*

assisted my fate. The Lord does work in mysterious ways and delivers prayers and miracles through others. You, Mr. President, are an "other." For through your grandiosity of self-appointment to my future, I did not receive final clearance from the FBI.

Yes, you may at this point be smiling and providing self-imposed accolades, but read on. The Central Intelligence Agency has recently secured my services for its war on terror. Most assuredly, your eternal surveillance will require my new public service skills. Therefore, might I suggest no future little fudging on your taxes or, heaven forbid, you might be noticed talking to that illegal alien housekeeper of yours. Sorry, I have to go now; national security is calling.

Your most humble of public servants,

Alicia had only applied to the CIA when President Skaggs received this letter. The letter became a turning point in her CIA background investigation for the humorous style of the letter and President Skaggs being indicted for tax evasion and immigration charges two months after Alicia mailed the letter. She never admitted to ensuring US Customs and to the IRS received supporting documentation from her related to his Latina live-in housecleaner. One of the CIA agents mentioned the competition between the FBI and CIA for new recruits after 9/11. They also liked her spunk.

Alicia's humdrum background, perfect grade point average, tenacity, persistence, and aloneness probably made her a better candidate for the CIA. She had dreams of touring the world, apprehending terrorists, and being a female 007. She even learned two additional foreign languages while waiting for training camp. Her disappointment was immeasurable when she found herself in an unobtrusive, windowless ex-broom closet somewhere on a side street off the Mall in Washington, DC.

Tonight, as the rain pelted down outside and the tourists had dispersed, Alicia found herself surfing the Internet and searching for terrorist activities in chat rooms. *Futile,* she would say to herself. *What self-respecting terrorist would be tracked on the Internet? Hell, they have their own damn website.* She would remind herself how everyone had to start somewhere, and her career had started and stayed at the bottom for the last four years. She was a bottom-feeder, the lowest molecule on the food chain. *I'm an aquatic protozoan, a damn amoeba. I'm plankton.*

The four-foot-eleven, ninety-eight-pound brunette who aspired to be an American 007 sat beleaguered in the bowels of the CIA.

That's interesting, she thought, stopping on a Yahoo News article out of Chicago. She often read the Internet news sections of MSN, Yahoo, and others, especially the sections under the headlines of "Odd" or "Strange but True." The headline that caught her eye read "Heartless Man Found in Starbucks." She read on with intrigue. Then she remembered a book she had read on the Hell's Angels and how even though no charges were filed, the Hell's Angels had attempted to bury a man who had similar unexplained injuries. The man's throat had been torn off. *What better way to pass off the night CIA research shift than to become a CIA forensics expert?*

⊣ ⊢

Apple thought she would be in some type of seclusion cell for the night. Nothing could be further from reality. She was placed in a large cell with six bunk beds. She thought it was how a caged wild animal must feel the first time freedom is removed. She stood with her back to the clinking, closing cell door. If it had been dark, it would have been reminiscent of her Tulsa hiding place.

"Close on number sixteen," yelled one of the matrons to an old, balding, fat man with a disastrous comb-over and Buddy Holly glasses. "Stand back from the door, sister—or that cute ass of yours will be no more."

All eyes were upon Apple as she stood with her arms folded across her chest. *This scene reminds me of being encircled by those damn Hell's Angels.* A moment later, the balding Buddy Holly limped down the run, handed her a pillow and blanket through the bars and said, "Here. You might need these tonight. By the way, if any of these ladies give you any problems, just call for me. My name is Officer Holly."

"No shit!" Apple caught herself saying.

"Yes, mum. No shit," he replied.

"You can have the top bunk over there," advised a middle-aged, well-groomed black woman. She had on a starched gray trustee-type uniform with perfect creases down the legs. Her hair was straight and short. She had a Bible in one hand and was clutching a rosary in the other as she leaned against her bunk.

"Listen, sweetie, you can come bunk with old Joyce over here," offered a hunched-over, leather-faced white woman with silver-blue hair. Joyce lit a cigar and blew smoke in Apple's direction.

"I told you no smoking!" ordered the well-groomed black woman.

"Kiss off," Joyce replied. "Laquitta, you don't rule the roost around here. Besides, Officer Holly said we could if we showed a little tit later. Remember this is the only shift when we compromised a guard to even let us smoke. You'll be back in your own cell tomorrow night anyway. You shouldn't even be in our cell. It ain't our fucking blame you got caught kiting valiums and lost your private suite, bitch."

Laquitta, without saying a word or giving any indication of her next move, calmly walked across the cell and backhanded Joyce, knocking her to the floor.

"The Lord is my shepherd, and my shepherd says I will be forgiven for kicking your ugly, wrinkled white ass. So do me a favor and get up so I can satisfy the Lord. Amen!" Laquitta said while clutching her Bible.

The other women backpedaled into their respective bunks and spaces, not wishing to be active members of this foray. Apple climbed up to her bunk and stared at the ceiling.

Joyce tried to wipe blood from the corners of her mouth.

Laquitta walked confidently away, knowing her communication was understood. Apple could smell the blood. She thought about her last blood delivery from Sabin. *Shit! Blood in the icebox will take some explaining.*

"Dear, what you in here for?" Laquitta settled into her bunk under Apple.

"I thought cellmates weren't supposed to divulge crimes and such," Apple replied.

"Sister, you been a watching too many movies. Now give it up."

Apple explained why she was in jail and continued to stay with the story she had given the two detectives. Even though she could not see Laquitta's face, she knew she was not buying this storyline.

After a long pause, Laquitta responded, "That's some bad shit there. Yes, mum, that's some damn bad shit. Now we goin' to pray about it. Lord, yes Lord, I am talking to you. This here girl needs your guidance. She has lost her way and needs to find it. Give us a sign that you are with us tonight." While praying, Laquitta managed to reach up and squeeze her hand between Apple's butt and the bunk. She then proceeded to erotically massage Apple's butt while praying.

"Yes, Lord. I feel you tonight. I know a sign is a comin'." All the other ladies but Joyce chimed in with a healthy amen.

Apple had never been with a woman and had no intentions of being with one tonight. *If she ever wanted to be with a woman, it would not be tonight, and certainly not with Laquitta.* Apple softly and gently took Laquitta's probing hand in hers. She squeezed it, and Laquitta's fingers were smashed together. Apple heard her take a deep breath and struggle to contain a muffled scream. She was sure Laquitta didn't want to falter in the eyes of her cellmates. Slowly, Apple applied more pressure until the cracking of bones echoed off the cell walls.

Laquitta said, "Yes, Lord. I feel your sign and will obey," she said through her clenched teeth. She whispered to Apple, "Please let go."

⊣ ⊢

Sabin and CC walked the streets of Chicago until CC had the bright idea of ducking into the House of Blues.

"Hell yeah! This is straight. The Hansons are doing a second show tonight," exclaimed CC.

"You got to be joking! Hanson? That boy band from Arkansas or someplace like that? You like that kind of music?" Sabin fired off the questions.

"Fuckin' a, those peckerwoods can play their own instruments and shit like that."

The bar wasn't crowded and Hanson didn't start for another hour. Sabin ordered a couple of beers. CC was asked for proof of age, but the bartender told him to forget it when CC started to create a scene.

"Hey, you guys Hanson fans too?" asked a robust, disheveled man in a white shirt, bow tie, and a leather Dallas Cowboy jacket.

Sabin pointed at CC and said, "Talk to him. He's the fan."

"Victor Veder, attorney at law." The man reached out, shook their hands, and handed out his business cards to everyone in the bar.

CHAPTER 13

The Price of Failure

"Where is she now?" The man's voice was low and gravelly. He sat in a dim office at the end of a large antique desk. A modern conference table extended from the desk, creating a T. Tall bookshelves surrounded the walls. The shelves were stocked with old leather-bound books, tattered books, and new books. Old portraits, photographs, and paintings of well-dressed men adorned the walls. Some were in suits, and others wore traditional Native American regalia. A computer monitor rested on a credenza behind the desk. A Dell computer equipped with a microphone, webcam, and large speakers hummed in the background. Video monitors hung from each corner in the office, displaying every entrance and exit to the building. The office was a fusion of antiquity and modern affluence.

"Please, everyone. Don't speak at once," the man said.

"Mr. Desheeta, sir ... she's in the Cook County jail," answered Bobby Riley.

"Let me see, Mr. Riley, that is if you will allow me to speak frankly?" Desheeta continued.

"Oh, certainly, sir. Please continue," Bobby Riley said. The others at the table nervously looked on.

"First it was Mr. White. Now, I agree the FBI infiltration was an excellent idea, and we diligently worked to have one of our own as an agent. Actually, having Phil Parks here as an administrator with the Social Security Administration was more difficult to pull off. Right, Phil?"

Phil Parks sat beside Bobby Riley as Desheeta spoke to the group. Phil gave Desheeta a nod of agreement.

"We are all elders here," Desheeta continued. "Elders are held to higher standards than those we have created through sharing our gifts. That is why I am so troubled tonight. Elders, we have lost two more of our best. Mr. Riley, did you not arrange for the extinction of this woman, which resulted in Mr. White's demise? And did you not arrange for her extinction a second time, which has resulted in two others falling from our ranks?" Desheeta glared at Bobby Riley, causing Teddy to lean back in his chair.

Teddy was wearing an expensive pinstriped suit with two diamond rings on each hand. In contrast, Desheeta was dressed in matching khaki shirt and pants. He wore a faded, green John Deere ball cap and scuffed work boots. The hat created a shadow over his face. The two men stared at each other while the others attempted to disguise their watchful eyes.

Teddy finally answered, "You know her assignment was mine. I underestimated her abilities. How was I supposed to know her gifts and strengths? I assumed she would be as the others we have exterminated: somewhat weaker than us, foolish, and unable to survive without a network of Spirit Walkers. Mark White obviously made some mistakes."

"Mistakes?" interrupted Desheeta. "He was sent alone. There was no backup plan, no strategy for the unexpected. You, Mr. Riley, made the mistake. Now, inform us of the Chicago debacle—or as you may wish to refer to it as that unfortunate incident."

"She must have had help. I assumed there would be no interference. Yes, Desheeta, we lost two of our warriors. We will eradicate her at the next opportunity," explained Bobby Riley.

"Next time ... I see. Well, are you sure there will be a next time?" asked Desheeta.

"Sure, there will be a next time. I mean, surely the police can't hold her. At best, it will appear that she was just defending herself. Besides, she might bond out. We'll get her as soon as she is released."

"Assume ... surely ... might. Gentlemen, do these sound like the words of a confident man? Gentlemen, do these sounds like words of a man who should be trusted with the lives of additional purebloods?" Desheeta made eye contact with everyone in the room. Each man but Bobby Riley made brief eye contact with Desheeta and nodded.

Bobby Riley started to speak but stopped when Desheeta motioned with his hand to indicate he was not finished.

"This woman, Apple, is nothing special. We have allowed her to live too long. I accept responsibility for that. Obviously, she has been underestimated. Obviously, she has created some sort of protective network. We can't afford another miscalculation."

The table of elders glanced at one another, knowing what Desheeta would order.

"Mr. Phil Parks, how long before Otis changes names and occupations?"

Phil Parks, who operated as Desheeta's first in command for the past fifteen decades, stood. "He has two to three years remaining before suspicion concerning his lack of aging will necessitate a change. Maybe even shorter now that the Patriot Act seems to have created a life of its own."

"Patriot Act? Do you actually believe it makes any difference for Otis? The man is a CIA operative. They have been watching their agents for years. They even kill their own agents. Let's not forget John Harper's disappearance after he made it inside the CIA. He was our first successful attempt to have a Spirit Walker inside. Neither he nor his blood were ever found. These days, it's an understatement to say no one trusts anyone. Otis paints a vivid picture of the power struggle between the FBI, CIA, Homeland Security, and all the other bureaucratic secret agencies. Some secret agencies have been created with the sole directive to watch other secret agencies. You know his last report about the new super unit he was in, Power Geysers, was almost unbelievable. Even for a man like me, who has experienced three centuries, I find what is happening to our country today quite disturbing. Snowden was just the beginning. There will be others who will skin this onion and let the people know the demise of true democracy. The sad thing is that we will be unable to hide our existence in this camera-ready and covert nation unless we morph with the changes."

"Sir, do you wish for Otis to be directed to handle our problem in Chicago?" asked Phil Parks.

"Yes, that will be fine," answered Desheeta. "Now we need to clean ourselves of another problem first."

Bobby Riley stood and backed away from the table. He nodded acceptance to his peers at the table.

"Desheeta, I fooled myself in believing the centuries had mellowed you somewhat. Guess it was just wishful thinking on my part. Anyway, without you, I would've died of old age many times over." Bobby Riley bowed to Desheeta and then to the other elders as he spoke.

A tall, lean man dressed in buckskin swiftly and quietly entered the room from behind Desheeta. He drew a bow, removed an arrow from the quiver on his back, and shot the arrow through Bobby Riley's heart. Bobby spread his arms and accepted his fate. Upon falling backward on the table, each elder drew a small bone-handled dagger and took turns stabbing Bobby's lifeless body.

The archer placed a large decorated bowl on the table. Bobby's blood raced across the table, ran up the bowl's side, and poured into it. Each elder produced a small silver cup. Each cup's animal likeness matched the animal engraved on the dagger. Each lowered a cup in the bowl of blood, held the cup high, and chanted in a tribal language. Each drank Bobby Riley's blood, allowing it to flow down the back of their throats. No one swallowed. Their glowing yellow eyes flared in the room.

CHAPTER 14

Friends in Low Places

Victor Veder awoke the next morning with an aching head and breath that could melt an alarm clock. He stumbled out of bed, took a three-minute piss, and gargled with baking soda. He noticed a yellow circle in front of his white underwear and thought how he needed to remember to shake it a few extra times. If not, the leakage stained his underwear. *What the hell?* It was just another sign of getting older. He had just turned fifty-eight last week, and the celebration continued. A faded Marine Corps insignia tattoo was barely noticeable beneath the white hair on his chest.

"One thousand dollars," he muttered to himself. "Now where did I get that?"

A longhaired calico cat welcomed Victor's awakened state with a slow brush against his ankles and a hungry meow.

"Suzy baby, is my little girl hungry?" Victor stumbled to the microwave, found a day-old chicken leg, and tossed it Suzy's way. Suzy attacked the chicken leg like a tiger devouring a monkey.

"Kick me! What time is it? Goddamn it. I should have been down at the jail three hours ago. I promised whatever the hell their names were I would get their girl. Now what the hell was her name? Some kind of damn fruit: orange, cherry, fig, well fuck," Victor Veder yelled while putting on clothes and searching for his car keys.

He ran out the door, jumped into his 1967 faded yellow Fastback Mustang, and spun out toward Cook County jail.

⚔ ⚔

Apple had not slept well. She was confident she had instilled the fear of the Lord into her bunkmate, but she didn't trust her other cellmates. She was relieved only a few days had passed since she last fed her gifts. She felt strong and didn't have any problem saying no thanks when a breakfast of runny eggs was served on a bed of stiff oatmeal. The other cellmates ate like it was the best food they had ever tasted. The coffee poured like Hershey's syrup, and the cream had more lumps than liquid.

"Your lawyer is here to see you." The jailer walked down the run, waking those who had court dates. "Yes, you darling." She pointed a finger at Apple.

"Lawyer? I have a lawyer?" Apple inquired.

"Guess so, sweetie. Let's go."

Apple backed up and placed her hands through the hole as instructed. The jailer placed handcuffs on her, asked her to back away from the door, and led her away.

⚔ ⚔

Detectives Dean and Dunn had spent the evening and most of the morning going through photographs, witness statements, and other items from the crime scene. They also read the morning paper, which contained an article about Apple. The article was slanted toward Apple possibly thwarting a robbery. The article contained a photo of Apple, handcuffed and being placed in a patrol car.

"That's all we need: a picture of a cute, young black woman being placed in a patrol car by white officers," Dean commented.

"Yeah, after reading this shit, it makes us look like we arrested the damn hero," Dunn added.

"Dunn, Dean, who wants to catch line three?" asked the secretary entering the room with a steaming coffeepot.

"Who is it? I told you we didn't want any calls this morning. We got that vigilante or whatever she is to figure out," responded Dean while holding his cup out for a refill.

"It's some reporter or someone from the newspaper. Says he has an old photograph of your girl. You know, your black female Bruce Lee."

Dean took the call and advised the man that it would probably be tomorrow before they would have time to visit with him.

"Dunn, this guy says he has a photo of this Apple chick posing with some gangsters from the late twenties," Dean said after hanging up.

"Yeah, right. What's the big deal about that? This guy must think we're stupid or something. The chick in the picture would have to be about a hundred years old or so by now."

"I don't know. The old man was convincing. Says he is a photographer, and he has an eye for detail. Says it's the eyes. Says no two women could have eyes like that. Big, round descriptive eyes," explained Dunn.

"I kind of thought she looked like that movie star. You know who I am talking about? What is her name?" Dean continued.

"You talking about Alfre Woodard?"

"Yeah, that's the one."

"Well, you ready for round two?" asked Dunn.

"Guess so. We'll see what she has to say about the forensics," Dean said while grabbing a file of photographs and witness statements.

The detectives walked in together. Apple was seated across from them with her hands resting in her lap and a pleasant smile. She was rubbing her wrist where the handcuffs had been.

"Good morning, Miss Lewis. Hope you are well rested. Did you find the accommodations satisfactory? Oh yes, I have a report from the jail administrator that one of your cellmates was treated in the infirmary this morning. Seems she broke three fingers last night. You wouldn't know anything about that, would you?" Dean asked.

Apple turned the corner of her mouth up and shrugged her right shoulder.

Dean pushed the photos toward Apple and asked if she recognized any of them. The two bodies were those of her attackers. Their dissected bodies were like mummies. Only their hair reflected someone, who just moments before the photos, had been alive. They waited for her to respond, watching for any facial expressions. None were shown.

Dunn slid copies of witness statements across the table. Apple gingerly placed her fingers on them, separating the pages in front of her. She read Max's statement first. He had seen nothing. He explained his blood-splattered clothes as being a government conspiracy. Max described the blood as having been freeze-dried and liquefied when he opened the letter it was contained in. He claimed the letter was from the Federal Railroad Retirement Board. *These men have not had time to check Max's mental health record.*

Roger Merit claimed to have seen the whole melee. He claimed there were ten assailants, and he helped Apple fight them off. He also claimed to be Apple's lover.

Mitzy attested to seeing the men come in but ran as soon as the fight started. She had asked for a lawyer and refused to answer any more questions.

Apple looked at the two detectives and asked, "Abduhla Kahn? Where's his statement? He was there also."

"I'm afraid he was carted away by the Homeland Security Task Force. He didn't have much to say anyway," Dunn responded.

"Look, Miss Lewis, we don't wish to waste your time or our time. There is a great deal that requires explanation here. Why don't you just help us all out?" implored Dean.

"I'm sorry, gentlemen. I told you all I knew yesterday," offered Apple.

"Okay, look here. We're going to keep you here as long as it takes. We're going to find out everything there is to know about you. If you have every stubbed your toe, we will find out where and when. Do you understand me?" Dean asked.

"If that's the case, I need a lawyer," replied Apple.

"Detectives, there's a gentleman out here claiming to be Miss Lewis's attorney. Shall I let him in?" interrupted the secretary.

"Hell, might as well. She's been asking for one," Dunn answered.

"Yes, yes. Thank you very much, Officer. Victor Veder, attorney at law, representing that girl right there." Victor wore a ruffled bright blue suit, a white belt, and a pair of black-and-white oxfords.

"Have a seat, Mr. Veder." Dunn pulled an additional chair from the corner.

Apple was carefully analyzing all that was happening around her. This was one time she wished her gift of smell would fail her. *This man stinks like a sewer rat on crack. Is this a joke? Is he just an ambulance chaser? Maybe he was sent by the Spirit Walkers to set me up with bad counsel.*

"Gentlemen, I believe it is customary to have a few minutes alone with my client, so if you will excuse me," Victor requested.

The two detectives reluctantly left the room, stood behind the two-way mirror, and turned the speaker volume up. Both were aware of the legality of eavesdropping on attorney-client conversations.

"Who the hell sent you here?" asked Apple.

"Look, I'm having difficultly this morning. Give me a break. I can't remember their names, but they paid a retainer fee, and here I am."

"What kind of attorney are you … can't remember names," scolded Apple.

"Haven't you ever been hungover?"

"No, I have not. I don't like being out of control."

"Well, honey. I was out of control last night at the House of Blues."

"What did they look like? You said they. Were there more than two of them?"

"Damn, lady. You would think you would be glad to see me. Maybe you ought to spend another day or two in jail."

Apple grabbed his arm and squeezed. "How many—and what did they look like?"

"Shit. That hurts!" Victor yelled while attempting to pull his arm from her grasp. "Some young black man and an old hippie!" yelled Victor.

Apple turned him loose and started to laugh. She then stared toward the two-way mirror. She knew she heard something. Victor quieted after noticing her intense stare into the mirror.

Dean and Dunn, startled by her stare, hurried from the room and stood in the hallway.

"They fit the description of the two suspects who ran out the back door of Starbucks," Dean proclaimed. "Maybe we should've confronted her about those two?"

"Sounds like that's our boys," agreed Dunn. "Let's put a tail on the lawyer when he leaves. He will need to report progress to his clients. It's probably best that we didn't ask her about the two who were seen running out the back door, especially now that this dumb-ass attorney will lead us to them."

"Where are they now?" whispered Apple, loosening her grip on Victor's arm.

"I don't know. I think I remember them saying something about contacting me. Hell, I don't know where they're at. They're your damn friends, not mine." Victor pulled his arm away and stood.

"All right then. I just needed to confirm who sent you. Now can you arrange for my release today?"

"Don't know. I just got here. The front desk says they have no record of an official charge, so there may be some hope. Now, did you do it?" Apple cut her eyes at him. He must have read her eyes correctly. "You know, as your attorney, I will represent you whether you are guilty or innocent. Inquiring minds want to know. How did you do it? I read the paper while waiting to see you. The carnage and all that horror shit they wrote. Is it true?"

Apple almost wanted to answer the fool, but she was not sure whether anyone else was listening. She wondered how she always attracted such oddball and misfit characters. She had not actually attracted this one, but her supply line of characters had. How in the hell Sabin and CC came up with this character was beyond her. "Don't always believe what you read in the paper," she finally responded.

-⧓ ⧓-

"CC, wake up, man. Time to put your groove on or something like that." Sabin shook CC, attempting to awaken him. They had spent the night in a Days Inn.

"Leave me the fuck alone, man. You crazy or something? You don't be jackin' with a brother while's he's asleep … shit!"

"I didn't know Spirit Walkers could drink, much less have a hangover. Now get up. We need to check with that attorney we hired last night. Apple may already be out of jail and looking for us."

"Yeah, you right, I'm a crazy Spirit Walker, and I'm goin' to get Neanderthal on your white ass if you don't shut up!"

"Hey, man, that's from *Pulp Fiction*, ain't it? That's what the big black gangster says after being sodomized by the white dudes."

"Sodomized, my ass, Sabin, the word is *punked*. When you goin' to escape the sixties, seventies, or whatever decade you are lost in?"

"Me? You're the one who's a walking cliché. Speaking of clichés, how did you become a Spirit Walker? You know, was it a family thing or what?"

CC rolled out of bed, pulled up his sagging Spider Man boxer shorts, and rubbed his eyes.

"I had this inoperable brain cancer. I shouldn't be telling you this. Guess it makes no difference now since I fucked up. They probably goin' to eradicate my ass now anyway.

"I said, 'Fuck it. If I am goin' to die, I might as well have a good time, hang with my homies, and that kind of shit.' I figured I could get away with just about anything I wanted to. It's not like they were goin' to keep me in jail for long with having to medicate my illness and shit like that. So I did some shit I ain't proud of, robbed a few dudes, and stole some shit."

"Is there a shorter version, like *Readers Digest* or something like that?" asked Sabin.

"Do you want to hear the fuckin' story or not?"

"It's cool, man. I'm just joking around with you."

"So it was like this. Shit didn't go down the way I thought it would. My health got worse sooner than expected, and I found myself homeless. Hell, I was even stealing from the street musicians, dancers, and shit like that. It was a two-box night."

"What's a two-box night?"

"It's the American version of a three-dog night. Since I didn't have no damn dogs, it take two boxes to try to stay warm. The wind was blowing off the lake through the back alleys. You see—I had to stay down on Michigan Avenue 'cause that's where all the money is at with tourists and all hangin' down there. Anyway, this dude grabbed my ankles and pulled me out of my boxes. I say to him, 'What in the fuck are you doin'?' He says I'll do just fine, pulls a knife with one hand, and has some kind of container, bottle, or some shit like that in the other. I tells the motherfucker if he wants to kill me, then go ahead and do it. 'I ain't afraid of your ugly ass,' I tell him. Crazy motherfucker says good or some shit like that, and how this will be easy and won't hurt. I say, 'Yeah right. You can kill me, but I may just try to fuck you up a little too.'"

"So you're standing having a conversation, debating with a man who is going to end your life?" asked Sabin.

"Straight shit I did. He grabs my throat and lifts me off the ground with one hand. If I could've talked right about then, I would've said, 'Shit, you a strong motherfucker for a skinny-ass nagger.' Then he starts flaring his nostrils and shit like that. His eyes turn yellow, and I start to think maybe this motherfucker is the devil himself. A long-ass fingernail comes out of his middle finger, and he uses it to scratch my face. He then licks this ugly-ass nail. He gets this shit-eating grin on his face and tells me how I am sick and already dead. I say, 'Fuck you, motherfucker. How you know that?' He says some shit about a gift, and I say, 'I got your motherfuckin' gift right here.'"

CC became more animated as he recounted his tale.

Sabin waited for CC to finish his story, while CC took several interludes to collect unused soap, toilet paper, and anything else of use in the motel room.

"Hey, man, don't look at me that away. I got brothers on the street who can use this stuff," CC snarled.

"So, I'm like being held in the air, kickin' and shit like that, and this fucker throws me to the ground. He starts to walk off, and I call him a pussy. 'Can't you finish what you started, you pussy,' I yelled at him. 'If I wasn't sick, I would fuck you up bad.' He turns back toward me and says, 'What did you say?' I said, 'You heard me right, asshole. You deaf or some shit like that?' The man starts laughing like he can't control himself. Then I start laughing. He says, 'You're the pussy, my friend.' By this time, I'm weak from all the shit, and I just stare at him. He says he can help me, but I am probably just another homeless coward. Then he asked me if I wanted to be rid of my illness. I tell him that's the most stupid fuckin' question anyone has ever asked. 'Stupid motherfucker, my cancer can't be cured. Sure as hell anyone would want to live as long as possible.' He tells me to be careful what you wish for. The man's eyes glowed more yellow, and he says he can purify my body, but there was a side effect. 'Sure, motherfucker. I'm worried about some damn side effect. I'm dying here, and you givin' me a lecture on side effects.' He tells me not to

175

hesitate when he offers his blood. 'Blood?' I say, 'What blood?' The crazy motherfucker slices his wrist with that long, ugly fingernail and drains some of his own blood in some sort of pretty bottle. He offers his blood for me to drink. I thought for a moment how silly this is. Then I thought, *Hell, I am dying anyway, so fuck it.* I grabbed the blood and shot it down like a smooth glass of Canadian Mist."

"That's a great story. We better get going," interrupted Sabin.

"You asked, so don't interrupt me. I'm not finished. I drank the shit. Then all of a sudden I got this ass-kickin' stomachache. I started rolling around on the ground. I must have passed out. When I opened my eyes, there was the man, patiently waiting on me. He said I was changed now and would be all right. Then I remember something about side effects, so I asked him. He smiled and said not to worry about it. The only side effect was I was going to live a long time. Then as he walked away, he turned back and told me to get used to how I looked 'cause I wouldn't be aging normally. I yelled, 'What does that mean?' He just laughed and walked away."

CC was now dressed and ready to go. The two cleaned the room of any items that might connect them to the room. They had paid cash when they registered, and there was no need to check out.

"One last thing, CC. I promise not to ask about Spirit Walkers again, but how did you come to be attached to Apple?"

"I know what you're getting at. It's not like I was trying to seduce her or anything like that. Now, if she would give me a chance, I would rock her world. I was having a good time, you know. Hell, I could see for miles when I wanted to. I could hear people talking on the twentieth floor from the street if I wanted to. I never even got a runny nose. Then it all came crashing down. It took about six months, and then I couldn't eat, drink, take a shit, or do anything like that. I thought the cancer had come back, and I was dying. The fucker found me again. This time I was in really bad shape and didn't have the energy to give him any shit. I just told him to leave me the fuck alone.

"He said he could make me well again, but I would have to help them. 'Fuck,' I said. 'I will do anything.' He had some other dude with him. This man said I needed to be the guardian over some chick in town named Apple Lewis. All I had to do was stay close to her, and they would come around every now and then to check on both of us. If any harm comes her way, I was supposed to stop it. Like some guardian angel bullshit. He let me in on a little secret. I had to drink blood every so often or die. If he would've laid that shit on me earlier, I would've preferred to die. They both laughed, said, 'This one is on us,' and handed me a pint of blood. It didn't take me long to tell those fuckers I wasn't drinking blood. They walked away, saying it was my call. Two days later, I grabbed that blood out of the icebox and drank it like a Colt 45. The rest is history. But I fucked up. Apple is in jail, and these men may come take me out."

CHAPTER 15

Meet Mr. Beaver

Alicia Overstreet couldn't wait to return to work. Excitement about work was a rarity for her. She had been thinking about work all day—even when she attempted to fall asleep. She had arrived home after fighting Beltway traffic. Normally, she would not have been on the Beltway, but she needed to go to Silver Springs, Maryland, to pick up a book she found listed at an antique bookstore that had references to the Tulsa race riots. Normally, she would take the Metro from her apartment in Alexandria, but with work being so boring these days, she allowed herself the luxury of mobility. She drove.

She knew her Internet activities at work were always subject to monitoring, but she believed a little heat could be faded if questioned about searching for old books on the Internet. Internet shopping was not uncommon for researchers like her. Besides, she didn't think the CIA had time to check their spyware and follow up on every Internet violation. Besides there were all the big fish to fry like Snowden and a host of other big security breaches with the NSA and others.

She fought the covers all afternoon. The covers, including the sheets, were on the floor. It was the mattress caressing her face that caused her to wake up.

She punched in two minutes on the microwave oven, placed a tea bag in a mug of hot water, watched the bag swim to the bottom, and hit cook. She stuffed one of three remaining Fig Newtons in her mouth, stopped the microwave with fifteen seconds remaining, dropped the other two in the tea, and then sat in a lime-green beanbag chair. She checked her Blackberry for e-mails. That was her wake-up routine.

Today's routine was somewhat different because she brought unauthorized work home. CIA policy disallowed the removal of documents generated at workstations without prior authorization. Asking and receiving permission from her supervisor, Ron Evans, wasn't complicated or difficult. Asking permission would generate his patented bureaucratic, holier-than-thou oral dissertation. Mostly, this included how even the most seemly insignificant paper, if fallen into the wrong hands, could cause worldly destruction or destroy democracy. Alicia didn't have time for a repeat performance from Mr. Evans. Also, this had the potential to make her look like the crazy one in the office.

The previous night's research created a renewed excitement about her value as an intelligent human being and as a viable terrorism task-force member. She had begun to question her usefulness as an Internet CIA nerd. Searching website after website, day after day, and finding nothing of significance, was providing her with little job satisfaction. Rarely was she able to connect conversations in chat rooms to national security. Now, however, she was on to something. She wasn't sure exactly what it was, but she was connecting the dots. She dared not ask permission to take the work home. She made the decision to beg for forgiveness if detected.

What she secretly procured included newspaper articles, death certificates, witness accounts, police reports, and autopsy findings on a series of unexplained deaths over the past seventy-six years. The journey started with the Chicago Starbucks killings, and purely from boredom, she started a word search utilizing descriptions of the deceased's wounds. After retrieving archives on related lethal wounds, the search extended to other unexplained deaths. The Tulsa River killings, as they were referred to in the 1927 newspaper clippings, occurred in the 1920s. Some accounts attributed the killings to a wild animal, and others indicted the KKK or blacks retaliating for the Tulsa race riots. Alicia was astonished by the lack of data and detail on the riot. It appeared that every detail about the riot was speculative. She printed everything she could find. It wasn't the research on terrorism she was being paid to do, but who knew where the trail might end.

She had found an article from a 1930s Chicago newspaper called "The Snow Murders," which had similarities to the Tulsa killings. At work, she would backtrack the dates from the Chicago article and then move forward again. There were several big questions; the most pressing was how killings over so many decades could be connected. Was there a very old serial killer out there somewhere, and if so, what did the woman currently being detained in Chicago have to do with anything? Maybe someone else had researched the older killings and decided to be a copycat killer.

Alicia pressed the start button to her laptop, pulled a plate of leftovers from the icebox, and attempted to create a sandwich. Normally, she would have walked down to the corner store but she was too preoccupied with the killings to dress, fetch food, and return.

Alicia had been trying to quit smoking and was preparing to light up an old generic menthol cigarette she found while moving the coffeemaker when the phone rang. She wasn't in a mood to talk to anyone and watched the phone until the caller identification appeared. The caller ID read "Caller Unknown," but she recognized the number. Alicia wondered why a top-notch CIA operative would allow his personal cell phone number to be identified. Something was missing in the equation. Maybe it was some sort of code number and not traceable. *Shit,* she thought, *it's Otis Beaver again.*

Otis Beaver worked in the same building as Alicia. He was

introduced to all coworkers as a statistician. Of course, no one at work bought this. The CIA was notorious for planting operatives in normal, dull, and inauspicious surroundings. This included utilizing the CIA's own basic nonfield operative offices as cover for agents. Alicia actually believed this process was ingenious and clever. *Who would actually look for an agent right in a CIA office?* It made sense to her. *Who would suspect an employee who came and went from the office for everyone to see?*

She listened to the phone ring and blended soy milk with coffee. What did Otis Beaver want from her? Alicia was no fool when it came to men. She knew she was somewhat cute but not overly attractive. Otis Beaver was too glorious to be chasing her. He was six feet tall, with thick dark hair, a perfect complexion, and a muscular build. Best of all, he was smart.

His intelligence had impressed Alicia the most. He knew everything about everything. He talked history as though he had witnessed it for the past several centuries. Initially, he sought her out to learn what she was able to teach him about computers, Internet research, and other web-based things. It was during these training sessions that she noticed two things. The first, strictly from a woman's perspective, was his excellent choice of Obsession cologne. The second was that his eyewear was fake. He didn't require corrective lenses. Glasses did make him even cuter, if that was possible.

She lit the cigarette, took a large gulp of hot latte, and debated whether to call him back. The red message flasher on the side of her phone was pulsating. He had left another message. She blew smoke rings toward her newest IKEA purchase, a solar crystal chandelier. She chose her men carefully, and there were many caution signs surrounding Otis Beaver.

Alicia saw men as disposable objects. They were to be used as needed, then discarded. Her sexual appetite was strong but not so strong she didn't have the strength to reject a suitor who might be inappropriate or out of her class. She never overestimated herself when it came to men. She knew the type of men who were attracted to her, and she took full advantage. Otis Beaver didn't fit her mode of operation. He also didn't seem discouraged or fooled by her fake lack of interest. She often thought he knew she was faking and somehow needed her for something or just wanted the challenge. He was probably unaccustomed to working this hard to get into a female geek's pants. Every time he tried, he was getting closer.

Arriving at work, she presented her fingers and palms for the usual biometric identification. An eye scan was being installed. Alicia was impressed that her little work team and office was becoming important enough for such an upgrade. Then again, with how the federal government operated, the upgrade was probably just another way to spend all the extra Homeland Security appropriations.

Alicia searched the Cook County felony docket but didn't locate any criminal charges being filed on an Apple Lewis. This caused her to believe that another suspect had been arrested or detained. She checked the Cook County booking list, which showed Apple Lewis in custody. She was reviewing a follow-up article in the *Chicago Sun* when a hand touched her shoulder. Startled, she turned to acknowledge the presence of Otis Beaver.

"Good evening, Miss Overstreet. I hope this beautiful evening finds you doing well."

"Thank you. I'm doing just fine this evening," Alicia responded in her customary way.

Seldom did anyone in the office address coworkers other than with proper etiquette. If anyone were to do otherwise, it would be Otis. His casual attitude toward office protocol was something new for the otherwise drab atmosphere. From his initial introduction, he appeared aloof. He had nicknames for everyone in the research section. Alicia had been patiently waiting for weeks to hear what name he had given her. Alicia often thought Otis got away with foolishness because he was a hotshot agent.

Rumor had it that he was a member of a small, local special operations unit called the Power Geysers. Supposedly, the unit's primary—and maybe only—function was to eradicate the DC area of terrorist suspects. Alicia wondered if management ever gave the CIA plankton, such as herself, credit for noticing the obvious.

"I left you a message on your phone earlier. Did you get it?" Otis asked.

"No. I guess I was already out for the day," replied Alicia, returning to her computer screen.

"By the way, Mr. Beaver, how long had you been looking over my shoulder?"

"Long enough to know you're not searching for terrorist web chatter," he slyly responded.

"You know, you should really stop that," Alicia remarked.

"Surely you should allow me to practice my sneaky skills. Who knows, someday I might be a real agent," Otis responded. His wink went unnoticed by anyone other than hidden cameras.

"Mr. Beaver, now why would you want to practice something you will never use in this CIA plankton pool? Now, what is it you do around here exactly? I mean, you're either sick a lot or have other duties I'm not aware of." Alicia realized she was taking a small risk. It was a controlled risk, unlike her college days.

"Why don't you have breakfast with me after work, and we can discuss all your questions? Besides, I'm curious about your current research," Otis suggested.

Alicia absorbed the aroma of his cologne. She was torn between curiosity for this man and her need to be realistic about her desires and chances for fulfillment. Her practicality indicated this was a mixed match at best. He either obliviously wanted something other than sex from her or he was the most insecure gorgeous man she had ever met.

"Sure, we can have a bite to eat in the morning," responded Alicia, finally looking up at Otis.

"Great," responded Otis. "I will meet you out front, and we can go to that little folksy diner down the street."

"So sorry, I thought you were going to pick me up at my place. There are several great breakfast venues in Alexandria. You know, those hard-to-find antitourism places." She thought this would deter him and the evenings' game would be over.

"Great, that will be fine. I will pick you up at your place about nine."

She hadn't expected such a quick and positive response. *He must be really hard up—or I'm stupid,* she thought. She was hesitant to give him her address. What the hell? He's a CIA agent for heaven's sake. Anyone could find out where I live. "Sure, that will be fine," she responded. She continued working but could feel his presence.

The work shift slowly faded toward daybreak. She exhausted all her options on killings that may have been related to the Chicago Starbucks but not before finding a possible related oddity. She discovered a coroner's report on a Hell's Angel death in 1970. The death certificate listed cause of death as homicide due to unknown causes. The report described the victim's throat as having been torn out. She listed this death as another possible connection to her serial killer or killers. No record of anyone being charged could be located.

Alicia walked outside and allowed the cool morning breeze whipping around the white granite building to have full access to her face. The breeze awakened her drowsiness.

As the Metro train sped parallel to the National Airport, she gazed out the window. As she saw the tall Masonic Temple reaching for the sky, she knew she was five minutes from her station. She departed the Metro, walked down three flights of stairs, crossed the street, and strolled past the numerous specialty shops Alexandria was noted for. She peered into several storefront windows in an effort to calm her nervousness. She was having second thoughts about her spontaneous agreement to have breakfast with Otis Beaver. *Maybe it wasn't so spontaneous.* She knew the mind could convince a person of anything. This was especially true for her when the topic was emotion or desires.

She arrived home at a quarter after eight and decided there was enough time to take a quick shower. A morning shower usually helped her sleep, but she was banking on it to keep her fresh and awake. If she was going to have to match wits with Otis, she had better be alert. Hot water pulsated across her back as she made the mental transition from work to relaxation. Stepping from the shower, she heard a knock at the door. She quickly glanced at the bedroom clock: 8:55. *Had she stayed in the shower that long?*

The doorbell rang as Alicia reached for a heavy terrycloth robe she had stolen from a Marriott several years earlier. Hastily, she tied the belt and peeked through the door eye. It was Otis.

"I'm not ready!" she yelled through the door.

"Sorry. I guess I may be about five minutes early. Do you mind if I come in while you get ready? It's a little odd standing out here at this time of day."

For a second, she almost asked him to go away—and they could try another day. There was something about him that conflicted with her ability to think completely rationally. She smelled him through the door—or at least imagined she did.

"I guess so," she responded while unlocking two deadbolts and a chain. She was surprised to see he had changed clothes. He wore faded jeans and an untucked black dress shirt. He wore a pair of black-and-white Adidas sport flip-flops and no glasses.

"I will just sit here and watch television, if you don't mind?"

"Sure, okay. That'll be fine," she said nervously while walking past him.

Otis reached and took her hand in his as she walked by. He gently encouraged her to spin around by giving the slightest tug on her arm. She turned to face him. He placed his hands on her hips and stared into her eyes. The whole world stood still. She stared back into his dark eyes and felt paralyzed. She felt hypnotized. She tried to move her arms, but nothing happened. She concentrated on taking a step backward, but her legs wouldn't obey.

Otis kissed her on one cheek then the other. He found her lips and gently caressed them with his. He removed one hand from her waist and touched her neck. She felt warmth begin in her neck, and it rushed through her entire body. He dropped to his knees, untied her robe, and slowly pushed it off her shoulders.

She tried to speak but couldn't. She watched helplessly while he kissed her stomach, circling his tongue around her pierced belly button. He kissed her breasts. She felt all the natural sensations of being seduced, caressed, and kissed, but she was unable to move.

He gently picked her up like a rag doll. He carried her into the bedroom and pulled back the covers. He whispered, "You can move now." Magically, she could move again, but she lacked the desire to do so. She wiggled her toes and placed her arms around him just to be sure she could actually move.

"Let the lovemaking begin," she whispered to herself.

Otis Beaver stood naked, viewing his latest conquest. She was resting peacefully in a deep sleep. He laughed loudly while thinking of the advantage he had over other men. Besides all the gifts bestowed upon him as a Spirit Walker, he possessed an additional gift of creating a trance in his victims. He found it more useful on women for his other gifts were more suited for ensuring a good kill. He admired the contour of her hips one last time and searched her apartment.

His searching was unsuccessful. He had been researching Apple Lewis and had planned a trip to Chicago. But he was surprised to see Alicia researching Apple. Otis had lived for more than two hundred years and was never surprised by anything. At first, he thought the CIA was on to him. Maybe Alicia was part of a test. He believed it was just a coincidence. Alicia must have stumbled across something that intrigued her. Maybe it was the carnage and sensational newspaper coverage. He had to know more.

He finished searching the apartment and walked back to the bedroom. Alicia had rolled over on her back but remained asleep.

"I will allow you to live for another day, my little victim. Who knows, we may engage our bodies again, but you will eventually have to be eliminated. Don't connect all the dots on Apple Lewis too soon."

☩ CHAPTER 16 ☩

Day in Court

Apple moved to a different cell on her second night. She and Victor Veder spent five hours the previous day reviewing her case. She was pleased that Sabin was somewhere in Chicago, trying to help her. She remained unsure about CC, but due to information obtained from Victor, she assumed CC was a friend and was helping Sabin. She also suspected CC was a Spirit Walker because of his actions at Starbucks. *USA Today* called the melee a "Massacre at the Coffee House."

Apple watched the activities of her new cellmates from her bunk. There were four others in the cell. Jail officials had conducted a quick screening on her yesterday afternoon. The frail white girl, who could have been no older than twenty, had explained it was a risk assessment to determine where she would be placed within the jail. Apple created a perfect childhood history with two loving, deceased parents and a brother who had died in Vietnam. She enjoyed spinning a web of innocent deceit for the assessor. However, spinning a Norman Rockwell picture of family life didn't override the risk points for a violent crime. Because of her risk assessment, she assumed her cellmates were also violent offenders. Apple had learned not to tell and not to ask about crimes.

Too much noise in the cellblock kept Apple from sleeping. Apple could hear the breakfast orderlies being removed from their cells at two in the morning. She could hear thumpings and sexual assaults occurring in cells on both sides of her cell.

Martha, the toughest woman Apple had ever met, explained what a blanket party was. She was serving a year in the county jail for an aggravated assault on an ex-boyfriend. Martha explained that she wasn't aggravated at all at her ex, but he just deserved a good ass kicking, and she gave him one. She represented herself at a plea bargain and attempted to advise the judge how poor dental hygiene caused her ex's teeth to fall out—and not her left hook. She had more difficulty explaining a chewed-off ear and an eyeball knocked out of the socket. *If Martha were to ever become a Spirit Walker, she would be the ultimate killing machine.* She knew other Spirit Walkers would kill her for being too noticeable.

Rebecca wore nothing but county-issued boxer shorts. Every time she moved, the plastic pad on her bunk squeaked and crackled, creating an unforgettable memory for Apple. Martha told Apple how Rebecca would dare someone to make a move on her. Rebecca wasn't her real name, but one she gave herself since no one could pronounce her real name. She was part Laotian and Sudanese. A dragon tattoo crawled down her back and disappeared into her shorts. She had matching scorpion tattoos starting at the elbows and stopping just short of her neck. Her hair was black and glistened when a stray light from another cell reached into theirs. Apple had to admit that the woman was pretty. Martha claimed to have run into her on the street, and that Rebecca was a low-rent assassin who swung both ways. Allegedly, she was in on a sting operation where she agreed to snuff someone. The person doing the hiring was an undercover cop.

The last cellmate was Cindy. She was a crying wreck of a woman who had killed her husband while he slept on the couch. She claimed self-defense after years of abuse, but the county had no record of abuse calls from her. She would awaken every few hours, plead her innocence to whoever was awake, and then cry herself to sleep again.

A fog of smells lingered in the cell as the predawn hours slowly passed. The nicotine-hued walls were indicative of livelier times when one could smoke the hours away. Now, only the debilitating atmosphere of freedom removed was available for contemplation assistance. Apple was thankful for her gift of night vision. She could pierce any darkened corner or hapless silhouette many yards in either direction.

Not wishing to cause trouble or bring attention to herself, Apple waited patiently for Rebecca to wash her face and comb her hair. Only she and Rebecca had motivation to prepare themselves for visitors that day. Rebecca had a court date, and Apple was hopeful she would be released until the investigation was completed. Rebecca paraded topless across the floor and shared a sinister grin with Martha. Apple caught both grins and wondered if it was a sign of mutual respect or a prelude to an altercation.

Apple was hoping for a shower but had been advised showers and a change of jumpsuits happened every three days. *I will be out of here before my next shower*, she thought. She had not forgotten the seventy-two hour rule. Apple attempted to comb her hair, and Rebecca offered a rubber band to Apple. Apple pulled her hair back into a tight ponytail, washed her face, looked into the shiny sheet metal posing as a mirror, and did her best Fonzy imitation. She chuckled to herself as she walked away. *They can't take my sense of humor away.*

"Rise and shine," came the announcement in maximum decibels from down the run. "I say rise and shine, you bitches!"

Apple heard doors popping and keys rattling as cells were opened and mates were instructed to go to chow.

"No, no, no, not you babes!" The guard pointed at Apple and the others. "You, the violent ones, the fantastic four. I just kill myself. Should have been a stand-up comic … shit."

"Stand back, you wild ones, you children of a lesser god." More chuckling. "Over here, my man." She directed a young man to park the food tray and handed four plates through the door.

"See that there, Kenny? That's some fine-looking women."

Apple felt a twinge of hostility toward the guard and her ignorance as she struggled to keep her mouth shut. "Your vernacular certainly improves the austerity of our humble abode, and your fat ass is tantamount to the four of us," Apple hurled the insult before she realized what she was doing.

"That some sort of cussing language, you little bitch? I could write your ass up for verbal assault on an officer!"

"Why, no, officer, I was just immersed with admiration for your physical dilapidation, enshrouded in spiraling layers of obesity, and mesmerized by your gorgonian face," replied Apple, unable to control herself.

"You trying to get fresh with me, ain't you? Well, I ain't that kind of woman. I got me a loving husband at home who takes good care of my needs," the guard responded defiantly.

"I bet he don't go down on the muffin," Martha yelled out as the guard and Kenny strolled to the next row of cells.

"Hell, you one educated bitch. Give me five," Martha said with a laugh.

Rebecca attempted to disguise a smile, turned her back, and finished dressing. She had a complete set of dress clothes for her court appearance. She dressed with her back to them in the darkest corner of the cell. When she stepped out of the corner, she appeared as a dark-haired Jane Fonda from the movie *Nine to Five*. She even had a pair of black, thick-framed glasses and a pink bow in her hair.

"Okay, License to Kill, you're next," said one of two uniformed women who arrived moments later. "Let's see what a jury does for you. I told you last month you should have taken the twenty-five years that young assistant district attorney offered you. You probably are going to get life now."

Rebecca backed into the cell door and placed her hands through the bars for the woman to handcuff her. The two officers escorted her away. Moments later, the two officers returned.

"Miss Apple Lewis, you're next. Guess you don't need any fancy clothes this time around," one of them announced.

Apple replicated Rebecca's procedure by backing to the bars to be handcuffed. As they walked away, Apple thought how she wasn't looking forward to being interrogated by the two detectives again. Choosing between visiting with the detectives and talking with her attorney would be a choice of the lesser of two evils. They walked past the pungent smells of drying mops and cleaning supplies and past the back docks of garbage. They arrived at a garage-type door, which opened when one of the officers inserted an identification card. The bright rays of light momentarily caught Apple by surprise.

"Where am I going?" asked Apple.

"Don't know for sure. We just got our orders to deliver you downtown."

Not another word was said as they drove toward the famous skyline of Chicago.

⊰ ⊱

"Apple Lewis."

"Yes, Your Honor."

"Are you represented by counsel today?"

"Appears that I am not, sir, I mean, Your Honor."

"And why is that, Miss Lewis?"

Apple perused the filled courtroom. Her two favorite detectives nodded and smiled at her. There was no Sabin or Victor Veder.

"Miss Lewis, if I could garner some of your attention, we might proceed." The young judge wore the traditional black robe. "This court doesn't have time to waste. As you can ascertain, there are at least fifty defendants in the room awaiting arraignments."

"Arraignment? Your Honor, am I being arraigned?" Apple asked.

"Young lady, the state of Illinois has charged you with second-degree murder. Now, do you or do you not have an attorney?"

"Yes, sir. I have an attorney of record. His name is Victor Veder, but I don't know where he is, sir." Apple saw a smiling man stand up across the room and walk toward the bench.

"Your Honor, if it pleases the court, the state would not object if a court-appointed attorney was provided at this time. We believe Miss Lewis would probably qualify as indigent. Also, Your Honor, I am certain the court is aware of Mr. Victor Veder's attendance record, as this is business as usual for him," remarked the state's attorney.

"Miss Lewis, do you wish to have an attorney appointed by this court to represent you?" asked the judge.

Apple applied pressure to her handcuffs and again perused the room.

"Your Honor, I believe my attorney was not properly notified of this hearing. If he had been, he certainly would have been here. I am not indigent and would prefer my own attorney."

"Clerk, check the record for notifications," demanded the judge.

"Mr. Assistant District Attorney, please step forward. I have been advised the court has no record of attorney notification of this hearing. What gives?"

The state's attorney quietly explained to the judge how the detectives had just brought him the case this morning and had assured him they had notified Mr. Veder. The judge asked what the rush was all about. He was informed that the case was receiving an unusual amount of media attention, and time for filing charges were running out.

Apple smiled, knowing they didn't have a clue that she could hear every word they were saying.

"Next case. Miss Lewis, you will remain here until two this afternoon, which should provide ample time for the state to correct their notification process."

Apple was escorted downstairs and placed in a human-sized crate, a so-called holding cell. A stainless steel toilet was attached to one side of the wire cage. She could cope staying in a large cell, but the cage was challenging. She tried to concentrate on something other than the size of the cage. There were plenty of distractions around her to assist with this endeavor. Defendants were being placed and removed from cages as their names were called for court action. Court officers were sneaking down to the cage area to have quick, unauthorized smokes. Several defendants, and even a few officers, recognized Apple from a mug shot that had been released to the news. Apple wasn't in the mood to be a conversationalist.

Apple's gifts grew restless as the dire reality of the situation sank in. Twice she found herself separating the cage wire with her fingers. Her eyes flashed yellow when moments of claustrophobia embraced her. Sweat beaded on her face and neck, and then it ran down to her zipper. Apple fixated on the sweat in an attempt to quell her gifts, but they intensified. She detected the trail of armpit smells as court officers rode the elevators. She could hear conversations through the walls. Through the wall to a room on her left, she heard a mother begging her son to plead guilty and ask for drug court. Farther away, in the catacomb of basement offices, she overheard a young man advising his attorney how he could do a deuce standing on his head. Down the darkened hallway at least fifty yards away, she could see cobwebs hanging on for life.

Apple entertained escaping. She could effortlessly rip the door off its hinges, knock out any officer present, and make a run for the stairs. *If only I weren't in a basement,* she thought. *I could fly out of a window on any floor and survive. Once on the street, no one could catch me.*

She flashed back to 1930s Chicago and how she had killed and escaped the assassins sent by Capone. Life was less complicated then.

Maybe I should just allow myself to die. Another couple of weeks, and I will start to weaken unless I pull some type of vampire shit and drink from one of my cellmates. What am I thinking? I will be released today or at least make bond. They don't have anything on me. At best, it was self-defense. Fuck it, I'm going to fight until the end. If I am going to die from lack of blood, I might as well make them kill me first. Then again, I can't live forever. Or can I? Why didn't this Spirit Walker thing come with a set of instructions? Damn Jesse and Bobby. I wish I had just died there in Tulsa with all the others.

"Apple Lewis, let's go. You're up." A court officer unlocked the cage door.

Apple glanced at the wall clock. Three hours had passed. She was escorted into the courtroom. Upon entering through two large swinging doors and past a sign that in Latin read, "An Eye for An Eye," she was greeted by Victor Veder.

"Apple, sweetheart, you must know that I wasn't contacted for this hearing. Hell, the last thing I knew, you were going to be released this morning for lack of evidence," Victor frantically explained.

"State versus Apple Lewis," announced the stoic bailiff.

Victor stepped forward and asked for a few minutes with his client.

"Permission denied, Mr. Veder. We have waited on this case since this morning, and neither you nor I will take any more time than necessary to arraign this case," barked the judge.

Victor stood beside Apple. The state's attorney stood on the other side of Victor.

"Mr. Veder, how does your client plead to the charges of two counts of second-degree murder?" asked the judge.

"Your Honor, if I could approach the bench?" Victor said.

"You most certainly may not, Mr. Veder. This is a simple arraignment. You will have ample time to present your case at the preliminary hearing—unless you choose to waive it at this time."

"Your Honor, you must hear me," pleaded Victor.

The judge held his palm up, but Victor kept talking as fast as he could. "Judge, I was told yesterday that the state wasn't going to charge my client, and in fact, it advised me she would be released this morning. I am totally flabbergasted by the state's action in this case. Judge, I believe the state owes us an explanation."

"Will the state please approach the bench? Is this true? Did you or your office advise Mr. Veder his client would be freed this morning? Come on now. The court does not have all day."

"Yes, Your Honor. The state did imply something to that effect, but more information has come to light on this defendant," the prosecutor whispered.

"And that evidence would be what?" The judge leaned over the bench within several inches of the prosecutor's face.

"Your Honor, that information is a matter of possible national security and should not be divulged at this time in open court," the prosecutor stammered.

"National security is it? The last time I checked, this was still a democracy—and we had a constitution. So give it up now, or I will dismiss this case."

"Your Honor, I will require consultation with my superiors and possible agents of the federal government. I implore you, sir. This is a serious matter of national security."

Victor took one step back from the bench and glanced at Apple. They looked at each other in bewildered amazement.

"Your Honor, obviously this is news to my client and me. Most certainly, we will require an opportunity to review the information and/or allegations they speak of," Victor chimed in.

"Your Honor, the state wishes to delay this case a few more days. We believe there may be a plot against the government or something else of dastardly proportions being planned. We have what we feel are two of the defendant's coconspirators in custody as we speak. We need to question them further, Your Honor."

"The court orders this case to be held over until tomorrow afternoon. The state had better have some evidence and explanations tomorrow—or I will hold you in contempt. Do you understand me, sir?"

"Yes, sir, but the state requests more time—"

"The court has ruled. Next case. Mr. Veder, if you are not on time tomorrow, I will hold you in contempt."

"But judge, we are entitled to bond, and the court has not even accepted the charges. My client was not given a chance to even plead not guilty."

"Your client pleads not guilty. Bond set at one million on each count!" The bang of the gavel rang out as the judge delivered his order.

"Yes, Your Honor."

Apple went back to the basement cage. She would have to wait for the next county van to transport her. Victor stood outside the cage, shaking his head.

"Conspirators? Who in the hell are my conspirators?" yelled Apple.

"Keep it down. Keep it down. There's ears everywhere down here."

"I don't give a shit. Do you understand me? I want the fuck out of here, Victor!"

"You don't look well. You look a little jaundiced. Your eyes are kind of yellow."

"What kind of attorney are you? They have nothing on me, yet here I sit like a goddamn animal in a fucking cage!"

"Now wait there just a minute. You will have to admit I was pretty good in there. I mean, no time for preparation—and then they laid that national security shit on me. What the hell was that all about?"

"You're asking me? You're the damn lawyer. You go figure it out—and let me know when you do!"

"Well, we could start with you telling me who these coconspirators are." Victor said through the cage wire.

Victor jumped back as Apple made a hideous growling noise. "I don't have any fucking coconspirators, you dipshit!"

"Well, the government says you do!"

"Get the hell out of here, and you better be here tomorrow. This had better be my last night in this godforsaken hellhole! And do me a favor, will you? Tell that damn Sabin to get me a new lawyer!"

"I haven't seen Sabin since I was hired. After tomorrow, you can have a new lawyer. I don't give a shit! Tomorrow's court appearance will just about square us up on that paltry little pittance of a retainer fee he gave me! What's it take to feel a little appreciation around here?" Victor banged his fist on the elevator button.

Apple laughed. She had no regrets about being hard on the man. She thought he deserved all of it—and probably much more. She would forgive his ignorance tomorrow if she was released.

The hours passed slowly as defendants came and went from the cages. Finally, two men in expensive suits came for her. *They look like characters from* Men in Black, *she thought. If only one was as cute as Will Smith. Wait a minute. Where are the usual overweight guards?*

It was late evening when the two men rushed Apple out the back of the courthouse. She was ushered into a black sedan. The car drove about three blocks and pulled up to the curb. The driver and the two escorts exited the vehicle, and she was alone for a brief moment. Before she could contemplate her next move, the back door swung open and closed as quickly.

They stared at each other. Apple knew but didn't understand why she knew. They continued to stare.

"So, you're the infamous, Apple," the well-dressed, dark, handsome man broke the silence. "Well, well, you don't look so tough. I mean, I guess I was expecting a Raquel Welch in her prime. Let me correct that, a black Raquel Welch. I would have even been impressed if you resembled Pam Grier in her prime. Hell, you look like a skinny Oprah." The man laughed at his own joke. "You don't look like you could rip anybody's heart out."

"Who are you? And what do you want?" asked Apple.

"Come on, baby. Give it back to me. It's not often people like you and I get to meet and have a little verbal judo. You can call me Mr. B.

"I'm not here for your pleasure—so get to it. You know, baby, keep it real."

"You could be for my pleasure if I wanted it to be that away. So don't get fucking cute with me. I am your worst nightmare!"

"Watching a little too much telly, have we, old chap? I bet you are just full of clichés."

"That's more like it. Give me your best shot."

"Take these handcuffs off, and I will show you my best shot."

"Baby, baby, baby. You obviously don't know who you are addressing. I'm a pureblood, a descendant of Desheeta. I'm the one who will kill you."

"Why kill me?"

"It has been that way since the beginning of time. You know Hitler got close to getting it right, but he wasn't part of a superior race. I'm talking ethnic cleansing of the purest form. We—the pure Spirit Walkers from original tribal blood—can be the only survivors. While you mixes and other humans take turns ethnically cleansing yourselves, we sit back and protect our purity. I have witnessed this over the last two centuries. Someday, we who discovered the secrets to immortality will control the weaker species. To some extent, we already do."

"Why kill me? If I'm not pure, surely I will die someday."

"You have left a miserable trail of carnage and stupidity. We can't have half-breed Spirit Walkers like you giving us a bad name. We can't have you creating a trail for others to follow. We have lived for centuries without evidence of our existence. We now have that damn book that your Tulsa boys created."

"Why were they allowed to live? Why didn't you just kill them before I came along?"

"We needed lawyers, business people, and others to modernize our existence. We may have immortality, but what is it worth without power and wealth? The white man was taking our land even in the 1920s. Treaties were being broken, and racism was running rampant. What better way to defeat your enemy than to become one of them? I knew Jesse and Bobby, and I was preparing to kill them a few years after they actually died. Guess the KKK did us all a favor. Too bad they didn't kill you. It would have saved us a lot of trouble. Mark White was my friend, and you killed him and burned his body in the desert. You remember Mark White, don't you? I'm not sure how you did it, but you killed him. His blood returned to us and made us stronger. The blood of the two you killed here has returned to us by now. Drinking blood from purebloods keeps us immortal. You, on the other hand, drink blood from anybody. That makes you no different than a scavenger eating dead carcasses."

"Then kill me now, you fucking bastard. Kill me handcuffed here now like the coward you are!"

"I can't kill you now. You must excuse me; we have not been properly introduced. My name is Otis Beaver, and CIA is my game. Don't you just love the Patriot Act? It made me what I am today. Oh, I almost forgot. I have your two little friends on ice in a safe house across town. That old hippie is a little on the crotchety side isn't he? And that young black man is the poorest excuse for a mixed Spirit Walker I have ever seen. I killed his bloodline two weeks ago. I guess for you that would mean the persons who turned him into a Spirit Walker. Anyway, you have a great evening. I'm going to allow these gentlemen to take you back to jail. I suspect there are two ways for you to die, and I am undecided which way is best. I could ensure your continued incarceration until you starve to death or get caught feeding your need for blood. That one could be a little risky. You know, too much media attention and stuff like that. Oh, by the way, you shouldn't allow yourself to be photographed. That picture of you from the 1930s has caused the death of a very nice old newspaperman. Aren't you ashamed of yourself?"

"Just how do you know so damn much?"

"Let's just say I have a new girlfriend back at the old CIA office who enjoys Internet research. And yes, the other way for me to ensure your death is for me to personally tear you apart and eat your fucking heart. I know that sounds hideous and unprofessional, but we can't be leaving any clues for CSI forensics, now can we, honey? Oh, I almost forgot. Have a nice evening."

CHAPTER 17

Government Work

"Sabin, man, you in there?"

"That you, CC?"

"You okay?"

"Where the hell are we?" asked CC.

"I don't know. It's your town."

"Yeah, you damn straight it's my town, and I told your hippie ass we should have laid low another day or two. Hell no, you had to act like some fuckin' spy or shit like that."

"CC! Think about it. You're a Spirit Walker. I've seen what Apple can do. Can't you break out of that room you're in and get us both out of here?" asked Sabin.

"Don't you think I've tried that? These motherfuckin' walls made out of some strong steel or shit like that. What was that shit they sprayed us with anyway?"

"I don't know, CC. They just came out of nowhere. The next thing I know, I'm here in this dark room. I heard you cussing like a sailor, and I knew you were close by. Guess there is at least a wall between us."

"No motherfuckin' shit, Sherlock. Yeah, you right, they come down on us real hard. If you hadn't been trippin' on wanting to sniff Apple's ass—"

Sabin said, "I wasn't trying to sniff her ass. I just wanted to ensure she was okay. How was I to know they wouldn't allow visitors? Besides, we were at least five blocks from the jail when they grabbed us. I don't think us being grabbed and my trying to see Apple are connected."

"You are one motherfuckin' cracker fool. Let's keep it real, okay?"

"Look, CC, you know they will be back soon. I think we will be okay. I know they're feds or something like that. They probably just want to question us. Just keep it real, and we'll be all right. It's not like the federal government goes around killing citizens."

"Yeah, you right, sure they're feds. And my mother was a Mother Teresa, and my father was the pope. Guess that makes me one saintly motherfucker. Hey, man, there's someone here."

Sabin was unable to see in the darkness, which came in waves over him.

CC whispered to Sabin, describing the footsteps only he could hear. He then described a man who was standing silent in the dark, looking through a small door window at him.

"Sabin," CC whispered. "The fucker is just standing there. I can't hear him breathing. I should be able to hear him breathing. My hearing has never failed me since I became a Spirit Walker."

"I hear you, Mr. CC—or whatever you call yourself."

CC saw the man smiling in the dark as he opened the door. The man slowly walked over and touched CC's forehead. CC felt the man's strength and anger. His hand was cold as ice as he wiped CC's brow.

"Are there more like you on the streets of Chicago?" asked the man.

"What's going on in there?" Sabin yelled.

"Hey, Sabin, it's all good. I can take this man if I need to," CC yelled back.

"This is your last chance to answer. Are there more like you out there?"

"Go fuck yourself," CC responded.

The man palmed CC's head like a basketball and picked him up off the floor. He held him at arm's length and off the floor.

CC felt tremendous pain on his temples. He had not felt pain since becoming a Spirit Walker. He kicked at his assailant.

The man threw CC against the steel wall with such force Sabin could hear bones breaking.

"Who in the fuck are you?" CC attempted to stand.

"Just call me Mr. Beaver. You won't be alive long enough for us to become close friends, so Mr. Beaver will do just fine."

"Leave him alone, you son of a bitch," Sabin screamed. "We have rights. We want an attorney."

A sinister laugh bounced and echoed off the steel walls. "Man, I'm the CIA, and you have no rights."

"That's right, Sabin. Keep him laughing." CC plowed his head into Beaver's stomach, wrapped his arms around him, and drove him backward. Their backward progress lasted about two feet before Beaver dug his fingers into CC's back and propelled him against the ceiling. CC bounced off the ceiling and landed on the floor with a thud that vibrated the walls. Blood streamed from eight finger holes in his back.

"Sabin, motherfuckers a strong-ass Spirit Walker." CC tried to crawl away from his attacker.

Beaver walked over to CC and embedded his foot into CC's side. The removal of his foot sounded like pulling a foot out of wet cement. Beaver snapped CC's head back, breaking his neck.

"You're still alive, aren't you? Think you a big, strong, wannabe Spirit Walker, don't you. Let's see you mend yourself out of this one," Beaver taunted.

Sabin heard the tearing of flesh and the breaking of bones. An hour must have passed before he heard another sound. His door opened, and a light went on. The well-dressed man was splattered with blood with a sealed body bag slung over his shoulder.

"You know, I really do hate doing things this way. Now don't get me wrong, I enjoy killing wannabe Spirit Walkers, but they are so damn messy. This CIA gig is really the shits. I mean, I had to clean all this shit up before my fellow agents return. Desheeta would be unforgiving if I screwed this placement up. I haven't let him down in two centuries, and I don't plan on starting now. You must be Mr. Sabin Brown. I would shake your hand, but as you can see, I'm a little messy and busy at the moment."

Sabin held his knees, locked his fingers, and stared at the ghastly sight. He had not moved from the corner. *Poor CC,* he thought, *I hope he had no pain.* "Are you going to kill me next?" Sabin whispered.

"I only kill these Spirit Walker wannabes. That's not to say I couldn't kill you or don't want to kill you. Now you're going to wish you were dead. You see—my fellow CIA agents think you are supporting terrorism. Now what would give them that idea? Glad you asked. Can you believe it? Someone has fabricated wiretaps, Internet blogs, money transfers to offshore accounts, and much more. Seems you have been very busy donating all that money to train insurgents. My fellow agents don't like you at all. You will soon be declared an enemy combatant of the United States."

"Why not just kill me now and get it over with?"

"Haven't you heard? We are a kinder and gentler agency now. No more torture, no more … well, the Patriot Act is still in effect, so I guess we can just lose you somewhere in one of our so-called holding areas. But seriously, no really, you will be like honey to ants. You see, Sabin, we may need you later. I don't suppose you will tell us who and where Apple's daughter lives? We have heard of her, and we will eventually find her, but you could make it easy. Thought not. Anyway, who knows how many people know she's a Spirit Walker? You remember Mark White, don't you? It doesn't really matter. What does matter is he told me about the daughter, and I assume she helped kill him—or maybe it was you. You might be good bait."

Otis Beaver left as quickly as he entered. Sabin sat motionless.

He could accept Apple being a Spirit Walker and the fact they had to kill White to survive, but now a CIA Spirit Walker? *How many Spirit Walkers are out there? Maybe they're everywhere in the government?* He heard multiple footsteps coming his way. He faked being asleep, but two agents pulled him to his feet and threw him in the back of a car. Soon, he was in an airplane.

CHAPTER 18

Blood Sisters

Apple sat quietly on the side of her bunk, swaying her feet to the rhythm of Pearl Jam's "Daughter." She was contemplating her own death and wondering how people in her life had faced death. *Is dying easier when it is unexpected and you only have a moment to anticipate its coming? Is death darker when one has time to prepare? Darker because you have time to explore what you will miss most about life?*

Otis Beaver had given her a death sentence, and it was time to think about what she would miss. *Even though my body aged slightly in the last fifty years, maybe my mind is aging at a normal rate.* She had never taken the time to slow down and examine her mental state. Had her mind changed so much she had lost the will to survive? Had Otis Beaver placed a spell on her? She started questioning her passion to survive and her mental state after being delivered to her cell by two CIA agents. *Were they Spirit Walkers also? No, I would have sensed they were Spirit Walkers, wouldn't I? Maybe all this mental processing is because I am feeling weak? I'm feeling weak. I shouldn't be feeling weak. I have more time. Yes, I have more time before I need to feed. My gifts are strong, but I feel tired and weak.*

"Clear the hall!" a jailer yelled. Rebecca and Martha were being led toward the cell in full restraints. The jailer removed their leg irons, belly chains, and handcuffs and ushered them into the cell. Rebecca made a hissing noise at the jailer and stuck her tongue out.

Martha walked slowly to Apple. "Just who in the hell are you? Rebecca from Sunny Brook Farm and I got our asses dragged out of here and fucking interrogated for three fucking hours about your sweet ass. So give it up!"

Rebecca strolled to Apple's bunk. "Apple, dear, if I were you, mum would be a key word in my vocabulary right about now. My trial was even delayed because of this today."

"Look, ladies, I should be asking the questions, especially if the topic of your three-hour vacation out of this hellhole was about me."

"I'll tell you what, Apple. I give a little, you give a little—and we will see what happens." Martha slipped her shoulders out of her jumpsuit and tied it around her waist.

"Damn, woman. Put that top back over that white belly and sagging tits before I go blind." Rebecca took a step back and formed a cross with her index fingers.

"I got my fucking bra on, you little bitch. Besides, wait a few years and see where your tits migrate to. They'll find a whole new resting place," Martha dished back to Rebecca.

"Excuse me, but I'm tired. If we are going to do tit-for-tat, I'm going to bed," Apple said.

"They were asking all kinds of shit about you," said Rebecca. "What have you said to us since you been here. Have you slept? Have you acted strange or done any weird shit."

"Weird shit?" asked Apple.

"You know, weird shit like voodoo shit—and stuff like that."

"Hell, Rebecca, if you're going to tell her that stuff, you might as well tell her we were offered a deal to ask her a bunch of questions. Remember what they said about her?" Martha asked.

"What deal? And what did they say about me?" asked Apple.

"Look here, Apple. I ain't stupid. I can't speak for this Lebanese, Sudanese, Cambodian-ese, or whatever the fuck she is, but I ain't givin' up nothing else without getting something back," Martha replied.

"That's okay, Apple. I will tell you everything," Rebecca added.

"You do, and I will get ugly all over your ass, bitch!" threatened Martha.

"Yeah, you do just that. You may whoop my ass in here, but when you get out, your white trash soul is mine!" countered Rebecca.

"Ladies, I don't give a damn anymore. I don't care what they said or what they offered you, okay."

"You damn well better care," replied Martha. "'Cause them talking about you being a terrorist with some kind of new drug inside of you or something like that."

"What do you want?" Apple asked.

"I want money—and lots of it. They say you probably got donors and stuff to support your activities. That means lots of money, and I want some of it," Martha demanded.

"I will tell you what I know, and we can work out the payment later." Rebecca winked at Martha and Apple.

"Don't you two know the same thing?" Apple asked.

"Don't know for sure. They had us together for a while—and then they split us up," Martha said.

"Who were they?"

"A fool could have figured them out. You had a couple of local dicks then some feds. Then this one crazy dude came in with wild-looking eyes and scared the shit out of me. The whole room turned cold—or maybe it was just me. Anyway, I got goose bumps and almost pissed my undies when he put his hand on my shoulder. He asked me a question and looked into my eyes, and then all I wanted to do was fuck him to death," Martha said.

"The man was cute. I will give him that much. You know cute in an evil, bad-boy way. You know I like the bad boys," Rebecca whispered. "Had I known the answers to his questions, Apple, I would have answered them in a heartbeat. You see—when he laid those eyes on me, I was helpless. Come to think of it, I wanted to fuck him too." A silly grin came over Rebecca's lips as she started swaying back and forth to some unheard Latin beat. "Come to think of it, the man never said a word."

"Do we have a deal?" Martha asked.

"Sure. Why not? What do I have to lose? I got money and lots of it. Maybe I will get out of here—and maybe I won't. What difference does it make? I can get more money."

"So you're a terrorist?" Martha's eyes were wide.

"Tell me what you know, and I will answer your questions later."

"At first, the two local dicks wanted to know if you had talked about the crime or those two you killed in self-defense or whatever. By the way, if you don't know, they don't have shit on you for those two deaths. If they did, they wouldn't be wasting their time asking those questions," explained Martha.

"Did you ever stop and think—I guess thinking is a little too much to ask—but maybe those questions were just a cover for their terrorist theory?" interrupted Rebecca.

"I'm goin' to knock you ass silly. Shut the fuck up and let me finish," barked Martha.

"Then it seems the dicks got bored or something and just went away. Then the feds came in all serious and shit. Wanted to know how old I thought you acted—and did you talk about things that were really old? I asked them what kind of old shit. They said shit like using generational words or phrases or slang from old eras. Wanted to know if you referred to yourself by any other names. They asked if you talked about any contacts on the outside. Said some old photographer reporter was snuffed. Seems they think you should know about it—or maybe you ordered the hit," Martha continued.

"Foreign languages. They wanted to know if you spoke any other languages around us," Rebecca chimed in.

"Anything else?" Apple asked.

"Same old bullshit like did you talk about any other killing. And

I almost forgot, they wanted to know if we saw you eat and go to the bathroom. I told them that was some sick shit … fucking perverts." Martha spit her toothpick across the room.

Rebecca looked at Martha and said, "Tell her how you tried to cut a deal for a quick ticket out of here. Tell her how you offered to snitch her out on made up bullshit!"

"Apple, I was just looking out for myself. You would have done the same. Besides, I don't know shit about you. What is there to tell? Rebecca, you better hope you can sleep with one eye opened tonight 'cause this shit ain't right, bitch!"

"Ladies, it's all good. Besides, I don't have anything to hide. I'm an innocent citizen. They're not going to let me out of here until they make up some conspiracy story that will stick. Prejudice is alive and well right here in Middle America. Sorry for asking, ladies, but it seems nothing they asked or told you will help me. I'm tired now. Go knock each other out, but keep it quiet."

When Rebecca strolled away, Martha stared at Apple. Her hands were clenched into tight fists, and she started grinding her teeth. "Smart-ass, you're just a fucking smart-ass. Thought you were one of us, but you ain't. I don't know what you are, but you're fucking weird. That's for sure. Don't ever speak to me that way again—or I will show you real prejudice," Martha threatened.

"Martha, honey, I'm tired—and that alone makes you one lucky lady tonight. I'm not even going to argue with you, but in another day and time, that little plea bargain you tried to cut at my expense would have gotten your heart cut out. Now, don't make me get retro and forget where I am!"

Apple detected no fear in Martha, but Martha sensed she was seconds away from pushing the envelope too far. Martha turned and walked away.

For two hours, Apple couldn't sleep. Her stomach ached, and her arms and legs were almost too heavy to raise more than an inch or two. Her heart was racing; sweat and chills swept across her body. As a distraction, she watched Rebecca making shadow figures against the ceiling with her hands. Martha's snoring sounded like a freight train climbing a mountain.

Sickness had never invaded her body. Was she sick? *Feeding her gifts could wait at least another two weeks,* she thought. Straining to lift herself, she rested on her elbows as the room began to spin. Sweat raced down her face, leaving trails before diving from her chin. *Could it be stress? Maybe this is the way life ends for someone who has cheated the aging process. Maybe my body has worn out from all the traumas and strengths I have asked it to perform. Stress, yes that must be it—stress from being in captivity.*

"You look like warmed-over shit."

While Apple was occupied analyzing her condition, Rebecca came upon her without detection. Apple strained and slowly turned her head toward Rebecca.

"Not bad," Apple laughingly whispered. "Not bad. An assassin cares for me."

"You're dying," Rebecca said.

"Apparently so," Apple whispered.

"Man, you don't look the least bit concerned. What's that all about?" Rebecca whispered.

"I lived a long and fruitful life. What choice do I have?"

"But you don't look much older than me."

"Sometimes things aren't what they appear. Besides, don't flatter yourself; I actually look younger than you."

"So before you kick off, why do your eyes flash on and off like a caution sign? That's why I noticed you were awake. I kept watching the flashing illumination off the walls and couldn't figure out what the hell was happening. I thought it was the detectives or something coming back to mess with us. Sometimes they keep us up all night, and then they drill us again while we're sleepy."

"You saw my eyes? I didn't realize they were glowing."

"Glowing ain't the word for it. They some evil-looking motion, and they still glowing right now."

"Aren't you afraid?" asked Apple.

"Hell no. Should I be? It's some type of voodoo or something like that, ain't it?"

"Yes, something like that." Apple felt weaker by the minute.

"So tell me?" Rebecca urgently asked.

"Tell you what?"

"Who—or what—are you?"

"You think I should squander my last dying breath telling you things you won't believe anyway?"

"What else you got to do? Lay it on me. At least give me the *Reader's Digest* version."

Apple faded in and out of consciousness several times.

Rebecca was holding her and wiping the sweat from her face.

Apple started to tremble and saw her yellow flashing eyes reflecting off the ceiling. She attempted a smile when she had a passing thought about her slow death having characteristics of a battery going dead. Apple began an abbreviated version of who she was.

Rebecca listened intensely.

Apple had no concept of time but knew she had told enough of her story to give Rebecca the concept of Spirit Walkers. She felt warm drops of sweat on her lips. *I can't even taste the salt any longer.* The sweat became heavier and streamed down her neck.

Rebecca's hands lifted Apple's head. "Drink, Apple. Please drink."

Apple believed she was in a dream. Her body was floating, and Rebecca was working feverishly to hold her down. She licked her lips. She licked them again. Her mouth opened to allow the sweat to pour in. She drank the fluid flowing into her mouth. She grabbed Rebecca's arm and started sucking. Her lips and tongue explored an open flowing wound, a spring of life.

"Drink as much as you need, Apple. I'm young and strong. You won't hurt me."

Apple opened her eyes and pushed Rebecca's arm a few inches away from her sucking lips. Rebecca was holding a razor blade in one hand. Like drinking ice water on an empty stomach, Apple felt Rebecca's blood racing through her stomach, searching for gifts to replenish. She reached for Rebecca's arm again, placed her mouth over the slashed wrist, and drank for a few more minutes. The sickness dissipated. "Why did you do that?" Apple felt enough strength to rise from the bed without assistance.

"I did it for both of us." Rebecca smiled.

"For both of us? What are you talking about?"

Rebecca lifted Apple's wrist, which was healing as they viewed the slash.

"I give you my blood—and take some of yours."

Apple noticed blood dripping from both corners of Rebecca's mouth.

"You cut and drank my blood?" Apple asked in astonishment.

"I didn't really believe your story, but I said to myself, 'What the hell? Let's give it a try. What did I have to lose? It's not like I'm going to get out of here for less than a life sentence.' When you started to show signs of regaining strength, I decided to cut your wrist and have a little drink myself."

"I didn't feel you cut my wrist."

They both looked at her wrist, which only had a small, off-colored scar remaining as evidence to what had occurred.

"I always have a razor blade handy. A girl never knows when she might need a close shave. Learned it while watching old movies. Bad girls always had some type of weapon in their hair."

"Rebecca, no one has ever drunk my blood. I don't know what, if anything, will happen to you. I'm a mix and not a pureblood. I don't think I can create a Spirit Walker."

"So we have nothing to lose, my new blood sister." Rebecca kissed her on the cheek and sashayed away.

"Someone's coming," Apple whispered.

"I don't hear anyone."

"Guess the blood didn't work for you," replied Apple.

Apple knew her gifts and strengths had returned. *Rebecca's blood must have been strong*, thought Apple while she smelled the air.

"Shit. It smells like Otis Beaver." Apple's nostrils flared as she detected his pheromones. His scent was a toxic mixture of thick Spirit Walker blood, sweat, and too much Obsession cologne. She smelled him before hearing his exceedingly light footsteps approaching.

Rebecca noticed Apple perk up and study the surroundings. Martha was asleep or at least acting like it. The other squalling, husband-killing cellmate never returned from her preliminary hearing.

"Apple, what gives? You look like you're ready to pounce on someone," Rebecca said.

"Damn it! He's a Spirit Walker—a real bad Spirit Walker—and not a mix like me."

"We can whoop his ass," Rebecca bravely interjected.

"No, I don't think so. He will be much too strong. Besides, you can't fight the government from this cell."

Otis and two other government agents arrived with one of the county deputy sheriffs. Otis was smiling, and a toothpick hung from the corner of his mouth. He was dressed in a wide black-and-gray pinstriped, double-breasted suit with black snakeskin, ankle-high, zip-up boots. He appeared much more conservative at their first meeting. He was allowing several strands of his cold black hair to lazily hang down across his cheeks.

He must think his hair gives him a certain ambiance associated with being an assassin, thought Apple. "Gentlemen, you guys looking for a good time? You know, in my other life, I was a massage therapist and could always guarantee a happy ending. Of course, the dollar amount decided how happy your ending would be."

All the men but Otis looked at Rebecca as if she had lost her mind. Rebecca's sarcasm did not distract Otis. He stared through the grayness of the cell and allowed his eyes to pierce Apple's thoughts. She hadn't experienced telepathic communication in many years. She felt Otis forcing communication to her brain. Rebecca must have sensed the evil present because she shut up and backed into the corner.

Before Otis could force communication to her brain, the deputy said, "Inmate Lewis? Inmate Apple Lewis, please step forward and identify yourself!"

Apple paused for a moment and then walked into the light provided by the dimly lit hall. "I'm Apple Lewis."

"Your custody is being transferred over to the federal government. You are remanded to the custody of these federal agents. Ma'am, please back up to the bean hole and place your arms through so you can be cuffed for transport."

"There has been some mistake. I have a court hearing tomorrow. I have not been formally arraigned," replied Apple.

"Ma'am, I don't know anything about all that. I have my orders, and the paperwork that says the state is giving up all rights on you and passing you over to the feds. So do as you are told."

"Look, there's a mistake. I need an opportunity to speak with my attorney."

"Here's the deal. It's late. I got called in as the duty officer, and I am not a happy man. Tell it to someone who cares, you enemy-combatant terrorist. Now, I am going to tell you one more time, and if you don't comply, I will call a cell entry team to drag you out. I guarantee you will not like it. At three in the morning, I am sure they will just use pepper spray or the Taser shield to expedite your extraction. So get the hell over here!"

Martha peered from her covers, and her eyes met Rebecca's. Martha winked and smiled at Rebecca. Maybe it was sharing the blood or her hatred for Martha, but she felt bonded to Apple and felt angry at Martha's smugness.

Apple felt the cuff's cold, stainless steel tightly embrace her wrists.

She stepped back from the bean hole, turned around, and faced Otis. His sneer reignited the fire inside of her. She restrained her gifts but flexed her muscles. The orange jumpsuit suddenly appeared too tight. Apple grinned, realizing she had regained some confidence lost due to stress and incarceration. Rebecca's blood must have been potent. She cut her eyes at Rebecca and could see her blood in the crevices of Rebecca's teeth.

"Don't forget, Mr. Beaver. I have to account for those jumpsuits, so drop it off after you get to wherever you guys are going," the deputy said.

"Send Congress the bill." Otis spit the toothpick across the cell toward Rebecca.

Walking defiantly, Apple was directed by the agents down the hall, past hundreds of sleeping inmates and into a waiting van.

Rebecca paced in the cell like a caged animal. Her muscles ached, her head pounded, and her heart raced. Her vision blurred and then came into focus. Her heart went from racing to beating once every fifteen seconds. Her well-manicured fingernails grew an inch. She walked to the bars, gripped them, and pulled. She felt them bend just a hair.

Martha stood beside her bed and watched Rebecca's actions.

Rebecca stood back and studied the bars. She was small and slender. She could never break or bend those bars enough to pass through. *I am strong. I have some Spirit Walker in me. I know I do.* "Hey, Martha, you bitch!"

Martha had been waiting for an excuse to fight Rebecca, and with Apple gone, it was the perfect opportunity. She took two quick, short steps toward Rebecca before Rebecca's backhand struck Martha's face. Martha was dead before she hit the floor.

Damn, I think I broke her fucking neck. Rebecca looked at her hand and then gazed in astonishment at Martha. She was limp on the floor with her head resting under her left armpit.

"Motherfucker, ain't that a riot?"

Rebecca gathered three soap bars from the sink. She stripped naked and threw her garments into the hall. She then wedged a bunk frame between two cell bars. With all her might, she was able to bend the bars another fraction before breaking the bed. She gripped the same two bars and again was able to bend them another hair. Utilizing the bars of soap and water, she lathered her hips, sides, back, butt, and head. Forming a running stance Gail Devers would have been proud of, Rebecca raced with amazing speed and leaped sideways between the bars.

"Shit. I'm stuck!" she screamed. The pain dissipated as quickly as it arrived. Her legs and an arm made it through to the other side. The bars were lodged against her hips and face. She determined her breasts and torso would be able to continue through if not for her head and hips. She was suspended. Her feet couldn't touch the floor.

"There's no turning back," she muttered.

"What the hell is going on down there? Some of us are trying to sleep around here!" an inmate yelled from the next cell.

Pushing as hard as she could and with a little wiggle, her hips reached freedom. Now all that remained in the cell was her head. She kicked, wiggled, and then stood, but she could not free her head. In final desperation, she created some slack by pushing her neck and head as far back toward the cell as possible. With all her might, she flung her head back toward the bars. A crunch vibrated down the hall. Rebecca fell to the cold concrete hall floor. She was out. Blood dripped from her nose and her ears.

Rebecca started to move and screamed, "I broke my nose. I broke my fucking nose!"

"Yeah, and I'm going to break your ass if you don't shut the fuck up!" the inmate yelled.

Rebecca walked to the next cell, reached through the bars, grabbed the inmate by the hair, and knocked her out against the bars. She grabbed her clothes and ran as fast as she could.

The van was idling about two blocks from the county jail. Otis was instructing the other two agents. Apple sat on an iron bench in back of the van with her handcuffs attached to an eye hook protruding from the bottom of the bench. A black sedan, similar to the one she had first sat in with Otis Beaver, was parked beside the van. The driver exited the sedan and exchanged keys with Otis. The agents unhooked Apple, removed her from the van, and placed her in the back of the sedan. They were starting to place leg irons and a belly chain on her when they became distracted.

A commotion came around the corner. Apple looked toward the noise and saw Rebecca running like the wind with two jailers giving chase. In a flash, Rebecca plowed into the two agents and knocked them off their feet. She showed no signs of slowing down.

Apple saw the opportunity and took advantage of it. She kicked the agent who had been preparing to place leg irons on her and ran after Rebecca. Gunshots sounded, and both women instinctively weaved and darted sideways. Tires screeched as Otis floored the sedan and gave chase. Apple and Rebecca ran for their lives into the Chicago darkness.

CHAPTER 19

Dismissed with Extreme Prejudice

Victor Veder couldn't remember much. His face was stinging from the punch that had knocked him unconscious. He tasted blood in his mouth and felt tightness around his wrist. His vision was blurred. Blinking only changed his sight from blurred to fuzzy. Drinking at the House of Blues was one of his last memories. He vaguely remembered walking past the valet, down the drive, and to his car, which was parked across the street. Having gotten into an argument last year with a cocky valet regarding customary tip amounts, Victor swore he would never use their valet parking again.

Victor heard someone in his bedroom. Attempting to roll over to possibly see who or what was making the noise, he knocked over his porcelain Siamese cat lamp. The lamp was partial payment for representing a pawnbroker for fencing stolen property. The lightbulb would glow through the cat's eyes. Staring at the glowing cat eyes often assisted him with correcting his vertigo after too much alcohol. Now it was broken, and the cat stared at him from just a few inches away.

Victor's body started sliding backward, causing splinters from the hardwood floor to embed in his face. He felt his body being lifted off the floor. He glimpsed a knee a second before it met his face. Another knee broke his nose. Blood spewed in a single, powerful shot, splattering on the broken porcelain cat. Whoever was holding him by his ankles started spinning him like a top. He vomited the gallons of beer and buffalo wings.

"You little bastard! I'll teach you to throw up on me!"

Victor felt his ribs break as he was thrown through the air toward his television. Gasping to regain his breath, Victor groaned. "Untie my hands, and I will kick your ass."

Laughter reverberated through the room. "You vile little shit. Amazing. It's simply amazing that you have survived this long."

Victor crumpled to the floor. "Who in the hell are you? What do you want with me?"

"Look at this place. I wouldn't let my dog stay in a trash hole like this. Come to think of it, this place kind of looks like a lawyer's lair. Get it? It's a joke. I made a joke." The man laughed while walking over and kicking Victor again.

"Take what you want. I don't have much money. Just take it and leave me alone."

"Lowlife, little shit … I wouldn't soil my hands touching this antiquated, seventies pop culture shit."

"Then leave me alone!" Victor clutched his ribs.

Victor raised his head and attempted to focus. He could see the silhouetted figure standing over him. He blinked, but his eyes were somewhere between out of focus and swollen shut. "Damn it! Who are you?"

"Guess I'm your malfeasant nightmare with a badge. Now tell me where she is."

"Where's who?"

"That little black bombshell client of yours, that's who. Don't you know she's the number one enemy of the state?"

"You talking about Apple?"

Otis Beaver took one step and kicked Victor in his broken ribs.

His polished shoe met with a crunch. "Yes, you dumb ass. Don't play stupid with me. Where is she?"

"She's in the Cook County Jail," cried Victor.

"Guess news travels a little slow in your neck of the woods. Oh, I forgot; don't think I called her escape in to the local authorities. Silly me. Public information is not my bag. Bag ... now that's an interesting word. Guess I picked it up from that old hippie, Sabin. Yeah, that's it. Papa's got a brand-new bag. Mr. James Brown, the king of soul. Now, I bet Sabin is having fun hanging out with all those camel jockeys. Damn, I can come up with some funny shit. Now, back to business. Where in the fuck is she?" Otis faked another kick to Victor's ribs.

"If she escaped, then I certainly wouldn't know where she's at." Victor was trying to breathe and speak simultaneously.

"Even in dying, you sound like a lawyer. Can't you lawyers ever get real?"

"Dying? Are you going to kill me?"

"Tell me where's she is, and I'll let you live."

"But I hardly know her. I only met her in the jail. She wouldn't even know where to find me."

"Guess you got a problem there, Mr. Lawyer," Otis said.

Victor attempted to get up. He finally found his balance and squatted on his knees. The pain from broken ribs and a broken nose superseded the pain from the handcuffs pinning his hands behind his back. He blinked until his assailant came into focus. "Didn't I see you in back of the courtroom today?"

A hard, backhand slap knocked Victor to the floor.

"I ask the fucking questions around here. Understand?"

Otis grabbed him by the handcuffs and started to lift him up. "Look here. Those are some nasty fingernails, you slob. Don't you respect yourself enough to practice good hygiene? Now what's that commercial with the little fungus monsters that live under your fingernails? You know that fungus that's unsightly but not lethal?"

"You're crazy, man. You need help," offered Victor.

Otis removed a small, lock-blade pocketknife, jammed the blade under Victor's left thumbnail, and popped the nail off.

"My God, you're insane!" Victor wrenched in pain.

Otis smelled the blood oozing from the thumb, laughed, and licked a drop of blood from the fingernail. "That's surprising. I would've thought you to have weak, sick blood—or at least a few undiagnosed diseases. You, my good man, are disease-free. Must be all that alcohol killing what ails you; of course, what helps us can also kill us." Otis laughed. "Now, one last chance to live. Where is she? No, wait a minute. Don't answer that. Give me a minute. Okay, here, answer one question out of three and you can live. Where is she? Where is she going? And who's she close to? That's right. I like games, don't you? This one is multiple choice. I made it easy for you."

"I only know the two who hired me, but I don't know where they're at."

"You, my good friend, are really living in the past. Kind of reminds me of that old hippie. Now, if you were going to mention Sabin or his little black sidekick, don't bother. It seems they're kind of not around anymore."

"Then I don't know anything," Victor cried. "Son of a bitch, please don't kill me."

Victor's other thumbnail propelled across the room, landing on a windowsill.

"Now, now, now. You can't pass out on me now." Otis poured a glass of water on Victor's face. "There. That's better. The way I see it, you really don't know anything."

"Then you will leave now and let me live?"

"Now, I didn't say that. Don't jump to conclusions, and don't interrupt me again. What I was about to say was that you have two things going against you. One is I hate lawyers, and the second is you can identify me. Excuse me, there's a third. Your blood is surprisingly healthy ... a little too much alcohol, but my body will filter that."

Before Victor could respond, Otis punctured his jugular with the pocketknife and held his fingers over the wound. "Look at this." Otis removed his fingers, and blood squirted from Victor's neck.

Victor watched in horror as Otis continued to play with the hole in his neck. Otis made a quick move to grab a glass from the kitchen. He returned, drank, and refilled the glass before allowing Victor to bleed out onto the floor.

"Must have been damn horrific, dying slowly while some Spirit Walker slowly drinks cups of your blood," Otis whispered into Victor's ear. "Should have listened to your mother and been a doctor." Otis laughed and walked out the front door.

⤬ CHAPTER 20 ⤬

Homeward Bound

"I haven't been here since I was a kid. Of course, all this wasn't here then. Well, some of it was here. That's a big Ferris wheel," Rebecca exclaimed.

Apple hadn't spoken a word after she and Rebecca had pulled themselves from the Chicago River. They walked the shoreline and decided to hide on Navy Pier. The sun would be rising soon. The lapping of waves against the pier maintained a rhythmic beat as a cool predawn breeze flapped the decorative flags strung throughout the amusement park area.

The two escapees had zigzagged through the streets and alleys before Apple relieved a cabby from his ride. They wrecked the car at the corner of Wacker and Michigan. Otis was quickly approaching when they jumped off the bridge into the dark river. Apparently, Otis had no idea they had jumped.

Apple said, "That's ironic. Congress of the American Correction Association. See that banner? Must be their convention here on the pier."

The two women were wet and needed to exchange their prison jumpsuits for civilian clothes.

Apple thought about where she would move if she could escape the Windy City.

Rebecca was more concerned with immediate needs. Testing her newfound strength, she broke a lock from a storage closet. Inside, she found an array of tools and a box of discarded janitorial shirts.

Apple watched as Rebecca stripped off her jumpsuit and tried on several shirts. Rebecca's body had been lean and defined before she drank Apple's blood, but Apple noticed more muscular definition as Rebecca styled each wrinkled, ragged shirt.

"Yes, this one will do." Rebecca performed a ballerina twirl. The shirt hung just a few inches above her knees. "Here, try this one on for size." Rebecca threw a shirt at Apple. "Tie the tail up like this and tuck it under. You'll have a custodial dress."

Apple perused the area, hoping to locate an alternative style of dress. She stepped out of her jumpsuit and reached for the shirt Rebecca had thrown at her.

Rebecca grabbed the shirt first and pulled it away. "Take my breath away, darling. That is one hard rockin' body you got there. Let me just take it all in," Rebecca said in a sultry, raspy voice.

"Don't go there." Apple pointed her finger at Rebecca. "You may have a little of my blood and a few gifts now, but I can still kick your ass. I will not hesitate to do so."

"Chill out, Apple, my newfound blood sister. I would only take if you offered. You can't blame a girl for admiring such a work of art. Besides, even if I weren't AC/DC, you could turn me in a heartbeat. Be still my beating heart."

Apple tied her shirt as demonstrated by Rebecca. Rebecca found two old hats; one had a Mack Truck patch on the front, and the other was a White Sox cap. Both were splattered with paint. When the sun rose, visitors and workers started arriving, and they exited their hiding place.

Rebecca and Apple promenaded down the pier, becoming immersed in the crowds of tourists, workers, and convention-going correctional officers. A few sailors turned to watch Rebecca and Apple walk away, but nobody else noticed them. They walked past the tour boats, food vendor carts, and Bubba Gump's Seafood restaurant.

"Now what?" asked Rebecca at the pier's end where taxis and buses dropped off conventioneers and tourist groups.

Apple walked over to a waiting cab. A few minutes later, she motioned for Rebecca. They jumped in the back of the cab and took off.

"You ain't got no money. Shit, these Chicago cabbies will have no tolerance. He will call the police when we can't pay. We should have jumped on one of those tour buses. What did you tell him anyway? And where are we going?" whispered Rebecca.

"You don't have to whisper. That damn Latino radio station he is listening to could drown out a machine gun. Besides, I told him you gave the best blow jobs in Chicago."

"You said what!" Rebecca snarled through her clenched teeth.

"Relax, my little sister. He took one look at you and said he preferred the money. I told him if he took me home, I would give him a hundred-dollar tip."

"You know, you really are a schizophrenic. Like, you're serious when I'm trying to be funny. And you're funny when you're supposed to be serious. I can't take this anymore!"

Apple instructed the driver to park several blocks from her residence. She told him Rebecca would stay while she retrieved the money. The driver appeared nervous, but the money outweighed any fears he had of being a crime victim. Rebecca was surprised by the driver's cooperation. She started to think that Apple really had promised some favor. What she didn't know was Apple was able to harness the gift of hypnotism, and a little of it went a long way with this driver.

Apple carefully cased the neighborhood and focused her sight and hearing to ensure no one was waiting to ambush her. She sniffed the air just in case Otis was present.

Her home was a wreck. Other than a few small items, possessions meant nothing to Apple. She was not bothered by the broken computer and other trashed items. She went straight for her bedroom, unscrewed a post from her canopy bed, and broke it over her knee. The post had been hollowed out and used for a safe storage of her emergency cash. She removed four rolls of bills, which had been stacked on top of one another inside the post.

As she was leaving, she noticed a blinking light underneath the sofa. The sofa had been cut to shreds and turned upside down. The blinking device turned out to be a cell phone, but it wasn't her phone. The screen blinked to indicate a text message. She hit the view button and read:

> *I assume, Miss Lewis, that if you are reading this, you have survived another of life's inconveniences, namely Otis Beaver. It is time we visited. Your next destination should be Oklahoma, specifically, Oklahoma City. Keep this phone, and upon your arrival in Oklahoma City, I will contact you.*

Apple stared at the phone and read the message several times. *It's a trick, an Otis Beaver trick.* She grabbed some clothes and a leather-beaded headband Sabin had given her, stuck the cell phone in her shirt pocket, and exited through the side window.

"What took you so long? This driver keeps smiling at me and talking some Spanish shit. I don't think he can speak or understand English at all," Rebecca said.

Apple spoke perfect Spanish to the driver and handed him two hundred dollars. He nodded and smiled.

"Hey, you gave him two hundred! What's the other hundred for?"

"He's going to allow us to change in the backseat. Here, take your pick from these clothes. By the way, he says he still expects his blow job."

"You can both just kiss my Laotian, Sudanese ass!" Rebecca laughed.

"Rebecca, these gifts you have from my blood ... be careful. Certain people like Otis Beaver will know this, hunt you down, and kill you. You're not immortal. Someday you will die of old age, maybe two hundred years from now, if they don't kill you first. Here, take this money." Apple peeled off a thousand dollars in hundred-dollar bills.

"I know what you told me about your story back in the county jail. I'm not like you. I need to live large. I'm not into all those books and shit. This girl just wants to have fun. *Comprende?*"

"Hey, it's your life. I'm just telling you there's a lot about this Spirit Walker stuff I don't know about, but I do know they will hunt you down and kill you."

"This is my town. I got friends—seriously Neanderthal friends—who can get caveman on Otis's ass. I say bring it on, Otis."

They changed clothes, aware that the driver had adjusted his mirror to watch them. Rebecca gave him a few special showings of what he would never touch. They said their good-byes.

Apple handed the driver another hundred, instructing him to take Rebecca wherever she wanted to go. Apple waved as the cab sped away, read the text message again, walked over to a low-end BMW, broke the window with her fist, cracked the steering column with one flick of her finger, started the car, and leisurely drove away.

Damn. My old gangster skills even work on today's cars.

≈ CHAPTER 21 ≈

Honey, I'm Home

Alicia Overstreet hadn't seen Otis Beaver for several days. She determined he was probably on some sort of secret mission related to that special operations team no one in the office was supposed to know about. *The New York Times* had written an article about the special unit on Monday, and the office manager's denial of its existence was a joke. Everyone was nervous and no one trusted anyone anymore.

The Cook County Jail records indicated no record of an Apple Lewis. She viewed the screens from the court network system, and even the arraignment ledger was void of any mention of an Apple Lewis. Just three days earlier, Apple's arraignment date was recorded. Now there was no record at all—like it never existed.

Alicia and several other researchers were given an assignment, which delayed her search for connections to Apple. Two private companies that contracted with the government to collect and store data on everything from credit reports to library reading preferences of citizens had been hacked into. Millions of people's credit card numbers and other records were stolen—or at least duplicated into an unknown, illegal parallel system. Alicia couldn't help but think there might be a connection with the missing records.

Cyberlinkend and Interconnect were the two companies whose security protocol had been violated. Initially, when the stories were leaked to the media, there was a public outcry. Alicia was disappointed—but not surprised—the outcry lasted only a couple of days. Even working for the CIA, Alicia was concerned about the privatization of citizen records. She was keenly aware of the public's disposable attitude and short attention span. Were people really that stupid? Did they actually think the so-called cloud was invincible and immune to hacking? Now she had an opportunity to search a vast database of mostly average Americans.

Her assignment was to determine the source, trail, and process utilized by the perpetrators. To enable her to do this, she was given the source codes and other system information to examine the data in the vast system. She was pleased that her superiors appointed her as lead on the project. At least she would have a few weeks to break away from the monotony of spying on chat rooms. Chat rooms were so out of fashion. The good stuff was much deeper in the web.

Search: Apple Lewis, black female, thirty years old, last known address Chicago.

Alicia's curiosity had gotten the best of her. Who would know, care, or question why she typed in Apple's name? First she tried the Cyberlinkend database. There was an Apple Lewis, age twenty-five, black female, Chicago, but from 1931. An old black-and-white photograph accompanied the data. Alicia was impressed with the scanned photo and the quality of the date arrangement. However, she believed it wasn't the Apple she had been tracking. She found nothing else about Apple in Cyberlinkend.

Two team members left work an hour early. The next shift would arrive shortly, so Alicia decided if she was going to search Interconnect for Apple's data, this was her opportunity. Even though the project was given priority and the data breach was dominating the news media, Alicia knew the project could be killed at any moment based upon political or other factors. The CIA had a long history of starting projects and not finishing them.

There it was. An Apple hit on Interconnect. Interconnect downloaded records from all criminal justice networks and court systems on a daily basis. The data files that had been closed and downloaded to the servers in Alicia's office from Interconnect must have collected Cook County records before someone deleted the originals. Alicia saved the Apple file to a portable jump drive. *There is too much data and not enough time to read—plus this is the CIA.* Alicia laughed to herself.

At home, Alicia prepared a double-shot espresso and soy milk. Once her computer warmed up, she inserted the jump drive and opened the Apple files. The software utilized by Interconnect had been designed to capture, collate, and file all information with common variables into one file. How else could she explain the numerous entries of a woman named Apple Lewis? There was an entry on an Apple Lewis collected from records held by the Greenwood Cultural Center in Tulsa, Oklahoma. This was a young girl listed as one of many missing after the Tulsa race riots. The entries on Apple Lewis started in Tulsa and ended in Chicago.

No way. This can't be! Apple's county jail booking photo looks just like the one from 1930s Chicago. Alicia's fingers raced across the keyboard. *Damn. I'm just tired and hallucinating.* Another picture appeared from a 1969 California driver's license. "It has to be the same woman—or she has a twin." Another photo in an old Peace Corps file had been captured by the Interconnect system. Alicia started to hit the print button. Records from Mexico and an adoption appeared and so did records for a name change on a child named Treasure Freeze. *This can't be one and the same! My theory of an occult of serial killers is better than this.*

In the CIA, secret databases, eavesdropping, and sleuthing were paramount, but nothing prepared Alicia for the complexity of the software and intricate detail of the information its data structure contained.

She typed *Treasure Freeze* and found another verifiable connection to Apple Lewis as the mother of record. A cross-reference to previous addresses indicated that Sabin Brown had listed his address as identical to Apple's for several years. Alicia processed this information. *Could Sabin be a husband, an occult member, or something unexplainable like Apple?*

The information was merged into three main categories and then flagged by government-interest activities. Alicia queried the data and ran parallel records on Sabin and Apple. Both appeared to have invested substantial funds in the same stocks and checked out similar books at libraries. Sabin Brown had purchased an airline ticket to Chicago and should have arrived the same day as the killings.

Time slipped away, and the noon chime on her kitchen clock startled Alicia. She stood, stretched her back, and poured her cold coffee down the sink.

"Shit! Oh shit!" She placed her hand over mouth in an effort to muffle her startled outburst. She dropped the coffee mug on the floor and ignored the broken glass that shattered across her bare feet. Otis Beaver was parking his car in front of her residence.

"No, no, no! Not again! He will not do this to me again!"

Otis patted his side, verifying the presence of a weapon. *Did he do this out of habit—or is he preparing to use his weapon? Maybe he's not here to force himself on me again.* She remembered sensing the evil in him. Maybe he was going to kill her. It was really a rape. That's it. He's afraid I will file a rape complaint. Alicia's mind was a kaleidoscope of thoughts and fears. She went over the episode with Otis Beaver again. She must have resisted. She knew he had gone through her apartment while she slept. None of what she was going through made any sense. He had never threatened to do anything to her. Maybe it was just all the stuff happening at the office, and everyone's paranoia was rubbing off on her. He must have known she was illegally mining the data from the two private companies. She had

gone beyond the scope of her assignments. The CIA had sent him
to clean up the situation.

Otis adjusted his wraparound sunglasses, spun in a slow circle,
evaluated his environment, and slowly walked toward Alicia's
apartment. Alicia locked the deadbolt, closed the blinds, and hid in
her closet.

The knocking was soft and gentle. The doorbell rang, and then
the intensity of the knocking increased. Alicia scarcely breathed as
her eyes adjusted to the darkness.

"Alicia, I know you're home." Otis's voice echoed through the
apartment. His voice was coming from all directions.

"Look, honey, let's not play games. You have nothing to be
afraid of. I just need to visit with you. You know, like last time. Just
stare into my eyes, and I will make all your worries disappear." His
laughter followed each sentence and caused Alicia's hands to shake.

Alicia's heart was begging to escape the confines of her chest. The
pounding was rapid and fierce. Her veins constricted, and her heart
labored to force the blood to flow.

"Look, little Alicia, baby. I know—and you know—that I know
you're in there. Does that make sense? I can smell you. How does the
old nursery rhyme go? Fe-fi-fo-fum, I smell the blood of my *honey*.
So come open the door, and let's get reacquainted. All my lovers are
repeat customers. Now, you wouldn't want to give me an inferiority
complex, would you?"

The knocking stopped, and an eternity passed. The quietness
caused her heart to race faster. She wanted to believe he was gone,
but she knew better.

Slam! The door flung open, causing the doorknob to slam into
the Sheetrock wall. Footsteps echoed across the entryway.

"Come out, come out, wherever you are. Otis wishes to play.
What do we have here? Looks like Alicia brought some work home.
I didn't know the CIA gave homework assignments. Apple Lewis and
Sabin Brown … that's an interesting homework assignment. I may

have underestimated you, my little darling. I knew you were smart 'cause that's why I wanted to hang with you, but for you to be onto me like this, now that's just downright impressive."

Alicia could barely hear what he was saying over the pounding of her heart. *What the hell is he talking about? I'm not onto him about anything. Damn, I left the computer on with the jump drive inside.* She heard the chair squeak when Otis sat at the computer. She heard the computer ping when he hit the wrong command key.

"This is bad, real bad. Yes, I had a stressful week and needed a little release, with your assistance. Thought you might even give it up freely, but this changes everything. Now how did a little CIA research geek like you find my trail and my prey? And where in the hell did you get a database like this. Looks like nothing I've ever seen the CIA use. This must be some kind of FBI secret weapon. Guess I got me one more killing to do this week. Desheeta is going to be exceptionally and mega-pissed about this. Alicia, darling, does the CIA know about Apple? You know besides little-old-me CIA. How much do you know, girl? Now, Otis, don't overreact. Allow your CIA training to kick in here. Let's see, little nerd geek girl brings big CIA work home against regulations. Why, it's elementary, my dear, you haven't told anyone yet, have you?" His laughter vibrated the closet door.

Alicia stood and softly climbed the wood shoe rack nailed to the back of her closet. She remembered a small opening in the ceiling. Once she had to call the landlord because of noises in her attic. He had shown her this entry to a small attic. A squirrel had entered the attic through an outside air vent. The landlord explained that the attic was just a small space for wiring, cable, and air circulation. The squirrel found his way in, but it needed assistance to get out. Now this small space might be her only salvation.

"Let's see, this needs to look like a burglary gone bad."

Alicia heard the breaking of glass and the throwing of furniture. She pushed the small piece of plywood aside and stood on the last shelf. Stretching, she was able to lock her fingertips on the edge and pull herself up. She restrained two sneezes. The dust was unbearable. Rays of light coming from where the squirrel had squeezed through the outside vent temporarily blinded her.

"Are we comfy up there?"

Her heart stopped, and her chest produced a suffocating pain. Otis was standing at the bottom of the closet and staring up at her. She tried to crawl away. Otis, without bending a knee, jumped straight up through the attic opening and grabbed her head. She twisted, kicked his face, and jerked her head, leaving Otis with two hands full of her hair. With her head free, Otis fell back to the closet floor.

Alicia scraped both knees as she crawled to the vent. Otis crawled after her. She felt the sting as she exited the attic after kicking the vent out. The gunshot sound came after the sting. The shot echo was deafening. Blood dripped across her toes as she ran across the rooftop. She tripped and fell through a neighbor's skylight. Another sting jarred her body.

⊰ ⊱

She was alone and cold in a bright room. Hoses, connections, and hanging bags came into focus. A blinking white light glowed above the bed and another blinking light connected to her index finger was red. She reached down and felt the catheter between her legs. She scratched the hardened wrap her head was encased in.

"Welcome back. You've had a long nap," a nurse said.

"How long have I been here?"

"Let's see … it will be two weeks tomorrow," she said as she reviewed her hospital chart.

CHAPTER 22

The End of the Beginning

Apple exchanged cars three times before leaving town. She drove the stolen car only far enough to find a used-car dealer. Walking up to the dealer, she offered the asking price of $2,500 cash for the 1972 Beetle. She gave the car and $5,000 to the grandson of an old mobster she had stayed in contact with in exchange for a 1992 Bonneville and three sets of new identifications. This aficionado in the art of fake identification was surprised when Apple wanted fakes. He explained how most of his sales involved processing stolen identification, social security numbers, bank accounts, Internet passwords, passports, and credit reports. Apple stayed with the old school of fakes, even though he made a good argument against it. She didn't want the possibility of anyone else hunting her. She believed the best way to do this was to go low-tech, and only a few old gangsters would still do it.

With the famous skyline silhouetted in the misty haze from the lake, Apple took one last look in the rearview mirror. She thumbed through the envelope of false IDs. Obviously a name change was in order, but what name? Even if Otis Beaver was working alone—and Illinois didn't want her—there could be others. *Coco Jones? The name had some potential.* She looked at another set of identification. *Lawanda*

June Porter? Now that name sounds tough. Chalice Blu Clay was the final option. She realized more time should've been allowed for name selection, and delegating the choice of names wasn't cool. Maybe she would use all three interchangeably.

Usually, a drive from Chicago to Oklahoma City wouldn't take more than a day or a day and a half at most. For Apple, it was a six-day journey. She stopped and read every historical marker and detoured through every small town along the way. She stopped at every antique store that even remotely appeared to have old books. After a few stops, the backseat was full of old, dusty books. Her favorite find was a 1914 New York City high school textbook of the complete works of Edgar Allan Poe. What intrigued her most were the children's notes written in the margins and text that was underlined. She had read a Poe book back in Tulsa. She remembered the little boy hiding with his family while Tulsa burned. He had held her Poe book in his hand.

Refreshed was the only way to truly describe how she felt. Another stop and three more books were added to the backseat library. The stores didn't have the usual display of political, literary giants that adorned the huge franchise booksellers. The glossy-covered, portrait-enhanced hardbound copies of Newt Gingrich, Michael Savage, and Bill O'Reilly were demoted to the discount bins. Thinking about the state of literature in America helped distract her from the uncertainty of her journey. Authors churned books out every month or so, and publishers were only interested in promoting the same few authors who could guarantee large sales. Even though their books were literary embarrassments, they dominated the market. Who was buying all these books on murder trials, athlete drug use, and other news headlines? Apple had a habit of turning around every Ann Coulter book she saw on the shelves or placing Al Franken books in front of them. *If one woman in America deserved the life of a Spirit Walker, it would be Ann Coulter. Of course, once I turned her, it would be a pleasure to kill her. Maybe I can write a book if life settles down for me in Oklahoma City or wherever my journey ends. My writing will be a cross between the erotica of Zane and the intelligent human insight of Ian McEwan.*

Treasure wasn't pleased when Apple finally called her from the road. Apple explained all she knew but was unable to satisfy Treasure's questions related to Sabin.

Treasure had yelled, "You better not have gotten Sabin killed."

Apple had to remind herself how Treasure was a normal human being and how her aging process was physical and mental. Treasure was showing signs of aging: worry, detail fixation, loss of patience, intolerance, and so on. They made arrangements for Treasure to sell some of Apple's stocks. The money would be transferred when Apple provided further instructions after arrival in Oklahoma.

In Saint Louis, she took a detour to Memphis. She had read about historical Beale Street and was intrigued by the indigenous blues and jazz of Memphis.

On the way, Apple's cell phone vibrated. The text read:

> *Where are you? Oklahoma City awaits your arrival. I assume, unless you have killed again or located a willing donor, your gifts will soon be demanding nourishment. Lesson number one: the need to feed increases as the years pass.*

Apple drove west on Interstate 40. *Could this be an Otis Beaver trick?* She didn't care anymore. If it were a trick, that would be fine with her. *Enough is enough. No one should be hunted like this. And if it isn't a trick, it could be an adventure.* Apple knew curiosity was her weakness, but she still wanted to follow the cell phone instructions.

Humidity, wind, and heat welcomed Apple to her home state. She was expecting another cell phone message by the time she arrived, but none came. Money was not an immediate concern— five thousand dollars remained in her possession—but she contacted

Treasure and had another ten thousand wired to a local payday cash loan company.

She was anxious for privacy that a car or hotel room couldn't fully provide. However, not knowing how long she would be in town, she located a peaceful and inconspicuous hotel called the Waterford. She flung herself across the king-sized bed and hugged the pillows. She had forgotten how wonderful cool sheets and fluffy pillows could feel. It was certainly a step up from the plastic-coated jail beds favored by Cook County. Indulging in a whirlpool bubble bath, she reflected on her history by associating each body scar with a passage in time. Settling into a huge, high-backed Victorian chair, she began to read one of her favorite Toni Morrison books, *Beloved*. Little did she know that across town, part of her history and possibly her future were being debated.

꘡ ꘡

"Did you kill her?"

"Desheeta, you know the answer to that."

"Otis, why don't you go ahead and tell us."

"I know what you're trying to do. You're doing that ancient custom of publicly ridiculing a failure. I've been here before, and trust me, it's not necessary this time," explained Otis.

"Trust is an interesting choice of words, Otis. The council appears to have lost trust in you," Desheeta remarked.

"Oh, it's not the council, Desheeta. It's you."

"Otis, I will remind you only once not to interrupt me," Desheeta said.

"But I have completed every dirty deed you and the council have requested of me."

Desheeta stood at the end of the long table of council elders. He slapped the palms of his hands on the table and stared with gut-wrenching intensity at Otis. Otis stared back, but Desheeta didn't blink or move a muscle. After a long pause, Otis looked away.

The other elders were becoming noticeably uneasy.

"Now, Otis, did you kill her?"

"No, I did not … sir!" Otis clenched his teeth in a sinister smile.

"All right," continued Otis. "I underestimated the girl. She's smart and stronger than I imagined. She's different and has adapted well to societal changes."

"Societal changes?" asked Desheeta.

"You know, like continually educating herself, working like a normal human, making loyal friends. She seems to have this charisma. Maybe it's her big round eyes."

"Sounds like you may be somewhat infatuated with her. Is that why you didn't kill her?"

"How can you question my motives? I have never failed to complete a mission. I have been your one-man final destination for many an adversary."

"Yes, you have. But I blame myself for what you've become."

"Desheeta, I am what you wanted me to be."

"I never wanted you to be what you are today."

"You made me an assassin."

"Yes, but an assassin with a cause, a constitution, and a mission to fulfill for purebloods—not some audacious fiend, spewing vilification. I made you to honor and protect our traditions and secrecy—not to take pleasure in the misery of your victim's plight," Desheeta clarified.

"Well, you get what you create. I am what I am, and I have served you well. I will kill her. She would already have been dead if you had not called me back to this godforsaken place."

"Because of your fondness for big cities, bright lights, whores, and other perversions, I'm not surprised your home state has lost its attractiveness."

The elders were doing their best to disguise their increasing apprehension. From past experience, they knew Desheeta would allow Otis Beaver a certain level of defiance and obstinate communication.

They also were aware how Otis was taking the flexibility previously granted by Desheeta to an unsafe, unpredictable level. Also, prior to Otis arriving at the council, Desheeta didn't request the traditional arrow-shooting assassin. The problem-ending archer would close the chapter on Otis Beaver with a heart-piercing arrow. If Desheeta hadn't planned on—or was unsure about—closing the chapter on Otis, then Otis was influencing his fate.

"My behavior and indiscretions have never been an issue before. If the mission was accomplished, what issue is it of yours what I do?"

"I would have thought maturity came with age. I thought you would improve your ways. You have grown worse."

"Worse? Only by your antiquated standards."

"I expected you to assimilate into a changing society—not to emulate all that is bad with each generation."

"You shouldn't get upset about things you can't change. I've been here for almost two hundred years, and I ain't changing now."

"Does that explain why you violated and killed your coworker? Alicia was her name, wasn't it?"

"I told you I had to kill her. She knew too much and was onto me. It wasn't my fault. She was brilliant and got lucky putting facts together. How was I to know she was connecting the dots on Apple Lewis? She had to die. She was getting close to identifying Apple as something other than human. I killed her, and that's that."

"Yes, but did you have to rape her?"

"I didn't rape her. She fancied me and wanted to have me."

"You always revert to older words like *fancied* when you lie," Desheeta said.

"You are the only one who can call me a liar and draw another breath, Desheeta."

"Thanks for the respect of allowing me to breathe. The fact is you didn't kill this woman. Otis, you're careless, and that carelessness is placing us all at risk. You didn't even question how I knew you had violated Alicia Overstreet—or how we even knew about her."

"I gave up a long time ago trying to figure out how you know so much. For all I know, you have a hundred Otis Beavers running around doing your dirty deeds."

"The woman is alive. She has spoken to the CIA, and they believe her story. She's in protective custody, and our information is that they are secretly looking for you. You are one of them, so they most assuredly don't wish to publicize they have a rogue agent suspected of aggravated assault and rape of a fellow employee."

"It's my word against hers. There were no witnesses. Besides, who are they going to believe: a seasoned agent or some country-bumpkin nerd?"

"Otis, I have a surprise for you. They are going to believe her. Have you ever heard of a webcam? Have you ever heard of a PC microphone? Seems your little country bumpkin left a record of your breaking and entering—not to mention attempted murder. By accident or not, the CIA now has a video of your escapades. The hit was on Apple Lewis, damn it, not on some CIA researcher!"

"Desheeta, calm down. Everything can be fixed. You know the CIA will keep this under wraps. You're right. They're not going to air dirty laundry. They never do." For the first time since the conversation began, Otis appeared nervous. His left eye was twitching. His foot patted nervously under the table.

"No, Otis. I don't want you to fix anything. As you are astutely aware, we don't air our dirty laundry either."

"Look, Desheeta. Let's not rush into anything. Give me another chance. I can get to her and Apple ... kill them both ... no problem. Okay?"

The elders attempted to disguise their glances at one another. No one dared attempt telepathic communication. Desheeta and Otis had strong gifts and could easily intercept such communication. Several believed Desheeta would never harm Otis. Desheeta had given Otis his own blood to make him stronger. He had treated him like a son. At one time, Otis was considered a natural to someday sit at the table of elders. Sure, Otis would need to be taught a lesson, maybe a harsh lesson, but he should never be cleansed.

"Otis Beaver, it's one thing to fail, but to come in here and lie to this council is unimaginable and unforgivable. Did you think we would let you come in here and insult us with untruths?"

"I guess not. I thought my unimpeachable service would carry more weight. Guess not. I can see where this is going."

As Otis stood and turned away as to walk out of the room, two elders brandished bone-handled hunting knives and sunk them into his back. Otis anticipated the stabs but allowed then to happen before he flung himself through a window, falling several stories to the pavement.

Desheeta remained seated as the elders cautiously peered down at the pavement. There was a splattering of blood but no Otis. Desheeta slowly walked over to where Otis had stood, reached down, and picked up pieces of a Kevlar vest.

"I expected as much," Desheeta commented while rubbing pieces of the vest between his fingers. "He's hurt, but he will heal. He knew we were going to close him out and cleanse him, but he came anyway. Why?"

"What now, Desheeta? Do we go after him?" one of the elders asked.

"Patience is a virtue, my friend. Be patient. He will return," Desheeta said. "He has nowhere to go, and he can't hide from us forever."

⚖

Apple finished her bath and attempted to read one of the books she had collected on the trip. Restlessness overcame her. She flipped through the channels and checked for text messages every few minutes, but the only item appearing was a low battery signal. She hoped the battery would last until she could purchase a charger in the morning.

The restlessness continued. She called the front desk and inquired about the restaurant hours. It was closed, but she could order a sandwich from the bar. Slipping on a pair of jeans and a tight white T-shirt, she proceeded to the bar.

The bartender seemed pleased to have someone to visit with. The only other person in the bar was a well-dressed, handsome man about her age. She noticed his blue eyes and light blond hair in the darkened room. She ordered a whiskey sour because she wanted to appear inconspicuous.

The Irish bartender was interested in Apple, and she was intrigued by the events that had brought him to Oklahoma. The vibration of her cell phone interrupted his story.

*If you're just going to play with your drink, come sit with
me. I'm sure we have lots to talk about.*

Apple stared in disbelief at the message. The cute white man in the corner was the only option. Her secret messenger who had brought her to Oklahoma was in the bar? She turned in his direction, but he didn't look up or return her gaze.

The bartender told her what time he would get off work and how he would enjoy her company. He also mentioned that his ego could handle being with a black woman.

Apple turned to him, and her glare spoke a thousand negatives. The man was no fool and nodded in acceptance.

"Is this seat taken?" asked Apple.

"No. As a matter of fact, I was saving it for you," the blond stranger replied. "I take it you had a pleasant journey?" he asked without making eye contact.

"My life has been a journey. I am not sure what you're referring to," replied Apple.

"Miss Lewis, I know who and what you are. I don't like to waste small talk. I'm not an enemy."

"Then who and what are you? And how did you know where to find me?"

"Slow down. First things first. Before we get started with questions—and I forget that briefcase by my foot is for you—we thought you might be hungry. Here's a little present for you." He slowly pushed the leather briefcase toward Apple. She cautiously unzipped the top. Inside, a unit of blood was wrapped in a special cold-retention medical carrier.

"How did I find you? There's a GPS device in your cell phone. I had it placed under your bed."

Apple was taken aback by the blood and wasn't listening too closely to what he was saying. "And your name is?"

"Well, that's kind of complicated. My current name is Daniel Baker."

"Daniel, pray tell, what would be your interest in me?"

"Let's just say I'm carrying out the wishes of my boss. I'm here to assist in your reacclimation to Oklahoma—and to be your personal advisor."

"And your boss would be?"

"The boss will choose if and when he reveals himself."

"Not good enough. I appreciate your offer of the liquid diet, but I have been taking care of myself forever and don't desire an advisor." Apple stood.

"Have it your way. Just a word of warning, Otis Beaver is in town—and I suspect he is really pissed at you. If I know my pureblood Spirit Walkers, and I think I know them fairly well, you're in a heap of shit."

Apple sat back down and said, "Now we're getting somewhere. For your information, I have been in a heap of shit my entire life. So you think you know Spirit Walkers? Please continue. Tell me more."

"Really, there's not too much to tell. I'm an attorney hired by a Spirit Walker to take care of his affairs. You see, Miss Lewis, you probably know more about Spirit Walkers than I do. I have only known one in my life, and he employs me. You, on the other hand, have killed several and fought with others. If I'm not grossly mistaken, you also created a cute little Rebecca Spirit Walker."

Apple studied Daniel's eyes and facial expressions. She had always been able to detect other Spirit Walkers, but Daniel was different. His skin was light with no noticeable scars, but she could sense he was dissimilar in other ways. The bartender interrupted her evaluation by reminding them of last call.

"Tell you what, Miss Lewis. I have other business to attend to tonight. Why don't I pick you up in the morning? We can go for a drive and discuss, among other things, the future." Daniel reached over and cupped his hands around hers, looked her in the eyes, and winked. He left the bartender a twenty-dollar tip and walked out without looking back.

Apple took the briefcase and strolled into the parking lot. The standard, warm Oklahoma wind kissed her face. She felt like she was home for the first time in ninety years.

⊶ ⊷

"So, where we going?" Apple asked as Daniel Baker opened the door to his black BMW SUV. The sun was warm, the humidity was high, and the wind was strong. Apple had slept well and had been on the curb waiting for Daniel since dawn.

"My, don't you clean up well?" Daniel admired her white shorts, sleeveless pullover blouse, and flip-flops. "Thought we might run up the turnpike to T-town."

"T-town?" Apple asked.

"You know, Tulsa. Like it's time to be on Tulsa time." Daniel smiled as he sped away from the valet parking area.

They made small talk as they sped over the rolling, tree-lined hills toward northeast Oklahoma. Chills floated across Apple's arms every time a road sign indicated the miles remaining until Tulsa.

"So, you ever been to Tulsa?"

"Yes," replied Apple. "I was born there, sometime around 1911."

They topped a hill and saw the Tulsa skyline. Crossing the Arkansas River Bridge, close to downtown, Apple was amazed by how much she remembered. The river was lined with more trees and vegetation than when she lived with Mrs. Johnson. The river had been there for the first ten years of her life, but she never had an occasion to venture toward it until the riot. The river was another reminder of segregation. People preferred to stay with their own kind back then also. *In that respect,* she thought, *things have not changed much.*

She stretched for a better look at downtown Tulsa. She loved the tall buildings and churches. On Greenwood Avenue, there was a new county jail, a halfway house, the Salvation Army, and manufacturing plants. A two-block area led to the Greenwood Cultural Center.

"What's this?" Apple pointed toward the center.

"You'll see," Daniel replied.

They walked past a two-story brick home with a plaque that read, "Only House Remaining from the Race Riot." Inside, Apple was speechless at the huge black-and-white photos of the 1921 race riot. Photos of her childhood neighborhood on fire decorated the stark walls. Lining the large lobby were photos of charred bodies, dead bodies stacked in the back of trucks, and the old lady in a rocking chair with devastation surrounding her. For the first time in her life, she felt a tear caress her face.

Daniel silently watched Apple move from one photo to the next and back again. She read through the books, viewed all the artifacts, and returned to the photos. She softly touched the photos and sensed the pain as her mind drifted back to the riots. She touched the photo where the church would have been. Her hand ran across an aerial photo of the devastation and stopped close to the old courthouse. She traced a circle across the glass encasement. "Jesse died here," she whispered.

Daniel stood behind her, took her left hand, and placed her index finger on a partially burned building. "And this, Apple Lewis, is where you first met me."

Apple stood silently, resisting the urge to face Daniel. "Somehow I knew I had met you before. You were the little white boy I couldn't shake loose."

"Oh, you shook me loose okay, but I didn't go far. I came back to look for you. I knew you would send me away again, so I followed and hid from you. I was in the church when Bobby was killed. I saw what he did for you, and I saw you drinking the blood. After you took off, I imitated what you did. Granted, there was not much to drink—and now I think how crazy I was to have done it. We were just children then, and somehow I thought it would save me. You were the bravest kid I had ever seen. It was natural for me to want to be like you. *Why not drink the blood?*"

Apple turned to face Daniel. "You're a Spirit Walker from the same bloodline as me?"

"Shh, not so loud. There are still a lot of old tales and mysteries about those days. Can you believe it? There are stories of zombies, the living dead, and old Indian tribes with the secrets of the fountains of youth."

"So you're really like me, a Spirit Walker?" Apple whispered.

"Not exactly. I've been told my initial dose of Spirit Walker, as I call it, was fairly weak. Even though I have to feed like you, it isn't very often, and I can't gain any additional strength. I understand feeding for you is akin to recharging batteries. Anyway, I have a few gifts but not equal to yours. And as you may have noticed, I appear a little older than you."

All this was too much for Apple. She took Daniel by the hand and directed him outside. She needed fresh air. They walked south on Greenwood Avenue.

"Apple, down these streets, Louis Armstrong, Dizzy Gillespie, Nat King Cole, and Cab Calloway used to play. Guess that might have been while you were into your Chicago gangster years."

"How do you know so much about me?"

"We only determined who you were about five years ago, and

then we weren't sure. Prior to 9/11, changing identification was routine and easy. Like you, I have had to change my name and identity several times. After 9/11, we had to reinvent ourselves. We had to diversify and retool the organization."

"What organization?"

"Patience, Apple, patience. We were in the information business. I ran a credit-rating company that collected data on people and sold it to other companies. This branched into mailing list sales, market research, and other depositories of collateral, informational databases on people's purchasing habits, consumption patterns, etc. Anytime a record was kept electronically, whether it was a credit card purchase or filling out a survey, we wanted it. Of course, we were not allowed access to bank records, voting records, or other sensitive, constitutionally protected information.

"We experienced a metamorphosis when the federal government contacted us. Our prayers had been answered. Concerned about the difficulty of changing identifications—and keeping track of pureblood Spirit Walkers—we were frantic for a solution. We became federal contractors, and the availability of data was unlimited. We were given access to everything that could be submitted electronically or digitally. If it was in the air, we had it. The Patriot Act couldn't be fed enough data. Apparently, there were no restrictions on what the government could collect. But all good things must come to an end. We hacked our own system. The boss believed the government was getting out of control with the database. They kept providing addendums to the contract, giving us access to more information. Our job—besides being a private storage for such information—was to connect the dots and identify possible "people of interest." Of course, our selection was to be based upon objective criteria. Once it was made known to us, the boss ordered a hack of our own program. Now the CIA and FBI are working with us to determine the origin of the breach."

"You said you found out about me five years ago?"

"Yes. We had encounters with Desheeta and his group over the years, and at times there was peace, love, and harmony. I'm joking. There were times he wasn't trying to eradicate us. He had respect for my boss—but not for me."

"How did you find me and determine I was actually a Spirit Walker?"

"At first, your name and profile were automatically saved in a file based upon your choice of books. I guess you were simply infatuated with the occult, witchcraft, and tribal medicines—or you were searching for your identity. But when three bookstores attempted to search for books containing Spirit Walkers, we caught on. Initially, we believed you were one of Desheeta's elite, a chosen one. How was I supposed to know you were a woman with a name like Apple? If I knew your name when we first met, I must've forgotten it. You see—Desheeta's clan has no females, at least none we know of. Many of Desheeta's purebloods choose bizarre and peculiar names. Of course, I didn't have confirmation you were a Spirit Walker until I briefed my boss. He was convinced you were a Spirit Walker, but he wouldn't explain how he knew. He suspected you were not connected to Desheeta. From there, it was easy. The new access to the database allowed us to search old scanned and microfilmed newspaper articles that had been destroyed, erased, or just eliminated from lack of space. Someone had listed you as missing from the Tulsa riots, and you were a suspect in a killing some years later. I find it somewhat ironic that you were listed as missing but were actually living with a wealthy, white family a dozen or so blocks from the riot. This really demonstrated the separation of the races in those days, doesn't it?"

They turned around at the bottom of the hill and strolled back toward the Greenwood Cultural Center. Apple stared at the ground and watched her feet take each step on the new pavement. She saw the ancient earth underneath and witnessed the dead reaching out to her, summoning her to join them in eternal rest. She felt their decaying hands reaching for her ankles and heard their screams as she and Daniel hid from the riots.

"Apple, are you all right?" Daniel asked, gripping her hand.

"Where are all the victims buried? Where are all the victims of the riot buried?" Apple asked.

"Nobody has ever been sure. Many were hauled off and buried in mass graves, others were burned, and some were given proper burials."

"They're here—in the ground—reaching out to me. They want something from me."

"Maybe you're feeling what I have felt over the years: guilt for surviving with Spirit Walker benefits."

"What about you, Daniel? This doesn't make sense. How could you live as a child and be a Spirit Walker with a slow-aging process and not be detected?"

"I was told my parents were killed in the riot. The boss found me, and we have been together ever since. I never saw my parents again, and I assumed what I was told was true."

"What do you mean the boss found you?"

"After the riot, a white kid on the street was unusual. I was homeless for several weeks, but they didn't put us in encampments like the blacks. Eventually, I was living in a shelter downtown. One day I was sitting on a park bench, whittling with an old pocketknife I had found. I was just sitting, whittling, and whistling, and the boss stops dead in his tracks and just starts staring at me. It was as if he knew something was different about me. He came over and smelled my hair. Somehow I knew I should go with him. We have been together ever since."

"So when will I meet the boss?"

"I thought maybe today, but he is a busy man. Maybe in a few days."

As they walked back to Daniel's SUV, Apple could feel the clawing and vibration of the tortured souls filtering through the red earth.

⊣ ⊢

"How many days has it been? Look here, you assholes. I know my rights. I have the right to an attorney, and I wish to exercise that right. I have a right to a phone call. Goddamn it. I have rights! Don't you fucking idiots understand English? Fuck, not again!"

The stinging, powerful spray of water hit him in the chest, thighs, and legs. He covered his face the best he could and curled into a fetal position. He had learned from experience that this position lessened the pain. He preferred the powerful sprays of water as an intermediate control measure even though it was painful. The alternatives, which he had also had the pleasure of experiencing, had extensive aftereffects. The pepper spray stayed in his eyes for days, and the electric shocks from Taser guns rattled his nerves for a week.

He could only guess what the foreign guards were saying to him. He had been there long enough to make a few things out, such as "Fuck you, you American traitor." Also, the word *terrorist* sounded remarkably similar in any language. He had been in federal custody for twelve hours, handcuffed to the seat of a small jet. He wasn't sure where they landed.

Sabin hadn't been afforded a bath or a shave since he was captured in Chicago. The CIA and FBI interrogated him before he was sent out of the country. He knew why he was out of the country: legalized torture. He maintained a ray of hope that this would be all over soon. Every morning, he cursed the nightmare that was reality.

⇥ ⇤

"Desheeta, how many years has it been since we met?"

"I would say about a hundred years," replied Desheeta.

The two old acquaintances were having lunch at Mickey Mantle's Steakhouse in Bricktown, just east of downtown Oklahoma City. The meeting location was previously negotiated and mutually agreed upon by their staffs. Daniel sat three tables down from the conversation while several purebloods sat at the bar.

"Why did you call this meeting? Not seeing or hearing from you is the best medicine for both of us," Desheeta said.

"You haven't changed at all. Always a man of few words and direct to the point. I have always appreciated that about you. It seems you continue to avoid saying my name. You know I haven't changed it from our days in Greenwood."

The two men sipped their coffee and glanced around the restaurant, pretending to be distracted. Both were keenly aware that distractions were not random. They had created many distractions for each other over the decades.

"The woman, Apple Lewis, I want you to stop hunting her."

"You have some interest in her, do you?"

"Now who's playing games? You are very much aware of my interest in this woman."

"Your language, I remember you sounding more hillbillyish— more countrified. Am I wrong?"

"Desheeta, like you, I have changed with the times, and I speak in a manner that best serves the situation. If you prefer countrified, you shall have it. I don't hear you mentioning speaking in forked tongues and saying, 'How, Pilgrim.'"

"You certainly haven't lost your sense of humor—or is that sarcasm I hear? Why should I allow this woman to live? She was never supposed to happen or be. She's an abomination."

"In a way, you created her."

"I don't see it."

"You created Jesse and Bobby."

"Yes, but we needed their types for our tribe's survival. We needed men who could assimilate into the world. Blacks were coming to Oklahoma in droves. Black townships were springing up all over the place. Blacks were more acceptable than us natives. I saw it coming: the riots, the discrimination, and the injustice of it all. It was so predictable. Once the blacks started to flourish, have influence, gain wealth, and demand equality, it was just a matter of time. The riot was inevitable."

"Desheeta, I don't want to debate the history of mankind with you. Just allow the woman to live in peace. I assure you she will not be a problem for you or what you believe in."

"She is reckless and irresponsible. She leaves a trail anyone can follow."

"And Otis Beaver hasn't?"

"Otis is not an issue here."

"I think he may be. The CIA is looking for him. You're searching for him. He has potential to become the biggest liability you have ever had—far more than Apple Lewis."

"We take care of our own and will do so again."

"Desheeta, leave the woman alone. I offer my assurances. She will not be a problem."

"And if I don't?"

"I have nothing to threaten you with, Desheeta. I ask this as your brother and for the sake of our mother who would not wish us to quarrel over such matters."

"Don't bring our mother into this. Your father brought black into the bloodline. I will give you this: I have matters more pressing at this time. I will not have her hunted for now. We will talk again."

"So she can walk this earth freely?"

"For now, but I make no guarantees for the future and none for the present as it relates to what Otis Beaver may or may not do. He is most assuredly out there somewhere."

⚔ ⚔

Umbrellas were a necessity when an unexpected thunderstorm flashed across the sky. For someone attempting to hide their identity, the weather and a large umbrella couldn't have been more costumed order for the occasion, even if the devil had placed the order himself. Staying with the horde of walking commuters, like a swarm of flies returning to their nests—nests of high-rise apartments, condominiums, and studio flats—he pursued his prey.

Rebecca had laid low for a few days after Apple left Chicago. After a few days of watching and waiting, she surmised she was not the hunted. She couldn't explain why Apple's escape never appeared in the newspapers or on television. She had a friend call the sheriff's office, and no warrants were on record. She described the escape in excruciating detail to all her criminal acquaintances, but none believed her. How could anyone break out of jail and no one report it or even care enough to come looking for her? Her previous pending charges had been dismissed.

She went shopping in the boutiques in the shadow of the Sears Tower. She decided to try the J. Lo look: tight, low-rider, bell-bottom jeans and a fluffy, sheer, sleeveless blouse tied just under her breast. The plan was to display as much stomach and hips as possible. She had purchased a new ring for her pierced belly button. She sashayed down the street, exaggerating the swing of her hips. She liked the wet look; therefore, an umbrella was a nuisance. Her newfound strengths and the few gifts she had discovered created an aura of invincibility. Through the sea of umbrellas, she walked without a care.

For Otis Beaver, she was easy prey. He was somewhat disappointed. He desired a challenge. He needed a challenge. A challenge would lessen the sting of having to bear the brunt of Desheeta's criticism— not to mention the attempted assassination from his own elders. What motivated him today was twofold. He was angry for having to kill Rebecca for her helping Apple to escape. He held Apple responsible for that need of a collateral kill. He also needed to demonstrate to Desheeta and the elders that he could clean up his own mistakes. Yes, he would prove his worthiness once more.

Otis had planned this well. He wasn't going to kill her quickly. Maybe she knew where Apple was. Maybe Apple was close by. Rebecca would surely know. He would enjoy killing her since revenge was the best medicine for the soul. If she didn't know the whereabouts of Apple, he would go after Alicia Overstreet. He would be the closer, the cleanser. Desheeta tried to close the chapter on him. He would close chapters of his own. If this was unacceptable to Desheeta, he might close out Desheeta.

Rebecca didn't see the evil until it was too late. If she had more time to experiment with her gifts, she might have detected the evil approaching. She was crossing an alley when hands wrapped around her neck. Her assailant flung her down a set of stairs with metal railings. Her head hit the last stair, splitting her forehead. She felt the blood rush from the wound. Peering up, she saw Otis Beaver standing with one foot on her chest and the other firmly planted underneath her chin. A sinister laugh echoed in her ears.

He was too strong for her to move. He smeared the blood oozing from her forehead across her chest and stomach. He raised his hand, studied the blood on it, and licked it clean.

"Where's Apple Lewis?" he demanded.

"Fuck you!" Rebecca yelled.

"Good enough," he replied. He thrust his foot into her neck, partially decapitating her.

⊰ ⊱

Apple was becoming part of the family of employees at the Waterford Hotel. She poured coffee in the mornings for the guests at the checkout counter and rearranged flowers on the reception room table. Daniel had warned her not to venture outside until he said it was safe. He only provided an inkling of what he would be doing. "Safety," he would say. "The boss and I are going to negotiate your safety."

Daniel returned after three days. He was extremely relaxed when he finally picked her up. "I like the name *Coco* the best."

"How did you know that was one of my options? I know what you're going to say. It's always the same answer, 'Patience, Apple, patience.' I'm putting you on notice today; my patience is running very thin. Now, where are we going?"

Daniel smiled and said they were going on a very short trip. They drove through a beautiful old neighborhood and a large park. A small stream ran through the park. Apple watched children swinging and elderly people walking their dogs. The morning sun was kissing all it touched.

At the south end of the park, an exit road delivered them to a single row of turn-of-the-century mansions. Daniel hit a remote control button under the dash, and two wrought-iron French-styled gates swung open. The home was enormous. A separate, smaller house was adjacent to it. Large oak and pecan trees bordered the driveway. The roof appeared to be brass or copper.

"I told you patience, Apple Lewis—or shall I call you Lawanda or Coco Lawanda? The boss man awaits you."

The huge wooden entrance doors swung open to a marble floor with two fireplaces. Tall windows started at the floor and reached the ceiling. They revealed an expansive, wooded conclave yard. Spiral staircases flanked both sides of the windows.

Rays of sunshine illuminated the dancing dust particles. The top of a hat was all she could see as they proceeded to the center of the room. The hat protruded slightly above an old, red high-backed Victorian chair.

Daniel said, "Apple, meet the boss."

She slowly walked around to the front of the chair.

"My dear Apple, you can call me Tom Duke or Old Tom Duke. I think you used to prefer the latter."

CHAPTER 23

The Pleasure of Violence

"Sloppy, sloppy, sloppy," Otis Beaver whispered. There was no one close enough to hear him, but he had become accustomed to talking to himself. It used to worry him, but Otis figured it came with his chosen profession. They were so easy to track that he believed it must have been a trap. But after careful analysis, he believed he was just that good. All it took was a few calls to friends with the feds, a little hacking of cameras at the Tulsa Riot Museum, and paying off a poorly paid state employee at the Turner Turnpike Authority for car and tag photos.

He never considered himself a hit man or an assassin. He considered himself more of a fixer, correcting bad behavior. The tribe took care of him. Money was never an issue. He was kind of on retainer and did not receive bonuses or payment by the job. Maybe after he cleaned up all this, his improved reputation would take him into the big leagues. No more working for the same pay every month from the tribe. No more having to dress the part and put up with being a federal agent. He would be a violence consultant. The thought of his new self-given title caused a wide grin to spread across his square, muscular face. He would be relevant like never before.

Otis was taking no chances this time. He had all the tools of the trade for a job in a somewhat populated area. At his immediate disposal were two bone-handled bowie knives, choking wire with polished white-oak grips, and a crossbow. He preferred to kill with weapons that provided a personal touch. His favorite was killing with a knife; it allowed the soul of the deceased to enter his body and give him their strength and wisdom. He also carried a Walther 380 with a silencer. He saw no security on the perimeter as he scaled the eight-foot concrete-and-rock fence with the gracefulness of a cat.

◁ ▷

"Mr. Duke, you look almost the same. Wow! Is it really you? I can't believe this. I am sorry, but—"

"Now, my little Apple. No need to get all tongue-tied. Yes, it really is me, and it is great to see you again. I look a little older. You may have figured out that I am kind of a mongrel mutt myself—and not one of them fancy purebloods. Daniel has been takin' good care of me. Everyone, sit down, take a load off, and we will have bunches of time to catch up. Oh, and did you call me Mr. Duke? Well, we gots to get rid of that type of welcome for old friends."

"But I never knew. I mean I never even thought about you being a Spirit Walker. Even after all these years; it never crossed my mind," Apple said.

"Well, it wasn't like I was going around trying to impress everybody with it. Remember how I just like to sit around, give advice to you youngsters, whittle a little bit, and let my boys Jesse and Bobby do any sophisticated stuff."

"But you are here now—in this mansion. You and Daniel. How did you survive the riot? And how are you here now?"

"Daniel helped me survive and prosper. He is one smart young man. It is all a very long story, you know. We should have a little tea-and-bourbon mixer and get into the deep stuff later."

"Here, I will go fix us drinks while you two make small talk.

Save the heavy stuff for me to hear also." Daniel raised the blinds and revealed large windows.

Tom and Apple squinted as the sunlight bounced off the floor, glanced off an old oak-and-glass china cabinet, and illuminated the room. The newfound light caused Apple to fixate her eyes on the tapestries on the walls. They all depicted scenes she remembered or would associate with the Tulsa race riot: burning churches, wagons hauling piles of the dead, and other gruesome sights. There were two wooden signs; one said Black Wall Street, and the other said the Black Holocaust.

⊰ ⊱

Daniel felt the cold steel of the knife instantaneously. The large bowie knife pierced through from the back left side and separated his ribs. Daniel moved just fast enough to avoid the slicing motion of the knife, which most assuredly would have resulted in death. He reached back and grabbed Otis's shirt. They both fell to the floor, slipping on the enormous amount of Daniel's blood.

Otis wrapped the choking wire around Daniel's neck, grabbed the ends of it, and pulled it tight. From behind, Otis tightened his grip and choked Daniel.

Daniel kicked, slid, and twisted in the pool of blood as he attempted to break the stranglehold.

Otis removed his grip after Daniel stopped moving and breathing for several minutes. *The little shit was stronger than I thought.* Otis sat silently in the pool of blood and watched it change colors. Otis smiled as the blood quickly turned from red to burgundy to almost black. Otis had an old habit of tasting the blood of his enemies. With one small taste, he could tell Daniel was a stronger Spirit Walker mix than he had believed. He could hear Apple and Tom talking down the hallway. Fortunately for Otis, the kitchen was twenty yards from the living room.

"Daniel tells me that there is a website now about Black Wall

261

Street in Tulsa back in the days when you and I were roaming around there. He says you can read about it on Wikipee," Tom explained.

"I think you mean Wikipedia," interrupted Apple.

"Anyways, it says we was the wealthiest black community in the whole USA. You know you can't change the past or predict the future, but we can control today. What's taking Daniel so long?"

"I'll go check on him. Plus I want to see the rest of this mansion."

"Let me go with you. I gots some prize possessions you might fancy. You know I been a few places since we last saw each other. I just didn't hang around these parts."

⇥ ⇤

Otis walked into the living room and pulled the trigger on the crossbow as Tom stood up. The target was the heart, but the arrow hit his lower rib cage.

When Tom fell to the floor, Otis turned the bow on Apple. The arrow caught her in the left arm as she dove behind a sofa.

Otis took a step back and pointed the bow toward the sofa. "Apple, it is you I want—not Tom! Tom is still alive, you know. I see him breathing. I can take this here bow of mine and shoot an arrow through his skull … no, let's make that his heart. I want to retrieve my arrow, and skulls are tough to do that with. Or you can stand up and die for him. What's it going to be?"

Stall, I need to stall for time, thought Apple. Her eyes searched the room. An iron fire poker was up against a wall to the right, about eight feet away.

Otis placed his left foot on Tom and pointed the bow at him. "What's it going to be? I'm going to kill you. How sad. You are going to make me finish old Tom here off, and you are still going to die. I was born with no patience past the count of three. Here we go. One, two—"

Otis fell backward as the slashing knife stroke of Tom cut through the Achilles tendon of his left leg. Tom let out a tribal war cry as he delivered the blow.

Apple grabbed the fire poker and ran toward Otis. Otis was pulling himself up off the floor when Apple jumped forward and sliced from his neck through his back.

"Is he dead? Is he dead? Apple, make sure he is dead." Tom's voice was weak. He looked down at the arrow protruding and was surprised to see little blood.

"He's dead. Look at him. We need to get you to a doctor. That arrow needs to come out."

"Check on Daniel. Where's Daniel!" cried Tom.

Apple looked at the arrow in her arm. She felt no pain. She helped Tom stand up. "I'm not leaving you, Tom. Lean on me. Let's go look for Daniel."

Daniel was still on the floor in the kitchen. He had lost a tremendous amount of blood.

Apple placed Tom in a chair and got on her knees to check for breathing. She found none.

Tom said, "Apple, check his pulse. He has Spirit Walker in him. The pulse is the only way to be sure."

"Okay, Tom, but I am not sure if I feel one."

"He's pale, but he still has color. Is he warm?"

"Maybe. Yes, I think so."

"Apple, call this number. Whoever answers, give them my name—and Daniel's name. Just say there is trouble at the house."

⊣ ⊢

Help arrived within minutes. No one spoke as they loaded Apple, Daniel, and Tom in a van and sped away. Two sedans escorted the van.

Apple put Tom's head in her lap and watched several men and a woman work on Daniel. Apple and Tom took the tube of blood that was offered. Apple sipped hers, and Tom drank his in one gulp.

Blood was poured down Daniel's throat while he was being given transfusions.

※ ※

"Did you check the whole house?" asked the man who appeared to be in charge.

One by one, each of the six men in the house yelled, "Yes, whole house is checked."

"Okay, cleaners, get your asses in gear. Let's finish this job and get the hell out of here. This place gives me the creeps. Call it in, Sam."

"Yeah, Sam here … finishing up. Clean as a whistle. No, I didn't know we had a body to dispose of. No one told us about a body. Guarantee it. Been all through this house. You know we do a good job. Been at it for years. Yeah, we did a good job on that mess at Desheeta's a while back. I know, I know. Don't mention names or locations. Sure, we can look around outside, but that will cost extra. I'm joking, man, just joking. We will look for free. This one is on us."